D0457646

Allison K. Hymas

ALADDIN
NEW YORK LONDON TORONTO SYDNEY NEW DELHI

This book is a work of fiction. Any references to historical events, real people, or real places are used fictitiously. Other names, characters, places, and events are products of the author's imagination, and any resemblance to actual events or places or persons, living or dead, is entirely coincidental.

ALADDIN
An imprint of Simon & Schuster Children's Publishing Division
1230 Avenue of the Americas, New York, New York 10020
First Aladdin hardcover edition February 2018

Also available in an Aladdin MAX paperback edition.

For information about special discounts for bulk purchases, please contact Simon & Schuster Special Sales at 1-866-506-1949 or business@simonandschuster.com.
The Simon & Schuster Speakers Bureau can bring authors to your live event. For more information or to book an event contact the Simon & Schuster Speakers Bureau at 1-866-248-3049 or visit our website at www.simonspeakers.com.
Jacket designed by Karin Paprocki
Interior designed by Mike Rosamilia
The text of this book was set in Adobe Caslon Pro.
Manufactured in the United States of America 0118 FFG
10 9 8 7 6 5 4 3 2 1
Library of Congress Cataloging-in-Publication Data
Names: Hymas, Allison K., author.
Title: Arts and thefts / Allison K. Hymas.
Description: New York : Aladdin, 2018. | Series: MAX | Summary: Middle school retrieval specialist Jeremy Wilderson again must work with his archrival, Becca Mills, when someone sabotages the Summer Art Show where Chase's work is being exhbited.
Identifiers: LCCN 2017016597 | ISBN 9781481463454 (pbk) |
ISBN 9781481463461 (hc) | ISBN 9781481463478 (eBook)
Subjects: | CYAC: Artists—Fiction. | Stealing—Fiction. | Cooperativeness—Fiction. |
Mystery and detective stories. | BISAC: JUVENILE FICTION / Action & Adventure / General. |
JUVENILE FICTION / Social Issues / Friendship.
Classification: LCC PZ7.1.H94 Art 2017 | DDC [Fic]—dc23
LC record available at https://lccn.loc.gov/2017016597

Dedicated to Brian Hymas and his "ugly mug":
pottery is not your medium, but your sense
of humor is always top-shelf.

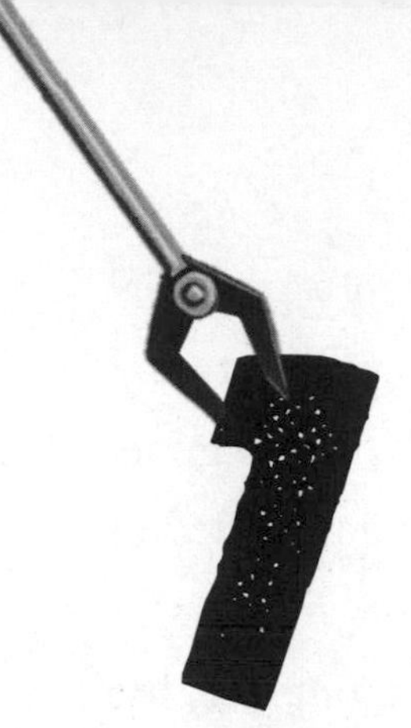

I HAD NO IDEA TROUBLE WAS brewing until Case busted through my back door at sunset one Thursday during summer vacation.

Hey, don't think that because I didn't have my thumb pressed to the pulse of Scottsville's criminal activity, I'd been slacking at my job. I'm not a crime lord, and I'm not a detective. My job starts *after* the crime has been committed, when the victim comes to me with a sob story and a slice of chocolate cake. That's when I sneak in and retrieve the stolen object from under the thief's nose.

But I had tried to pay a little more attention that summer. If I'd been more attentive during the school year, I'd have known that Mark Chandler was a dirty criminal psychopath posing as an innocent victim—definitely not someone who needed my help.

My contacts who usually told me when a potential client was looking for my skills, or any information I needed to retrieve something successfully, were gone. Cricket had packed up his impressive collection of denim clothing and left with his family for a few months in Canada, and Tomboy Tate had given me one last list of kids who were feuding (and thus may steal from one another) before going to summer camp.

The silence on the underground wasn't too odd, or even worrying. Summers are generally pretty chill work-wise for me, so on the sunny July day when our story begins, I had biked, swum, and played video games with Case and Hack. Then Case went off to meet Elena Trujillo at Comet Cream, which is an ice cream parlor that he frequents because it's a good place to find clients from all over town. I avoid it because Becca Mills—the tiny yet terrifying private detective whose goal was to see me in detention for life—knows this fact.

Fast-forward to an hour later, when Case burst into my house without knocking, eyes wild.

"Dude," I said. I had been sitting near the back door, waiting for a job if one came along and wasting time with summer reading (*To Kill a Mockingbird*), so I was there to greet him. "Next time, don't hold back. Just kick the door off its hinges."

"We have a problem," he said, shutting the door behind him.

"Yes," a voice said. "A devious kid, wearing fingerless Eagles gloves and a shifty look, just infiltrated our house through the back door." My seventeen-year-old brother, Rick, had made an appearance, coming in from the kitchen with a can of root beer. "Yet another illicit exchange for our Dr. Evil, and I appear to have stepped right into the middle. Oh my, what am I to do?"

"How about shut up and go away?" I said as Case pulled a pencil out of the back of one his Philadelphia Eagles gloves (which he always wore to protect his artist hands) and anxiously tucked it over his ear.

"How about no?"

"J," Case said, peering out the back door's window. "We don't have time for this."

"It's summer," I said. "We have all the time in the world."

"She's *right outside.*"

I went to the window and looked. Becca Mills was in my backyard, arms folded, grinning at Case and me through the window.

"I'm sorry, man," Case said. "I didn't know she followed me."

"I expected better of your criminal friends, Wilderson,"

she called. "Your forger should have known not to come straight here."

I turned back to Rick, who was taking a long gulp from his can of soda. He didn't seem to have heard. But I had to get rid of him before words like "criminal" and "forger" infiltrated his thick skull.

"Don't you have homework or some college pamphlets to read?" I asked my brother.

He swallowed. "I'll read the pamphlets tomorrow. And summer work is better done in the heat of desperation during the last week of August," Rick said. "Preferably in my spare time between scrimmages."

Oh, right. Football camp. Like he hadn't mentioned that six times a day all summer.

Rick gestured to the window with his can. "Isn't that the girl from across the street? You *are* in trouble."

"Nope. I can handle her."

Becca was still outside. I'd hoped she'd leave, but it looked like she wasn't moving until she got what she wanted. I groaned and opened the back door. "Come on, Case."

Rick shrugged and walked back to the kitchen. "Be careful out there."

"Stay behind me," I told Case.

"Happy to."

Becca smirked at us. "Hello, Wilderson. Seems like

you're still waiting for your first growth spurt."

I ignored the jab at my less than generous height. "What do you want?"

She ignored me and looked around the yard. "So this is why I've never seen you take jobs from home. They come here to the back door. I'll have to watch you better."

"This is my house, not yours. I believe that means you're trespassing," I said. "Not a great move for a law-abiding detective like you."

"Is that what you say to everyone who comes back here to hire you? If your clients are allowed, then I'm allowed to come talk to a pair of thieves."

"We aren't thieves!" Case said over my shoulder.

Becca's evil smile grew. "Felony in all fifty states," she said, and Case tried to push past me.

"Hold on, man," I said, holding him back. "Don't let her get to you."

"No one likes you, snitch!" he called to Becca.

"That's enough." I pushed Case inside my house. Turning back to Becca, I said, "I'd love to continue this chat, but unless you have something to say, I recommend you go. I have summer reading to do."

Her smile slipped into a bitter scowl. "I know you did it. Case coming here proves it."

"Proves what? I have no idea what you're talking

about, but I can't wait until you tell everyone that going to a friend's house is a crime. Now, good-bye." I stepped back inside and closed the door.

"You can't hide forever!" Becca called, but I ignored her again.

Case had his face against the glass. "She's leaving."

"Good." I turned around to see Rick leaning against the stair's banister. Oh, great.

"What did you hear?"

"Not a lot," he admitted. "But you having a secret meeting in the backyard with a girl? That's suspicious. The question is, should I tell Mom about this little get-together now, or should I hold out for a better offer? My integrity is strong, but it can be bought." He grinned at me. "For the right price."

Case glanced from Rick to me, breathing hard. He thought Rick was serious. But I'm familiar with my bonehead brother's ways. He knew nothing, and therefore his threat was as empty as the top half of a bag of chips.

I pointed a thumb at the stairs. "Come on, Case. Let's talk in my room. Rick's not allowed to bother me there." I glared at my brother.

"Wouldn't dream of walking into your evil lair. I'd probably step on your fluffy cat's tail, and ruin the joy of any diabolic stroking when you're taunting your victims.

I'd hate to put my baby brother out like that."

"Oh, you got me a fluffy cat? You shouldn't have. No, really, you shouldn't have. I'm a dog person."

Rick laughed. "Joke now, if you want. But if I see blood coming from under your door or smoke from above, I'm calling the authorities."

"That was one time!" I called as I hurried Case away.

In case you were wondering, it was smoke. Case, Hack, and I were experimenting with invisible inks. Most of them are made visible with heat. We had a little accident.

"Okay," I said once I'd closed the door. "What was that? Why was Becca here, and what was all that about a felony?"

"That's what forgery is. A felony in all fifty states." Case sat down on my bed, his dark skin paler than usual. "She made me tell them everything."

"Hold on." I ran downstairs, grabbed a can of root beer, and hurried back to my room. "Here," I said, offering it to Case. "Drink up, and tell me what happened." Case was high-strung, but he had never run into my house without the requisite social niceties before. Like knocking, or taking the time to catch his breath.

As Case chugged the soda, I thought about Becca's appearance at my house. Now she knew where I conducted my business. That wasn't good. I also didn't like her threatening Case. Sure, Case was a forger. He was a talented artist who used his skills with pen and brush to create fake hall passes, late notes, and the occasional school project, but always for a good cause. Like me, he used his talents to help people. I'd never steal something outright, and he'd never fake an assignment to help a cheater or to give someone false credit. The way we worked was hardly a felony.

Well, I guess there was my last big job. I'd been tricked into stealing, outright *stealing*, the master key that unlocked every locker in the school for a guy named Mark, who used it to steal from everyone in the school—Case, Hack, and me included. I had to team up with Becca Mills to stop Mark and return the key to the teachers.

But Case couldn't possibly know about the fact that I had worked with Becca. He and Hack hated Becca, and if they knew I'd worked with her Case wouldn't be over here downing a soda in my room. He'd be screaming at me, vocalizing his betrayal in the loudest way possible. That, or avoiding me completely. Which was why I'd never told him or Hack about Becca's involvement in that job.

It couldn't be about a more recent job either. Since school had ended, I'd only retrieved a few retainers left at the public pool after closing time.

Like I said, work was slow over the summer.

Case slammed the empty can on my side table and belched. "Excuse me. Okay." He sounded calmer, but I detected a small twitch in his fingers. Maybe it was just the soda.

"Okay," I said. "What's up? You look like someone stole your art supplies."

"Not mine," Case said. "But someone *did* steal brushes, and paints, and it's bad. I'm sorry."

"Nothing to be sorry about. Just tell me what happened."

"I was at Comet, sharing a Black Hole sundae with Elena, when Becca Mills came through the door."

"Well, she does like to get information there," I said. "Did she see you?"

"Would I be here if she didn't? She sat down next to me, trapping me in the booth between her and Elena. And here's the thing: Elena helped her! They caught me like a rat in a trap, and then they played with me like . . . like . . ."

"Cats?"

Case nodded. "I didn't even know the snitch *had* friends."

"It's not too unbelievable." Case gave me an odd look, and I added, "We've seen her at school. She sits with a group."

"I always thought they just took pity on her," Case said. His fists clenched.

"You okay?" I asked, pointing at them.

Case frowned at his gloved hands but didn't unclench them. "She's such a monster," he said. "I mean, she's always been, but today she crossed a line. She trapped me, J. *They* trapped me, Elena and Becca. Elena's such a nice girl, most of the time. But then Becca showed up and they sat on either side of me, keeping me from moving. Becca was smiling the whole time, like she enjoyed seeing me squirm."

"She probably did."

"And Elena was just like her, in that moment. She didn't say anything, but that *smile* was just like Becca's. The snitch is poison; she taints everyone around her. You should have heard her. Becca, I mean. When I tried to get away, she mentioned the other schools I work at, naming people I've done jobs for. That's when she mentioned how forgery is a felony and I should really sit back down."

I thought of Becca standing near the edge of my backyard, reminding Case of their conversation. She definitely had a mean streak.

"I . . . I couldn't take it, J. It was like I couldn't breathe. I told her all about the stolen brushes."

Um, what? "Stolen brushes?"

"You know, Heather Caballero's stolen brushes. Heather hired Becca to find some art supplies that were stolen from her."

"No, I didn't know. Stolen brushes? Heather? And what do you mean you told her everything?"

"Becca had a list that Heather gave her of the brushes she had stolen. They're good brushes, and she had a variety. A bright, a fan, an oval wash, a highliner, a round, and a one stroke," Case said, counting them off on his fingers.

"I don't know what any of that means."

"Neither did Becca, but I did. She could have just asked Heather or looked up the different brush types online, but she asked me."

"Heather might have told her what they looked like. She probably asked you just to see how you'd react."

"I think you're right. I wanted to be helpful so she wouldn't bring up felonies again, so I gave her detailed descriptions of each kind of brush stolen. Heck, I drew pictures! But now she knows what to look for. She'll recognize them when she sees them." Case's eyes scanned my room, like he thought the brushes would be lying on my dresser.

"Case. Case!" I grabbed his shoulders. "Calm down. I'm really confused. Why is this a problem for me?"

Case frowned. "You mean, you didn't take the brushes?"

"Not my gig."

"Oh." Case looked relieved. "I mean, I know you don't

steal, but I thought it could be a case of misinterpreted ownership, and then after all that junk with Mark—"

"I swear, if I ever have a job like that again, I will tell you everything." I'd promised my friends that I would inform them of any future jobs I took. Keeping the truth from Case and Hack while stopping Mark had been too hard, and, since it seemed unlikely I'd ever work with Becca again, it shouldn't matter.

It seemed Becca had similar thoughts. Never mind her animosity during our backyard visit—the hatred had been obvious for weeks. On the last day of school and every time I ran into her around the neighborhood, she shot poisonous glances my way. Yesterday I'd seen her glare at my house. I was at my window, reading. She couldn't see me, but it was like, to her, my house was evil because I lived there.

I had no idea why she was mad at me. I mean, we caught Mark, didn't we? I may have broken a few rules in the process, but hey, she seemed fine with that in the end. Right up until she wasn't. So what had happened?

I had a feeling this whole stolen-brush thing was going to come back around to punch me in the face. I sighed. "What happened with Heather?"

"Heather had a party yesterday, just for fun, but also as a release for everyone who's participating in the art contest. Swimming, sodas, that kind of thing. According to the snitch, after the party, Heather noticed that some of her brushes and paints were missing. Her guests had already left, so she couldn't ask them about it. So she hired Becca to find them."

"Huh."

Why didn't she come to me instead of Becca? Heather knew me; I'd done a couple of jobs for her in the past. Also, I charged way less than Becca for services rendered. Detective Becca Mills charged *cash money* for summer work. Why wouldn't Heather hire me for a quick retrieval when all I asked for in return was that my name get passed on and maybe a slice of chocolate cake? Was there some kind of extenuating circumstance that made me unfit for Heather's job, like a conflict of interest or something?

A nasty thought pulled me out of my trance. "You didn't do it, did you?"

"Of course not. Why would I take someone else's brushes when I have my own?"

"Sorry, man. I wasn't thinking." I rubbed my eyes. "Great. Another thief on the loose."

"Story of your life," Case said. "But if Becca listened to me, she'll know not to accuse you." When I raised an eyebrow at him, Case added, "I stuck up for you, you know. After I told the snitch all about the brushes. I mentioned how the brushes stolen were all specialized brushes, used for different purposes. An artist might know the differences between them, but you wouldn't. I explained this, and I told her all about every kind of stroke each brush could make."

I bet she loved that, I thought, smirking. Case tended to wax eloquent when it came to art. Also forgery, though he wouldn't dare discuss that side of his craft with Scottsville Middle's number one under-thirteen private investigator.

"She said she asked me because I'm an expert on art," Case continued, "and because I was in the art contest and everything, but if that were true, she wouldn't have threatened me. She suspects *you*. She had that evil grin she gets when she thinks you're one step away from getting sent to military school. And now she let me go and followed me here, just because she was sure I'd tell you the game was up. I didn't mean to lead her to you. I was just nervous. What if you had taken the brushes for a client who did know their art and which brushes to take?"

"I didn't. And don't worry about it. Becca would have come here eventually."

"Yeah, she would. She's convinced you stole the brushes and she's coming after you."

"She's coming for *us*." When Case gaped at me, I explained, "Think about it: just now, she called us 'a *pair* of thieves.' She knows you're participating in the contest. I'd say she thinks we're in this together and that I stole the brushes to give you an advantage."

Case's shocked expression turned into a mask of rage. He stood up so fast the soda can on the side table shook. "After I helped her and everything, that . . . *busybody* . . . thinks *I'm* the culprit? Me? Why would I steal someone else's brushes? The contest? Does she think I think I can't compete on my own merits and have to *steal* to make myself feel better about the competition?"

"You *are* nervous about it."

"Everyone is. You know what this contest is like."

I did. The Scottsville Youth Art Show and Competition was *the* biggest competitive event Scottsville held over the summer. Sure, you had your occasional street carnival and the Fourth of July was always exciting, with barbecues and parades and the fireworks, and of course, Rick and I dominating the Wilderson Family Picnic water balloon toss. But the art show meant not only outdoor festivities in the park, but prizes and glory for the competitors and bragging rights for their parents. Depending on how many sponsors they had, scholarship money could be even awarded to the winning artists. Those years always went down in history, and not always for the right reasons.

As far as I knew, the prizes this year were minimal. A picture of the winners in the local paper, the *Scottsville Gazette*, and some top-notch art supplies for each of the winners in three divisions: painting, photography, and sculpture. There was a Best Overall Art prize that was awarded to someone whose art was deemed the best in the whole contest out of all three divisions, and they also got art supplies, a picture in the paper, and the honor of having their art on display in Scottsville's art museum until next year's competition.

That last item might explain Case's anxiety. My friend was such an *artiste* that he needed his work to be perfection before anyone saw it, which made him a good forger but a difficult person sometimes. The idea of his painting hanging in a museum for all to see probably gave him insomnia. I guessed the other artists were the same way, but Case took it to a level that proved that freaking out can be its own art.

"It's guilt by association," I told him. "Becca hates me, so she's taking it out on you."

"Oh, that's a great detective strategy. Really sound logic, right there." Case fumed and paced the floor, then added, "Heather's not even competing this year. And if she were, she would have turned in her work weeks ago like the rest of us. It would be pointless for anyone to steal her brushes now. But no, that won't matter to that monster Becca. Right now she's probably out finding skewed evidence on both of us. Well, when I see her, I'm gonna—"

I grabbed his shoulder. "Okay, calm down. You didn't do anything. Remember, she thinks *I'm* a thief, not you. She might think you're involved, but if anyone's on the hook for stealing brushes, it's me."

"Right." Case took a deep breath and sat back down. "Right. You're the one she'll focus on. I should worry about helping you."

"Don't worry about it. Seriously." I sat beside Case and smiled. "Yeah, she'll come after me, but Becca's a good-enough detective that after she works the angles and realizes it couldn't be us, she'll move on."

Case looked skeptical. "You think?"

"She may want me roasted with barbecue sauce, but she has professional pride. She'll find the right person eventually. And, anyway, you saw how good I am at dealing with her."

He smiled. "You *have* had lots of practice."

"I'm a master at Becca-wrangling. Leave this to me. You worry about the contest."

"Then that's okay." Case flopped back on my bed. "I'm sorry I freaked out."

"You're wound tight because of Saturday."

"I'm not wound tight. I'm exactly as anxious as I should be. Do you know how long I've been working on that painting?"

"At least as long as I've been hearing about it."

"Months. And oh man, today is Thursday." Case sat up as though he'd been kicked. "The contest is Saturday. Saturday is the contest. I need to go get ready."

"What do you have to do? The painting is turned in. All you have to do is show up."

"Show up and see everyone else's art, all my competitors. And you've heard about things that happen at this contest."

I frowned and raised a finger. "You mean like that time the two kids started brawling because—"

"Because one guy said the other's painting looked a little 'sloppy in the details,' yes. They were both disqualified."

"That was years ago. We were seven."

"But you still remember it, right?" Case twisted the edge of his Baltimore Ravens jersey. "When we were eight, a girl made a sculpture that everyone said looked like it was made of earwax. We still call it the 'Earwax Statue.' And remember last year?"

"Some guy's painting got made fun of. He lost. Right?" I honestly didn't know too much about that one; after the contest no one talked about it again.

"Right! What if that happens to me? Or what if I spill lemonade on my pants, like that sculptor girl two years ago? She got her picture taken for the paper with a wet stain across her lap. That's it—I have to go home and practice walking with a full glass." Case stood and ran out of my room, downstairs, and out the back door. I heard the door slam.

"Thanks for the intel," I said to my empty room. Then I lay back on the bed.

Case running off without a good-bye illustrated how freaked out he was about this contest. Sure, things happened at the art show, but not every year. Sometimes it was just an art show. An art show with nervous contestants and some quality prizes, but an art show. Maybe Case would calm down a little.

Right, and maybe he'd invite Becca over to play some Madden with Hack and me.

After seeing Case lose it over Becca's interrogation and his almost-fight in the backyard, I was glad I'd never told him or Hack about my time working with Scottsville Middle's most feared detective. I'd never be able to explain it in a way that would prevent Case from feeling betrayed.

But that was an old problem, neatly avoided. I had bigger things to worry about. I hadn't lied when I said Becca was good enough to catch the real thief, but I also knew that she hated me enough to only see the clues that led to me, or worse, to Case and then to me. At least she would at first. She might move on, but only after harassing both of us for days. In fact, I couldn't believe she wasn't already knocking on my door, hand-drawn warrant in hand, ready to accuse me. That could get awkward if Mom and Dad and Rick saw. They wouldn't understand. They'd think she was my girlfriend or something.

Ugh. Can you imagine, Becca and me? We'd get along like two betta fish in the same tank. At least, we would now. There was a moment at the end of the Mark job that I thought Becca and I could be . . . well, no longer enemies, but that passed quickly.

The best plan was to relax. When the detective came, I'd tell her the truth and send her on her way. Case and I were innocent, so we wouldn't be in any trouble.

But trouble has a way of kicking in my door, no matter how many bolts I use.

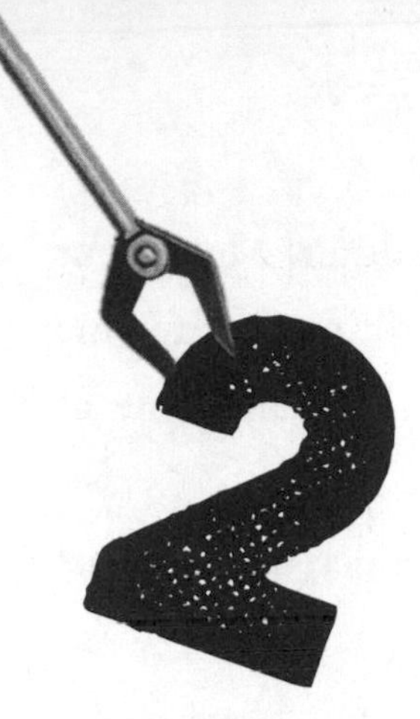

TO MY ASTONISHMENT, BECCA didn't bang on my door that night. Or on Friday. Or on Saturday morning as I put on the blue button-down shirt and khaki shorts Mom has laid out for me—a clear sign that I would dress nicely for the art contest or I wasn't going.

(I'd fought Mom on this. I'd protested that Case was the one hoping to get his picture in the *Scottsville Gazette*, not me, and that no one would care what I looked like as long as my jeans weren't torn. But Mom insisted that "the Scottsville Art Show is a semiformal event and it shows respect to the artists and the community to dress nicely." I know when to pick my battles.)

I frowned at myself (at least I didn't have to wear a tie) and waited for Becca to kick down my door as my family left to pick up Hack and then go to the art show. It didn't happen. Maybe it wouldn't. Maybe our time together had left her with enough respect for me to check her suspicions before she threatened me at home.

Or maybe she was waiting to pounce at the most annoying possible moment.

"Are you ready?" Mom called.

"I got to wear jeans last year. Tell me why I can't now," I said after I'd come downstairs.

"Because we all know you and Hack will rush the stage if Casey wins anything," Dad said. "If you're going to act wild, you may as well look nice for it."

I shrugged. "As long as there's a reason."

Rick came downstairs wearing a tie. "At least you got a reason. I'm still waiting for mine."

I would be the only one attending the show. Mom and Dad were taking Rick to visit some local colleges. Just as well—I didn't need his moronic comments about whether a monkey or a two-year-old human could create better art than the stuff on display.

Mom smiled at him. "You look very nice. It's important to make a good impression when we talk to your future professors."

"Yeah, but isn't it basically lying? They'll never see me wearing a tie again," Rick said. "I'd hate to mislead them."

"You're wearing it," Dad told him. "Lie or not. Now let's go before Hack gets himself grounded again."

Rick leaned down to me. "Dr. Evil, how long, in your professional opinion, can I go before I ditch the tie and no one notices?"

I smiled. "Take it off in the car and claim you'll put it back on later. They'll be distracted by the campus."

"I knew I could count on your nefarious mind."

The Family Wilderson got into the car and went to pick up Hack. His nickname comes from the time he first showed Case and me how he could get into his mom's e-mail and social network accounts, then later when he "accidentally" got every Scottsville Middle School computer stuck on a video of a dancing banana on the first day of online math testing. Most adults called him by his given name, Paul, but my parents had heard us use his nickname so often they had adopted it too.

Hack hopped in beside Rick and me, grinning widely. "Free to go," he said. "I was extra careful not to get grounded for Case's big day."

I snorted. "You'll wish you were under house arrest once Case gets to talking about art."

"Which he will."

"As sure as balloon animals are pointless."

"Was that a pun?"

"Not intended, but I'll take credit anyway."

Hack buckled up and peered at me through smudged glasses. "Has . . . Becca talked to you lately?"

"Why would she do that?"

"Case called my house Thursday, freaking out. Mom was home, but she was busy, and I'm not allowed near the phone without parental supervision, though I heard the voice mail later. All I picked out was 'sorry' and 'Becca' and 'trouble.' Care to elaborate?"

"Shh!" I peeked at my family. Dad glanced at me but then turned his attention back to the road. Rick raised an eyebrow, smirked, and shook his head before looking out the window.

"They can't know," I whispered. "I'll tell you later."

"We're here," Mom said. I looked out the window and saw the Edgar T. Fitzsimmons Memorial Park, right next to the Grecian-style art museum that looked impressive but was smaller than you'd expect. Welcome to the annual Scottsville Youth Art Show and Competition, held every year outside in the park so visitors could enjoy the summer sun along with their kids' artwork.

As soon as the engine ceased, Hack and I unhooked our seat belts and hopped out of the car. "Bye! See ya! Gotta go find Case."

"Hold on," Mom said. "We can't just leave you here. We need to make an emergency plan."

It didn't take long to decide that Case's parents were in charge. Mom gave me her cell phone and wanted me to call every hour, but Dad talked her out of it. The deal changed to me calling if there was any trouble or if our plans changed.

"We'll be back at five," Mom said. "Will you be okay?"

"Sure, Mom. It's an art show. How much trouble could we get into?"

Mom narrowed her eyes at Hack. I clapped my hands and said, "Better go find Case! Love you!" Then I turned to leave, pulling Hack behind me, as Rick and my parents left.

Hack and I ran through the park to the Contestants' Tent, where Case and his family would be waiting for us.

"So," Hack asked as we walked, "what happened with Becca?"

"Okay, here's the deal. Case came by and told me, *still* freaking out, that Becca is working a stolen art supplies case and she thinks I'm involved."

"Surprise, surprise." Hack rubbed his head, mussing his once well-combed red hair. "You weren't, were you?"

I stared at him and he raised his hands as we wove through crowds of pastel-clad visitors. "Sorry, sorry," he said. "After that Mark thing—"

"I swear, I'll tell you everything. That was one time. Anyway, it got better. Becca followed Case to my house and threatened us both from my backyard. Rick almost heard her."

Hack made a face. "I'm sorry you have to deal with her so much. She's such a witch. Did you know the parental locks on my school computer account were *her* idea?"

"Like those stop you."

"Yeah, but it's the principle of the thing."

"Well, it's a nice day. Try to forget about Becca and enjoy it. That's what I'm going to do."

It was a perfect morning. The sun shone, bright and yellow, in a blue sky, and the wind blowing through carried just enough of the past spring's chill to counter the warmth of the summer sun without raising goose bumps. I'd have to enjoy it while it lasted; it would get hotter and more humid as the day went on. I noted a stand labeled SNOW CONES! CHEAP! with a hand-painted sign and decided I'd have to come back later when the day felt more seasonal. Maybe a few times.

Inexpensive snow cones, no Becca, and a whole day of hanging out with my friends: life was perfect.

When we reached the Contestants' Tent, a big white-and-green striped canvas pavilion, a woman tried to stop us from entering. After we told her our names, she let us in. Case had already pulled strings to get us on "the list."

That would sound so much cooler if it wasn't for a community art show.

"Ouch," Hack said once we were inside. He took off his glasses and used them to scratch his head.

"No kidding." I stuck my hands in my pockets (stocked with a few dollars, a pack of gum, and my homemade lock-pick set) to keep from sympathetically fidgeting.

That's because the atmosphere in the tent was tense. Case's attitude at my house Thursday night was devil-may care compared to this. Although the tent was comfortable, the tablecloths and flower centerpieces bright and festive, and the refreshment table stacked high with everything from celery sticks to iced brownies (not chocolate cake, but beggars can't be choosers), the people milling around acted like prisoners on death row.

A girl at one table chewed on a twisted napkin, her eyes vacant. A boy paced up and down the side of the tent, muttering to himself in a way that wouldn't be out of place in a *Lord of the Rings* movie. Several girls were crying, and all around I saw helicopter parents whirring over their offspring. Shoulders were hunched and the air was full of the sound of grinding teeth. Man, this place was going to reek of sweat and desperation by the time the judges announced the winners later that afternoon.

Not everyone was a mess, I realized. Two girls were talking cheerfully. A skinny boy in a vest and a bow tie was even whistling. What was wrong with *him*?

"J! Over here." Hack waved me over to a shaking Case, who was sitting with his family at a table beside the refreshments. His parents were talking to some other child artist's parents.

"Move over," Hack said, nudging Case's ten-year-old sister, Mia. She scowled at him and stood up, emptying the seat for me, before walking over to join her parents and the other two mini Kingstons: Brielle, age seven, and Case's one and only brother, Bradley, age two.

"Thanks, Mia!" I called, and she glared at me as I hurried over.

"Don't be like this, man," I said, passing Case and Hack to grab a plate, a brownie, and three forks off the refreshment table. I handed out the forks. "The art is in. It's over. It's like when you hand a test in but it's not graded. There's nothing to do but wait, so why worry?"

Case looked up at me. He rubbed his hands, which, despite the summer heat and his shirt and 49ers logo tie, were still in his Eagles gloves. A pen rested in its usual place above his ear. "Waiting for a grade. That's supposed to make me feel better?"

"Let me try again. It's like you're a kicker for the NFL. You've kicked the ball, and it's up and hanging in the air. There's nothing you or anyone else can do but wait."

Case groaned and put his face down on the table. "Somehow that's even worse."

Hack draped an arm around Case's shoulders as I picked up a flyer lying on the table. "Come on," he said cheerfully, cutting out a piece of the brownie with his fork. "How about you, me, and J go out there and make fun of all the art that makes no sense?" He popped the brownie bite into his mouth.

"Yeah," I said, nudging Case to take his piece of the brownie. Not a chocolate cake, so not really right, but it was better than nothing. At least it was iced. I held up the flyer. "With a theme of 'Dreamscapes and Nightmares,' there's got to be a lot to mock."

Case snatched the flyer out of my hand. "It's bad taste to mock another's artwork, unless it's like that painting last year. Why do you think I'm in here?" He took a bite of the brownie and licked the icing off the fork. "I don't want to accidentally run into someone while I'm looking at their work because then I'd have to comment on it. What if I don't like it?"

"Lie," Hack and I said in unison.

Case gave us death glares. "Maybe you can tell a convincing lie off-the-cuff, but there's a reason why I do work where I can try again if I make a mistake."

I aimed my fork for a corner of the brownie, and Case and Hack both dueled me off with their forks. "Fine. Take it. What do I care? Okay, Case, how about I go back out there and scope it out? Tell you which pieces to avoid and where they are. Is there a map of this place?"

Case handed me a map of the park with lines and little numbered squares where the art would be on display along the sidewalks. A key on the back revealed which art belonged to which artist. "Thanks. I'll check it out. I only pray that after listening to you for years and years I can tell the good art from the less-good art."

Case's gaze sharpened. "Was that a shot?"

I stood. "Just a statement of fact. Back in a few. If I'm not, assume Becca found me and threw me into a snow-cone stand."

Hack's head snapped up. "They have those?"

"We passed one on the way in, just past the park gate." I waved. "See you later."

I escaped out into the sunshine. The aura of anxiety in the tent was suffocating. Had it been that bad last year, when Case wasn't in the competition? I mean, I understood that people were nervous about their art being judged; the contest officials hadn't let the judges see the art until today, so no one knew how they'd react. But why worry when there was nothing more you could do?

Outside, I could breathe freely. I wandered through the sculpture "garden," an empty area at the center of the park where the sculptor contestants' pieces stood on pedestals. They were made of everything from paper to clay, wax to metal. I didn't understand the point of most of them and some looked hastily made, but a few were exquisite (love that word). I peered at a wax statue of a woman that was hollow on the back side. On the inside, the artist had carved many tiny pictures of people, animals, cities, and landscapes. The name card read, "*A World Within* by Sandra Lynn, 8th grade." I liked it, so I circled that piece on the map for Case.

From there I moved to the paintings. While the sculptures had their own little garden in the center of the park, the photographs and paintings hung on temporary walls, bulletin board–like things that folded like accordions, along the paths of the park. Each wall was assigned a letter.

Maybe the paintings were just more accessible to me, or maybe I'd picked up more about painting because Case was, first and foremost, a painter, but I had an easier time spotting the really good paintings. On Wall E, I found a painting of a girl dressed as a superhero that was so realistic I thought I'd strayed into the photographs. I made a note on the map. But another on Wall A looked like someone had microwaved a cat (not a fluffy one) and painted the results, so I put an *X* over that one. Another looked like something I'd find hanging outside a kindergarten room, but much more intricate. I didn't know how to respond to that one, so I put a question mark on the map next to it.

I found Case's work on Wall C: a black-and-white painting of a moonlit beach that ran more impressionist than realist (what? Sometimes I actually listen to Case when he talks), which meant I had to stand back from it to get the full effect. The only color was in the places where light would shine. The moon, the light on the waves, and the fire were all painted in a spectrum of vibrant colors. He'd titled it *Visible Light*. I admired it for a while, and moved on down the paved path.

As I was looking at a well-crafted but somewhat strange painting of an army of demon zombie hamsters on Wall B, I heard loud footsteps approaching me from behind. My neck prickled. I knew those footsteps.

I whirled around to find Becca Mills, in a pink blouse and a skirt with blue flowers on it, coming at me like a runaway train. Her grin was the smile a mouse sees right before the cobra strikes.

THE TRICK TO DEALING WITH warpath Becca Mills is to never let her smell fear. Despite my shock, I just rolled my eyes and plastered myself to the temporary wall, between the hamster painting and vivid picture of a sunrise. Or sunset. Whatever.

"What do you think you're doing?" Becca hissed, her face close to mine.

"Assuming the position," I said. "You know, so you don't have to slam me against the wall. Between you and me, I don't think these things are structurally sound. Shall we test it?" I leaned back, making the wall wobble.

Becca's eyes bugged and she reached out to stabilize the wall. Before she touched it, the rocking stopped. I laughed, and she recoiled like I had thrown boiling water at her face.

Scowling, Becca said, "I mean, what are you doing

here? Aren't thieves supposed to lay low after the job is done?"

"Ah." Leave it to her to forget even after I'd explained it a hundred times. I raised a finger. "Maybe they are. But I am not a thief. I'm a—"

"Retrieval specialist, I know. I could call a duck a grizzly bear, but that doesn't mean I'll play dead when it goes quacking by."

"You should. It would be fun to watch." I nodded, like we'd just made a plan, and fixed my eyes on hers. I kept mine soft, like chocolate warmed by a toasted marshmallow.

Her own gray ones blazed like dry beach sand in August. "You know what else would be fun to watch? You, handing over six brushes and two bottles of tempera paint."

Cocking my head, I said, "Wait, I'm confused. Are you robbing me? Am I still the thief?"

"Absolutely." Becca placed her arm against my neck, not choking me but barring me from moving away from the wall. "Don't play dumb. I know you and Casey came up with some plan after he ran to your house, but this is just sad. Time to come clean about the burglary. Heather Caballero? Wouldn't have been hard, with all those people. Just walk in, walk out . . . So, what are they going to be used for? Is Casey working on something behind the scenes?"

Not good. Time to tell her the truth and send her packing. "No, and neither am I. Sure, I know about the theft. After you grilled him, Case told me that Heather's art supplies were stolen. That's what friends *do*. But that's all I know. Why didn't Heather call me if she had something stolen from her? I thought she appreciated my work."

Becca rolled her eyes. "*Of course* you've worked for her in the past. If you must know, a friend told her that I was the right person to call to solve this crime."

"And that friend would be?"

"Look, Wilderson, you're not the only show in town. A lot of people prefer getting help from an *honest* professional, instead of someone who steals art supplies to help his crooked friend."

"Case has more paintbrushes than a pizza place has pepperoni. Why would he steal art supplies?"

"The pool party must have made things convenient. You could slip in and out with the stolen brushes and paints, and no one would see you."

"Are you even listening to me?"

"Casey attended Heather's party. The same Casey that has an entry in this very art contest. Sounds like means and motive to me."

I laughed. "That's where you're wrong. Case was

invited, but he didn't attend. He was with me Saturday. Hack got a new game, and Case and I were trying to figure out the cheat codes so there would be at least some competition when we played him on Sunday. No one was at any party."

Becca smiled. "Liar."

"Not this time. I think you need to check your facts before you make wild accusations. You know me. Am I lying about this?"

Becca's eyes were like a laser scan, reading me up and down and turning my guilt levels into decodable numbers. That girl knows lies better than anyone; she can usually see through mine even if she can't find hard evidence.

Finally her gaze dropped. "You didn't steal from Heather." I shook my head and she sighed. She really wanted it to be me. "I guess I'll have to double-check my sources," she said.

"You can check our alibis with our moms, if you want. Also, you haven't thought through this theory of yours. How would stealing Heather's art supplies help Case? He, and the rest of the contestants, turned in their art weeks ago. Why take supplies now?"

Becca glared at me. "I've thought it through, Wilderson. First off, the brushes were high-quality. The prizes at the competition are the best of the best. Polished wood handles, natural bristles—Heather says they were expensive and any artist would want them."

"Then why only take a few different brushes and not the whole set? If the thief envied Heather's prize brushes, they'd take all of them, not just some."

"Yes, Wilderson, I thought of that too," Becca said with mock patience. "It made sense to me when your *friend* told me the brushes can make any kind of stroke. You see, the art may be in, but the judges haven't seen it yet, and final judging isn't until four this afternoon. The art is just hanging out where everyone can access it. That opens a nice window for sabotage, using stolen brushes that can make any kind of mark, don't you think?"

"Okay, listen, I know you think I'm a creep, but I would never in a million years stoop to something as low as sabotage—" I stopped as the word caught in my mouth. "Wait. You think the brushes and paints were stolen to be used for *sabotage*?" Case was in the contest. Sabotage . . .

My heart raced on behalf of my high-strung friend. Becca was a good PI. If she thought someone had stolen those brushes and paints to damage the best pieces of art before the judges could see them, then Case might be in trouble. For all his worry, he was a good artist. He might even be a favorite.

A group of high school kids walked past, and one guy

gave us an odd look. Becca and I both glanced at her arm, still pressed against my neck. She dropped it and stepped back.

Freed, I made a show of straightening up. I ran my hand through my hair, making it stick up. It probably looked cool; I'd keep it.

"Seriously, sabotage?" I asked.

Becca rolled her eyes. "You're not the thief this time. My thoughts on *my* case are none of your business. By the way, your hair looks like a dead hedgehog." She walked away without another word. It felt weird, not being the one she was chasing.

So I patted my hair flat and followed Becca. She turned left and so did I, keeping a reasonable tailing distance between us. If she wouldn't work with me, I'd have to catch the thief myself. Her leads could be a start.

When we'd reached the sculpture garden, Becca stopped and turned around. "Did you think I wouldn't notice you following me?"

"Do you think sabotage is a real possibility? Tell me the truth, and I swear, I'll leave you alone."

Becca rolled her eyes again. "It's a possibility I can't rule out. The art show is the only reason someone would steal Heather's paints and just a few brushes, but it's too late to use them to make something to submit. So, another motive would be to tamper with the art that's here. Still only one possibility of many, but serious enough that I wanted to be here to stop it."

I nodded. Becca was a good detective, and she had a point. Sabotage was serious, and I couldn't let it slide. But what was I going to do about it? I was a retrieval specialist, not a detective. My skills lay in finding stolen objects and returning them, not putting clues together to catch a criminal. For that, I needed a detective. I needed Becca.

I stuck my thumbs in my pockets, letting my hands hang free. "I want in."

"Oh no. Not again." She turned and sped into a crowd.

So I hurried after her, dodging passersby as she tried to lose me. It wasn't hard to keep up; I just had to follow the aura of ice-cold fury wafting through the summer day. Didn't hurt that I was also a sprinter on the school's track team. "Hear me out," I said, running beside her. "You're after a stolen set of brushes and paints, right? And you want to get them back? It's a retrieval job. That's what I do. You know I'm good at it."

She aimed a shove at me, which I dodged. "You said you'd leave me alone if I answered your question. Go find your friends and stay out of my way."

I thought about doing just that; Case and Hack were

probably wondering where I was, and I had sworn to both of them that the next time I worked a job, they'd know every detail. Getting into this one meant that not only could I not tell them that Becca and I were teaming up again, but I couldn't tell them I was working a job, period. Not easy to do, especially when I'd promised to support Case today.

But that word haunted me like yesterday's bean burrito. *Sabotage.* No one deserved that, especially not Case. Speeding up, I passed Becca and turned on my heel, literally getting in her way. I spread my arms out, blocking her as thoroughly as I could. "I'm not taking no for an answer on this one, not when you think the thief may use those brushes for sabotage."

"What does it matter to you? You're innocent. This time."

"Case is entered in the competition. His painting is hanging on one of these walls."

Her eyes widened slightly and she bit her lip. "You think the saboteur could attack him."

I nodded. "I'm here for my friend. If you let me, I could help you. You know I could."

She hunched her shoulders and glared at me. "I hate you."

"I know." I waited with bated breath. (Another

expression I don't understand. It's not spelled like *bait*, so that's not related.)

Becca opened her mouth, and for a moment I thought she'd say yes, that I could help her, but then she shook her head. "Nope. Not this. Not again."

Oh, come on! "Why not? We got our man last time."

"Remember what happened after, though?"

"Uh, you hated me again?"

"Yeah. That."

I shrugged. I still wasn't sure what the big deal was. I'd deleted some pictures on her camera because they incriminated Case, and suddenly it was like *I* was the thief who stole the master key *and* perpetrated the worst crime wave Scottsville Middle had seen during my sixth-grade year.

"That was then. This is now. And you need my help. There are too many people here, too many suspects."

Becca scoffed but then looked around the park, those laser eyes trying to read the guilt of the people walking around. Her shoulders tightened. Too many people to interrogate, no clear place to start.

What if I offered a gimme? "I could take you where I'd start first, if this were my job."

"Tell me."

"No. Show only." I had to get on this job somehow.

Becca glared at me. I knew what she saw: a thief, a common criminal. But I hoped she understood me enough to know that I would do whatever it took to keep Case safe.

"This is my world," I reminded her. "I know thieves. I know what they do, how they act, and where they'd go first."

"Takes one to know one." She sighed. "Fine. But that doesn't mean we're working together on this."

Whatever floats your boat. Didn't matter what she called it—in was in. "Sounds great. Follow me."

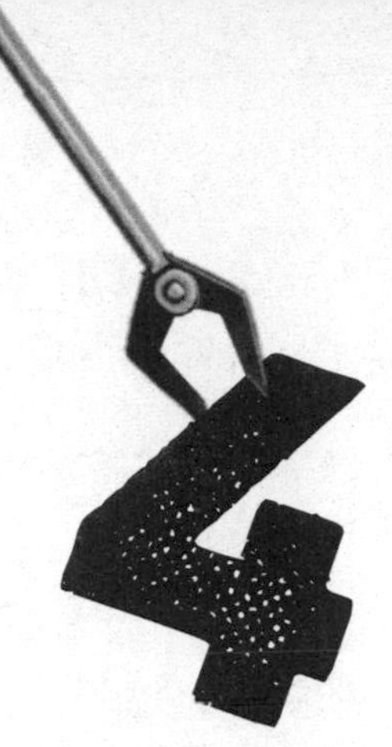

I LED BECCA THROUGH THE park, grinning like I was in a toothpaste commercial. I'd won. I mean, I *had* put myself in a position where, once again, my every move would be scrutinized by the wickedly observant Becca Mills, not to mention my best friend might be in danger of sabotage, but I'd *won*. I'd gotten Becca to do something she didn't want to do. Now I could take her to the tent and show her all those lovely high-strung suspects and . . . oh.

I couldn't take her to the tent. Case and Hack were in the tent, and Case was already upset. If I came in with Becca Mills—without her dragging me against my will—forget *upset*. Forget angry. They'd be rabid-dog, exploding-Vesuvius, school-janitor-after-a-food-fight *furious*. Worse than Case's outburst on Thursday. Especially after I promised to tell them everything about every job from now on.

"What?" Becca was scowling at me. I realized I'd stopped walking.

I couldn't go in that tent with her. As soon as I showed my face, Case and Hack would see me. With *her*. I'd never be able to explain to them why, when I heard of potential danger, I went to her and not them. I could hardly explain it to myself. Why did I join up with the girl who wanted me locked in in-school suspension until I graduated high school, the girl who harassed my friends, instead of the guys who always had my back?

"Well?" Becca said, her frown deepening.

Come on, Wilderson, think fast. There had to be somewhere else I could take her. I pulled out the map of the park, hoping the map's bird's-eye view would give me an idea.

Bird's-eye view. That was it!

"This way," I said, grabbing Becca's hand and pulling her toward the art museum.

She yanked it out of my grasp. "Don't. Touch. Me."

The touch had done the trick. Becca was so annoyed at my sticky fingers touching her long arm of the law that she focused on that and not on my hesitation. She followed me toward the museum without asking questions.

Which was all for the best, anyway. Going to the tent, like I planned, would make my friends mad. My second step, going and, uh, *taking a tour* of those suspects' personal belongings, wasn't likely to thrill my new partner. She already didn't trust me any farther than she could throw me. (Though, to be fair, she could probably throw me farther than most people could, despite her short height. Being on the Scottsville Middle field team for shot put has to count for something.)

But I digress. The point is, if Plan A was a bust, have a Plan B. That's the secret to good retrieving.

As I led the way, Becca eyed all the sheds, pavilions, and Dumpsters we passed. *She thinks I'm taking her to where I believe the thief hid the stolen goods*, I thought. But I was no amateur. This early in the job, with such a small, easily hidden payload, I had no idea where the thief was keeping the art supplies. On most jobs, I know who did it and where they stashed it; my clients tell me. It's the retrieval they pay me for. I don't solve mysteries, like a certain tiny, scary snitch I could name.

"This way," I said, beckoning the tiny, scary snitch over to the museum.

Becca stopped and looked up at the white marble building. "You're kidding. You think the thief stashed the stuff in here?"

"Here?" I asked as we climbed the stairs to the front doors. "Among the Van Goghs and Picassos? This is a museum for paintings, not painting supplies. Well, except for the gift shop. But I think a store may be a little insecure, don't you?" When we reached the doors, I opened one and held it for her. Mom raised a gentleman, after all. Without looking at me, Becca opened the other one and let herself inside. So I shrugged and followed her in.

"Although," I said as we walked into the atrium, "hiding something in the Lost and Found here isn't that bad an idea."

Becca raised an eyebrow at me. "Not like you've ever done that."

"Of course not. That would be underhanded." I grinned at her. She responded by scrunching up her face at me. I could feel her desire to punch me in the face like . . . well, a punch in the face. Then she closed her eyes, took a deep breath, and nodded for me to keep showing her the way.

I couldn't keep leading Becca forever. I'd have to get back to Case soon, or he'd suspect something was amiss. But first I had to get Becca chasing a lead long enough so I could go back to the tent, check in with my friends, and do a little snooping of my own.

"So, master thief," Becca said, "you think the art supplies are hidden in the Lost and Found?"

"Not today. With the contest, the place is going to be full of people looking for their lost hat or glasses or baby bottle or whatever. The supplies would get noticed. But if you'd like to go in there and check—"

"Maybe later. So where, then?"

I led Becca past the Lost and Found, past the room with the museum's rentable lockers (otherwise known as "a good place to practice safecracking, since most of them are empty"), and to the museum's sweeping central staircase.

Then I realized I should have sold the Lost and Found more. I could have left Becca neck-deep in people's lost items while I hurried to the Contestants' Tent, talked to Case and Hack, and drew up a suspect list. Then I could have returned, apologized for leaving Becca in a fruitless job, and introduced her to the suspects without having to go near the tent. But now I had to take Becca to my bird's-eye view. I hate it when a good idea comes too late.

"Up there," I said, pointing at the stairs. "Overlook on the fourth floor."

"This museum has an overlook? Why?"

"You'll see."

"Lead on." She climbed the first staircase and tilted her head. "How do you know about the overlook? I never took you for an art guy. Unless . . . unless you're planning something big." She glared at me as we continued our climb.

"By 'big,' you mean 'thief-y.'" I laughed and shook my head. "Even if I was a thief, this would be above my pay grade. They have security devices on the art, you know."

"Then how do you know about the overlook?"

"Case." Becca raised an eyebrow at me, and I explained. "When you're friends with an art nerd like Case, you learn things you never wanted to know. Like, how the park outside the museum is actually also a work of art. It was designed by Edgar T. Fitzsimmons, the man they named the park after, in the 1930s, and his family donated the plans and the money to make it happen after his death. And, as Case made sure I knew, you can see the whole thing from a special observation deck." I grinned at Becca. "The whole park, easily visible."

We reached the fourth floor and I pointed down a hall at a pair of French doors leading to a balcony. Becca looked, then smirked at me. "If this was your case, the first thing you'd do is go see an art exhibit? Classy of you."

"It is an art show, after all." Smooth as always. I wished I had a tie I could straighten. I settled for opening a door for Becca. Once again, she ignored me and opened the other. "That's getting old, by the way," I said.

"Stop acting like a gentleman. I know what you are." Becca walked to the balcony railing and leaned on it, peering out over the park. I joined her, careful not to stand where I could be seen from the ground. This bird's-eye view thing had a catch: if Case and Hack saw me up here with Becca, I'd be dead. Dead, buried, with little white maggots crawling up my nose to eat my brain.

Becca sighed, this time with pleasure, and I smiled. Mr. Fitzsimmons's park was beautiful from above. Even the trees contributed to the design. It looked better when the temporary walls for the art exhibits were down, like it was the first time Case forced me up here. But the walls couldn't hide how the paths curved in gentle arcs away from a center piazza, where the art show's sculpture garden was. Paintings and photographs followed each path, each arm, all of which ended in a circle around a flower bed of a different color.

"Kind of looks like an octopus juggling, right?" I said. "Anyway, from here you can see the whole park. And everyone in it."

"Including the thief." Becca smiled. "Or anything out of the ordinary."

"You can watch for patterns. Most people are wandering from artwork to artwork—"

"But the thief would be different," Becca interrupted. "They'd be part of the flow, but they'd make mistakes. Act nervous. Stop too often. Glance around too much." Becca looked at me. "You'd really come here first?"

I shrugged, acting smooth. "Can't do a job without intel. And few thieves are smooth after their job. They act guilty because they are."

"You don't act guilty."

"That's because I'm not a thief, *and* I'm the best at what I do." Before you go critiquing my humility, I'm not bragging. It's a statement of fact. I'm not a thief, and I *am* the best at what I do. The fact that I am the only retrieval specialist in Scottsville is irrelevant.

"Thief."

"Retrieval specialist."

Becca groaned and turned her attention back to the park below. I pulled out the crumpled map of the park and handed it to her. "Here. The paintings are along these paths," I said, pointing them out. "If your thief took painting supplies, this is where he'd be."

"Or she."

"Or she. It may take a few minutes, but I guarantee the guilty party will make their move." I started to pull away, but Becca, without looking at me, hooked my arm and yanked me back. Getting away to go talk to Case and Hack wasn't going to be as easy as I'd hoped.

She looked over the map and then at the park. "What are these circles and *X*s on the map for?" she asked. "Are these pieces you're planning to hit, or lift, or whatever?"

"You make retrieving sound like a day at the gym," I said. "It's something for Case. Ignore the marks."

Becca pointed at the paper. "These? Or those *marks* down below?"

I snatched the map back. "If you're going to mock retrieval jargon, at least use it correctly."

"People who you're intending to con or steal from? That's not the definition?"

"It is, but I'm not planning anything, so no one is a mark." Frustrated, I waved at the park. "Just keep looking for the odd one out. I'll be back."

"Where are you going?"

"Bathroom. Keep looking. The thief will appear."

She sighed. "Sounds so easy. Why do I get the feeling it won't be?"

"Because it never is, especially when you're involved."

Becca pointed. "Is that person acting guilty to you?"

I glanced over the railing just enough to see, then stepped back before anyone could spot me. Then I noticed Becca had been watching me the whole time.

She gave me her snake smile. "So, *that's* why you have to go to the 'bathroom.' Because I'm the complication in your work. Can't be seen with me, huh? Don't want it to get out that Wilderson's working with the fuzz?"

"The fuzzy what? And do *you* want it to get out that

Jeremy Wilderson and Becca Mills are an item?"

She reddened. "Just remember Mark and who came to who for help with a job gone bad."

"Whom."

"What?"

"Who came to *whom*."

"No one cares but you and your Language Arts–teacher mom. Just stay close from now on."

I sighed, trying to work out how to get away before Becca noticed the—

"What's that?"

And *that* was the part where my brilliant plan to keep Becca away from Case and Hack blew up in my face. Becca was pointing at the Contestants' Tent.

"Nothing important. Just some tent."

"Really." She held out her hand. "Give me the map."

"That's not necessary. Let's keep looking. We'll see something suspicious if we keep looking." I had to get out of there!

"I see something suspicious now," Becca said, narrowing her eyes at me. "Give me the map, or I'll charge you with obstruction of justice."

"With what authority? School's out; you're not a peer mentor anymore."

Becca jabbed a finger at my face. "You wanted an

invite to this party, Wilderson. You fought to help me in this case. I wanted nothing to do with you. Still don't. So, if you aren't going to help me, get out of my way."

So that was the ultimatum. Next time, I'd like a job where I actually enjoy myself.

Glaring at Becca, I tossed her the wadded-up map. "It's the Contestants' Tent," I said. "Where the artists hang out when they're not out admiring or ragging on one another's art."

Becca gaped at me. "Why, why, *why* did we not go there first? All those suspects, witnesses . . . Why are we up here when we could be down there? Why would you come to a balcony when you could be there, finding your thief?"

"What does it matter? You have your lead." I felt kind of annoyed. Partially because I'd had to give up important, difficult information to Becca without hearing so much as a "please" and "thank you," but also because I had possibly cost us valuable time in catching the thief by leading Becca here when we could have gotten some real intel at the tent. As much as I wanted to keep our collaboration a secret, if Case got sabotaged because of this detour, I'd wish I strutted into the tent, Becca on my arm, and let the chips fall wherever.

(Okay, so Becca wouldn't take my arm unless she was

twisting it behind my head, but you get the picture.)

Becca grabbed my arm and torqued it, hauling me away from the balcony's railing in the most painful way possible (see what I mean?). "Come on, then. We've wasted enough time on your fool's errand. Or is that what you wanted?" she asked, squinting at me.

"And we're back to 'suspicious of Wilderson.'" I groaned. "I'm not involved."

"Really? Those marks on your map would be a convenient way to keep track of what you'd like to sabotage later."

"That's insulting. I would never sabotage anything."

"But maybe your friend Casey would. You did say the marks on the map were for him."

"Case isn't a saboteur or a thief."

"He could have hired someone to steal Heather's stuff and tricked you into marking the good art for him."

"He wouldn't do that."

"Are you sure he tells you everything? Like you tell him everything?"

She had me there. I fumed a little and shrugged hard, pulling my arm out of her grip. "You know what? You're right. I don't tell him everything. He probably doesn't tell me everything. But I know Case, and he'd freak out if you hinted he'd sabotage anyone. Case is an honest artist."

"If he's so honest, he should have no problem explaining himself to me."

Oh, sure. That would go well. Becca storms in, and then Case instantly goes on the defensive. Doesn't matter that he's innocent. It wouldn't look good.

"Why don't you stay up here?" I said. "Look at the patterns and find clues. I can use my connections to identify suspects at the tent."

Becca snorted. "Like I'd let you out of my sight."

I raised my arms. "Sooner or later you're going to have to. How about this? You search for clues around the paintings, and I talk up the artists in the tent. It won't seem strange that I'm there because I'm listed under 'friends and family.'"

"I thought you wanted to be on this case."

"Stop playing that card. I want to help, but I can't be seen with you." How could I work with Becca but keep my friends from finding out? Splitting up was the only option.

"You're good at spotting clues other people don't see, and you know what they prove," I continued. "Do that and let me work my own angle."

"No, you don't." Becca grabbed my arm, right behind the elbow, like a real cop. "I don't trust your *angles*. Next thing I know, you could have stolen half the art in this museum."

"Despite their security systems, and with no planning? I'm flattered. What else? Do you have a picture of me under your pillow?"

"Sure do. I drew thick black bars over your face. It helps me sleep at night." Becca tightened her grip on my arm and pulled me forward. "Come on. You're just going to have to get used to the idea of having no friends."

"I thought that was your shtick."

At that, Becca dug her fingers into my arm, making me gasp. "Okay," I said, trying to pull her nails out of my skin. "That was out of line. But I need to be the one in the tent, and I can't be seen with you. I become less valuable to you if people know we're working together. Some people are more willing to talk to someone . . . on the outside."

"On the underground, you mean."

I sighed. "Like it or not, I hear different things than you do because of who I am. That's why you let me help, right?"

That should sell it.

Becca pursed her lips and let go of my arm. "So you can't be seen with me and I won't let you out of my sight. We may as well call the job now, tell Heather she's not getting her stuff back. As for the contest, forget it. Sabotage galore."

"Not acceptable. I know." I paced the balcony, massaging the little red crescents Becca's nails had left in my flesh. What could I do? I couldn't be seen with Becca. Wait: *I* couldn't be seen with Becca. But if I was someone else . . .

"I have an idea," I said. "It's a little radical, but it should work. We'll be able to pass in and out of the Contestants' Tent with no one, not even my friends, the wiser."

Becca nodded. "Lay it on me."

"I'll tell you on the way," I said.

We went back to the balcony doors. I held one open for Becca because it annoyed her so much. She ignored it, but after she was inside the museum, she spun around and closed the door on me. She laughed through the glass and hurried away, leaving me to catch up.

"I HATE YOUR PLAN," BECCA grumbled. "A lot."

"Trust me. No one will look twice at us," I said.

"Oh yes, they will."

Becca and I had ransacked the museum's Lost and Found and located a couple of disguises. She'd leaned toward dark jackets and hats, but I'd talked her into something more . . . colorful.

Becca was wearing a bright blue muumuu and orange hat, along with some mismatched shoes we'd found to change her gait. I had buttons in my shoe for the same reason (it was her idea; I had no clue she knew that trick).

"Okay, maybe they will." I was wearing a gray trilby hat (a brimmed hat smaller than a fedora; thank my dad's old movies for teaching me that) and a huge red, black, and green poncho that, judging by the crusty bits near the neck, someone had blown their nose on. "But that's the point. They'll notice the costume and not our faces. It's like my Boy Scout uniform. Have you ever noticed that people in uniform don't get seen? The uniform is seen and processed but not the face. People in uniform blend in to the background."

I'd tried to explain this to her in the Lost and Found, and I'd thought I'd succeeded. Dressing in a uniform gives you an identity based on that uniform. If I'm wearing my Boy Scout gear, people see a Boy Scout, not me. Weird costumes meant people would see and remember weird costumes, not our faces. I can be pretty brilliant sometimes.

"That makes sense when there are other Boy Scouts in the world, but no one dresses like this, Wilderson," she said.

"We're at an art show. If anyone does, they'd do it here. Come on, at least pretend you chose these clothes when you got up this morning." Raising my chin and strutting, actually *strutting*, I took off the hat and spun it on my finger.

"The hat doesn't work if you're not wearing it," Becca muttered.

"Doesn't matter when I have this poncho," I said.

The poncho also hid the way my middle was somewhat bulgier than it should have been. I had to ditch

Becca so I could get back to my friends somehow, and like I said, always have a Plan B in your pocket. In my case, literally.

We arrived at the Contestants' Tent. Game time. I put the hat back on and pulled it low over my face. There was a parent outside the tent, checking names like before, but I breathed easier when I saw that the shift had changed. This parent, someone else's mother, didn't know me.

"We'll do bad cop/good cop," I said to Becca. "I'm bad cop."

"Wait. I don't know what you mean—"

I ignored Becca—she'd figure it out—and stepped up to the parent, who was sitting in a foldable metal chair outside the tent. She glanced up from her phone and visibly flinched when she saw my getup. I suppressed a smile: her eyes kept being drawn back to the clothes any time they reached for my face.

"Names?" she said.

"Gibson Malarkey," I said. "And that's my partner in crime, Valkyrie Rainn O'Connor." I smiled back at Becca and tried not to laugh when I saw how red her face had turned under that orange hat. She looked like a three-flavor snow cone.

The mother checked the list and, of course, didn't

find the names. "You're not on the list," she said. "Either of you." Her eyes narrowed but with exhaustion, not suspicion. "Kids, you can't get inside unless you're contestants or on the friends and family lists."

"But we are contestants!" I groaned and rolled my eyes. "I should have known this would happen. Everywhere we go, blocked."

Becca nudged me and I gently pushed her back. "Look," I said. "I'm not on the list." I jabbed my finger at the still-glowering Becca. "She's not on the list. We're not on the list. Anywhere. Neither of us is in any program, and why? Because we *joined late*. I sent my application in on time! It's not my fault if my vision is beyond their scope. For crying out loud, I did as much work as any paint jockey at this show."

Yes, I sounded like a jerk. That's the point. People don't think straight when you fluster them. Once you put them on the defensive, they're more likely to give you what you want, as long as what you want isn't ludicrous. (Except for Becca. Push her and she pushes back.)

"Oh." The mother glanced over the list again. "So you two are artists?"

"Yes," I said, sounding totally exasperated. "But we're also the art, and no one understands that! We *are* the sculptures."

"It's performance art," Becca said. Yes! She'd caught on, just like I knew she would. "Since dreamscapes are always changing, we wanted our art to change too. The only way we could do that is if we dressed up and acted as the art."

"Exactly!" I said. "Why would we want to make static images of dreams when we could *be* the dreams? But, as a result of our creative endeavor, those morons who run the contest took their sweet time deciding what to do with us. Are we paintings? No. Photographs? Of course not, though people have been taking a few of us. We ought to charge them for that, actually," I said over my shoulder at Becca, and she nodded half-heartedly. "They finally placed us in 'sculpture,' though that's wrong," I said, and sighed. "Business types, trying to narrow the field of art. I'm all about pushing boundaries."

"Ah, there's the element of truth," Becca muttered, and I elbowed her. Speaking of Becca, it was time for Good Cop to step in again.

I glanced at her and she nodded. Turning to the flustered mother, she said, "Don't listen to Gibson. He's just annoyed because the contest officials wouldn't issue him a name card, like they have all the other art. It's a difficult day. I bet the memo got lost on the way to you. They probably only passed on our names by word of mouth."

The setup was perfect. Now it was time for the con to work.

It didn't. "I'm sorry, kids. I can't let you in if you're not on the list," the mother said. "We've had too many people trying to sneak in here today."

"Really?" Becca said. "At an art show?" The mother nodded, and Becca nodded too, looking sympathetic by mirroring her actions (another trick I had no idea she knew). "We won't be any trouble," she said. "I promise Gibson will calm down once he gets some lemonade in him. These outfits are hot, and we'd like a chance to recover."

"I'm sorry. Why don't you visit the museum? It's air-conditioned."

Becca started to leave, but I grabbed her arm.

"Come on, *Gibson*," she hissed at me. "We aren't welcome here."

"But we *need to get inside*," I muttered back. "Remember?"

Becca frowned and I could feel her tensing, getting ready to level me with some scathing comment that would flay open our disguises, when a voice behind us said, "It's okay, Ms. Windling, they're with me."

Becca and I turned to see a tall guy about our age. He had brown hair and wore a polo.

The woman, Ms. Windling, raised an eyebrow at him. "Friends of yours, Aaron?"

"Personal guests. I'm allowed them."

"Well, they're not on the list."

Aaron shrugged. "I didn't think they'd actually compete like this, so I didn't request ahead. But it's okay. I'll keep an eye on them."

Ms. Windling looked at the list and then at Aaron, and she nodded. "Fine. It's not like it really matters," she said, and gestured at the tent's opening. Aaron stepped forward and waved us behind him.

"Thank you," Becca said to our new friend once we were inside. "You didn't have to do that."

"It's okay" he said. "It wasn't cool for her to leave you out in the heat just because your art is *a little different* than most people's." He smiled. "If we don't help each other, who will?" He waved and left us standing at the mouth of the tent.

Becca grabbed me by the collar of my poncho. "Valkyrie Rainn O'Connor?" she growled as we looked around the tent. *"Partner in crime?"*

"I knew you'd like that bit." I scanned for Case and Hack and found them at a table, playing table football.

Case loves football, but he'll never play because he's afraid he'd damage his hands, his "delicate instruments" of forgery. Hack must have gotten him into a game to distract him from the contest, because when Case is playing any form of football, he totally zones out. There is nothing but the game.

Which means there is no traitor friend J working with the detective. I hoped the disguise would be enough to fool Hack.

Becca punched my shoulder. "Thanks for throwing me into your bad cop/good cop scheme without telling me what you were planning, *partner*."

I smiled. "I knew you'd catch on. Besides, I didn't think you'd agree to it. It was technically a con."

Becca looked stunned, like she couldn't figure out what part of that to attack first. Finally she said, "Why did you try to con your way into the tent when you could have just used your name? It's on the list."

"Case could get you in, but I couldn't. Not as a guest myself. And it was fun."

"You're so lucky that kid Aaron was there to let us in."

I shrugged. "Maybe. Don't tell me you didn't have a little fun."

"Fine, I won't tell you. And I was just trying to fix what *you* broke. Like always." Becca simmered. Then her face softened to thoughtful. "Hmm."

"What?"

"A couple of things. First, I think Aaron was Aaron Baxter."

"Who?"

"The kid who got laughed out of the contest last year."

"So that's what his name was." It was nice to see him back at the easel, so to speak. "What was the other thing?"

"What that woman said. 'It's not like it really matters.' That means nothing is here that needs securing. No personal items. Wherever the stolen items are, they're not here."

"Oh, right." I should have mentioned that before we put on silly disguises to get inside. "The contestants and their families get free access to the museum lockers today. After we talk to suspects for a little while, let's go crack those lockers and find the brushes and paints." If I could get Becca out of here quickly, then Case and Hack would have less of a chance to see through my disguise.

Becca laughed. "Safecrack? You really think I'd go for that?"

"Why not? You did just take part in a con." I smiled at her and she scowled.

"Against my will. And anyway, that's more like . . . undercover work. Safecracking is actual thieving. No, let's focus our attention here. Talk to people."

I squirmed with frustration. Case and Hack wouldn't be distracted or fooled for long. "Why? Isn't your plan to find the stolen goods and return them?"

"Through the proper channels and using the right methods. *I* don't just go through people's bags until I find what I'm looking for. That's a breach of privacy. Of trust." Becca's face pressed up into my big sunglasses, her lip curled into a snarl. "I didn't ask you to help me. You invited yourself. If you don't like my methods, there's the door."

I raised my hands and backed off. "Okay, calm down. I get it. This is your case. We'll do things your way."

"That's all I ask."

"But if you stayed here and talked to people and I went to wherever they're keeping everyone's personal belongings—"

"No. You're not leaving my sight."

I sighed. "You're inhibiting my basic human rights. I haven't done anything; I deserve to be free to roam wherever the wind or a chance for free chocolate takes me."

But she wasn't listening. As I moaned, Becca looked over the tent, seeing everything I had seen earlier. The level of tension had increased; before, everyone had been pale, but now the standard complexion was "green." I listened to the subdued muttering in the tent as parents tried to comfort their children and as the contestants stared blankly into space and twitched occasionally. A small pile of shredded fingernails lay on the table beside me. I brushed it to the ground.

"I may be wrong," Becca said, "but I thought the prizes for the contest this year were fairly minimal. A photo shoot for the local paper and art supplies for each division."

"Yeah. That's what Case told me." A picture and art supplies, and a chance to "do it for the art," was what Case actually told me. But I didn't think so many kids were freaking out due to artistic sentiments. And if Becca commented on the tension, then it was worth noticing. Something wasn't right.

"Best Overall also gets their art displayed in the museum, but you can see the physical prizes over there," I added, pointing at a table toward the back of the tent. Cellophane-wrapped packets of prizes for the three judging divisions—brushes for Best Painting, film for Best Photograph, and sculpting tools for Best Sculpture—were laid out for the contestants to fawn over. They were high-quality; they always were. But were they really worth this level of anxiety?

Becca looked at the meager display and nodded. "Something doesn't add up, then. No money, and the art supplies and museum display are always part of the prize. You'd think the contestants would be ready for this."

"You'd think. What did the thief take from Heather this year?"

"Some brushes and paints."

"Yeah, I got that. Case told me. But I need details if I'm going to interrogate people, and I don't have them. I wasn't involved, remember?"

Becca smirked. "For once." She reached up a sleeve and pulled out a wad of what looked like a napkin. "The brushes listed here, and two bottles, one each, of red and yellow tempera paint."

I looked over the notes written in Case's handwriting on a napkin from Comet Cream. Six brushes. Fine wood and non-synthetic bristles, probably belonging to the set Heather had won from last year's contest. Like Case had said, there were six different kinds of brushes stolen, each one with a different purpose. Together, they could do just about anything. Becca's napkin had drawings of each brush, probably Case's work. This would be helpful if I came across the brushes, though I wouldn't if I was limited to searching this tent.

I looked up to see Becca watching me. "Notice anything interesting?" she asked.

I handed the notes back to her. "Your average thief

wouldn't have been this careful in selecting the brushes. This was deliberate and planned."

"Wow. With observations like that, it's amazing the thief isn't already in custody."

I rolled my eyes. "What's amazing is that you haven't seen why these contestants would be so panicked."

"They shouldn't be panicked at all. A photo and some brushes aren't worth stealing over."

"Good point, but look at the parents."

Becca did, watching a mom smile encouragingly at her asparagus-colored son before moving to a dad telling his daughter, "When you win, we'll go get pizza to celebrate."

She nodded. "Helicopter much?"

"The photo gives exposure, and a win looks good on a college application." But that seemed too weak an explanation too. Sure, parental pressure might contribute, but I've seen parents fuss at school plays or spelling bees, and there wasn't this level of anxiety. Had it been this bad last year?

"Parents these days," Becca said. "We're in middle school, for crying out loud. But touché. Parental pressure has driven kids to desperation before." She looked at all the people in the tent. "Anyone could be the culprit. We're going to have to split up."

She waved a finger in my face. "If you leave the tent, I'll notice. You're as obvious as the Scooby-Doo van. But we'll cover more ground apart. Walk around. Talk to people. Find out who would be capable of stealing."

"And how am I supposed to do that?"

"You're a criminal. Birds of a feather. So, go flock." Becca shoved me at a group of guys our age. They looked at me like I was nuts, so I smiled, adjusted my borrowed trilby, and said, "Sorry for tripping. Not used to this poncho yet."

When I looked over my shoulder, Becca was gone, out looking for her first suspect to terrorize.

Perfect. I excused myself from the guys Becca wanted me to interrogate first and eased over to the refreshment table. I ducked under the tablecloth, which hung to the floor on all sides. An ideal place to hide. I stripped off the poncho, hat, and sunglasses, then rolled them into a ball and stuffed them next to the table's legs. Next I poured the buttons out of my shoe.

Then I pulled out the plaid button-down and baseball cap I'd borrowed from the museum's Lost and Found and stowed under my poncho: the shirt around my waist and the cap in my pocket. Disguise Number Two. The Scooby-Doo van was now a rusty Chevy.

I couldn't be seen in the company of Becca Mills, but

the truth was this: Jeremy Wilderson, retrieval specialist and best friend of Casey Kingston, contest entrant, could find suspects a lot faster than Gibson Malarkey could. Leaving Becca to wander the tent as the lone Technicolor dresser was just a bonus.

Besides, I had some friends to check in with.

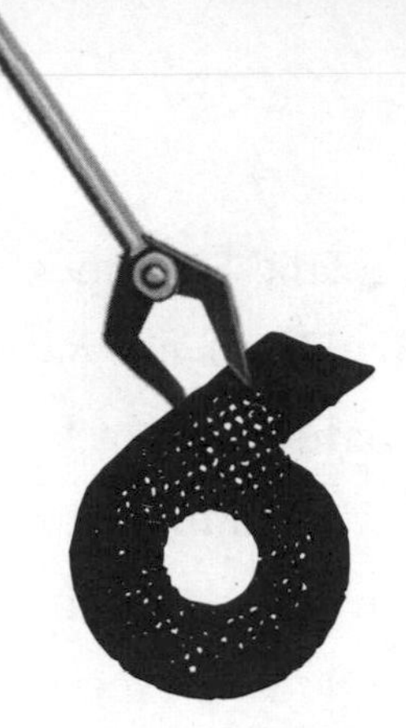

CASE WAS "KICKING" HIS paper football just short of Hack's fingers, missing a field goal, when I plopped into the chair next to Hack. "So, what did I miss?" I asked. The plaid shirt, buttoned up, covered my blue shirt and was big enough to alter my shape a little. The hat I kept pulled down low over my eyes.

"Where were you?" Hack asked as he flicked the football back. Case didn't acknowledge my presence (see what I mean about the football thing? Totally zoned out). "I thought you were going to look at the art and report back. And what are you wearing?"

"Long story." I had already come up with an excuse that hid the fact that I was on a job and that Becca and I had, once again, against our better judgment, joined forces. The best part was, I didn't have to lie.

I probably could have lied, a little. In the end, the job I was working was for them, and anything I did to stop a saboteur would justify the means, right? But Hack and Case knew when I was lying, and they'd call me out. Besides, they were my friends. I owed them as much truth as I could give.

"Did you find a job?" Hack asked.

"Not this time." Technically, the job found *me*.

"Oh." Hack sounded disappointed. "Just thought you might. I've had three people ask me about finding glitches in their new video games so they can beat it." He looked past me, waved, and nodded. "Make that four. Not like giving up a couple of tips will take me very long, if you have more interesting work to throw my way." He smiled hopefully at me as Case returned the ball.

"Keep hoping. And who knows, maybe one of your clients will have a really tricky glitch they want to . . ." I stopped. "Wait. Do they want you to fix the glitches in their games or teach them how to use glitches to win?"

Hack grinned and flicked the paper football back at Case. "What do you think?"

"I think I'm making you talk before I ever play anything with you again."

At that moment, the paper football came flying between Hack's thumbs. Case pumped his fists. "Yes!"

His eyes focused on me. "Oh hey, J. What took you so long?"

"Nice to see you again too."

"What are you wearing? Do you have a—"

"He doesn't have a job," Hack cut in.

Case groaned and banged his head against the table. "Can't you go find one?"

"Can't you?"

"A forger at an art show. Yeah, that would look good. Do you want me to self-destruct?" The desperation crept back into his eyes.

"Okay, okay. No job, sorry." Weird how my friends seemed so desperate to get out of the cushy tent, with its shade and food and comfortable seats, for a job in the midst of crowds and heat and melting snow cones. "All right, that's it. What's going on?"

Case looked up at me. "What do you mean?" he asked miserably.

"Well, for starters, why do you want a job so badly?"

"Maybe for the same reason it took you so long to get back here. Maybe for the same reason you feel the need to hunch down, wearing a shirt and hat that make you look like you're fixin' to hunt some possums."

"Mountain lions, actually. Is Becca Mills pestering you, too?"

Two disguises: one to hide from my friends, one to hide from Becca while I talked to my friends. Becca was looking for a guy wearing a stupid, brightly colored poncho. She wasn't looking for plaid.

Sometimes I am that good.

Case raised himself on one gloved hand. "So that's why you're wearing that."

"No, I just decided I'd do a little shopping at the museum's Lost and Found. What do you think happened? Becca found me by the paintings and accused me of stealing Heather's art supplies, just like you said she would. She's been harassing me all day."

True story. At least I gave as good as I got.

"Think she won't see through *that*?" Hack asked, slapping my baseball hat down over my face. "She's better than that."

"I know!" I fixed the hat. Oh boy, did I know it. "This getup's just supposed to buy me a little time so I can escape before she gets too close." I leaned forward. "Just so you know, I might have to disappear throughout the day."

"What? Why?" Case looked one step away from ranting. I held up my hands.

"That gumshoe doesn't know how to let it go. I'm sorry, man, but she took the map from me."

Case snorted. "She probably thought it was your master plan to steal all the art at the show."

He had no idea. "Something like that, probably. But it means I have to be distant today. It's just better if she doesn't see me again at all."

"So what if she does?" Hack tried to look tough. "We're here. You're our friend. You're innocent. We'll back you up."

Case didn't say anything, but he didn't have to. I knew he wanted me there. I knew that my job, as his friend, was to be there for him. I wasn't doing my job if I kept ducking out to meet with Becca Mills.

But then, I wasn't doing my job if I worried him with sabotage threats and let him lose his painting to a criminal's destructive handiwork.

"Becca suspects Case as my partner in crime," I said.

"She *what*?" Hack yelled, making people stare. I ducked under the table until the attention faded.

Sitting up again, I looked at Case, who had kept quiet but was shaking with pent-up anger. "If she catches up with me, she'll attack you next," I said, "and you don't need that kind of publicity today."

"That little—I'm going to—" Case looked like he was going to explode.

"Do nothing. You're innocent. Act like it. Focus on the contest and I'll stop in whenever I can."

Case kicked the table leg. "This is great. The snitch had to find you today, of all days. I don't need this."

I hit the table with both hands, making Case jump. "That's it. What in the world is going on? I can't remember seeing so many kids this freaked out, especially when the prizes are same-old, same-old."

"Same-old? What about Best Overall?" Case said, his eyes wild.

"What about it? I don't get it. You've been talking about this competition for months. Hack and I know everything about it, from the contest theme—"

"To the layout of the park," Hack added.

"To the kind of canvas the competitors use—"

"Down to the thread count—"

"Point made," Case snapped. "So?"

"So nowhere in any of that did you mention that the Best Overall prize is worth freaking out over."

"Yeah. A picture in the local paper, some art supplies, and a year of display in the museum, right?" Hack said. "Artists sure care a lot about publicity."

Case shook his head. "I forgot. You weren't there. You didn't hear the announcement."

"So fill us in now." I leaned across the table. "What is up with Best Overall this year, and why is everyone acting like an asteroid is going to hit the town?"

Case took a deep breath. "It may as well be an asteroid. The judges came in this morning to talk to the competitors before the guests arrived. They've changed the prizes this year."

"Changed how?" I asked.

"I guess they had more donors than they expected, and then the Harris Art Academy got involved at the last minute." Case took the pen out from behind his ear, twirled it, and put it back.

"Calm down," Hack said. "How does any of this matter?"

"We thought the winner of Best Overall Art in any of the three categories would get the picture and some art supplies, like the winners in each division, with the added distinction of having their art displayed for a year in the art museum. This year the winners of each division get the art supplies and picture, but Best Overall gets those things, a place in the museum for a year, *and* a check for five hundred dollars plus a scholarship for a summer art camp at the Harris Art Academy."

The news smashed into Hack and me like Rick during football season. Five *hundred* dollars?

"Five hundred dollars?" Hack gasped. "Why have I never listened to you when you told me I should take up art?"

"Because you never listen to me, ever."

"I do. Ask me anything."

"Fine. Who is considered the father of Cubism?"

"Anything but that."

While Hack and Case bantered, I rested my elbow on the table and grappled with Case's news. The judges were weighting the Best Overall heavily this year instead of divvying the prizes more evenly among the three divisions. That made Best Overall a seriously desirable win, far above those of the three divisions.

Did I believe in Becca's sabotage theory? Did I think these art geeks would have the guts to commit heinous acts against their fellow artists for just a prayer of studying at HAA, even if just at a summer camp? You bet I did. The five hundred dollars was enough on its own to tempt sabotage, but the Harris Art Academy was the most prestigious art school in the area.

That was motive. Five hundred dollars. Holy cow.

I looked around the room. So much fear, so much anxiety. How many people could potentially become saboteurs with that kind of pressure? And who might have known about the change of plans early enough to steal Heather's brushes?

Hack followed my gaze. "Wow, is that girl over there cosplaying as something?"

I turned around and saw Becca talking to a girl who

looked seconds from bursting into tears (though if she was that upset when Becca found her, I'd never know). Hah. Well, it was nice to know the disguises worked. Cosplaying. I wished I could rub her face in that one later. "Who knows?"

"She's probably one of *those* artists," Case said darkly. "Don't pay any attention to her; that's what she wants."

"Wait. What do you mean by *those artists*?" I thought about what Aaron had said. "Are there some artists that aren't as accepted as others?"

"Some artists don't take their work seriously," Case said. "They try to pass all kinds of things as serious art, which takes focus away from the rest of us who actually try. Dressing in bizarre costumes? Please. That doesn't take much effort. But just watch. She'll win Best Overall instead of someone who deserves it."

I kicked his chair. "That's it. Get out of the tent. The despair in here is bringing you down. Go out into the sunlight. Look around. Get a snow cone . . ." I trailed off as my gaze landed on the bow tie–wearing boy that I'd seen earlier. He leaned back in his chair and sipped a cup of lemonade while other contestants picked at their food, and his movements were smooth, not a shudder or a twitch in sight. Odd in this anxious crowd.

"Why isn't that guy panicking?"

Hack narrowed his eyes at me. "You sure you're not on a job?"

"As sure as I can be." What? It's not a lie. "But I don't shut down just because I'm not working."

Hack raised a finger. "That's technically the definition—"

"I'm not a computer, Hack." I shook my head. "Look. Case is a mess—"

"May you look this good when *you're* a mess," Case interjected.

"—and so is everyone else because of this surprise Best Overall award thing. Why not Bow Tie Guy?" I stood. "Be right back."

My motivations for going over to talk to the confident kid were twofold: on the one hand, I wanted to help Case feel more confident, and if this guy had a Zen way of staying calm, I wanted to know what it was. On the other hand, confidence raised all kinds of alarms for me. As someone who had worn self-assurance as a facade and had dealt with many, many people who radiated it because they thought they'd gotten away with theft, I knew confidence could be a cover story.

It could be that I was about to talk to the most well-adjusted kid in the tent. Or I was about to interview a thief who had something to hide.

"Hey," I said, sliding into a chair next to Bow Tie Guy. "Mind if I sit here?"

"Go ahead." Bow Tie Guy looked me over. "You a contestant?"

"A friend of one. I'm Jeremy."

"Explains the outfit. Lee Moffat." He held out a hand and I shook it. "This is my friend Ethan," he said, motioning at a boy with shaggy hair hanging in his eyes, sitting next to him. I hadn't realized they were together. "So, what does your friend do?" Lee asked.

"He paints."

Lee sniffed and straightened his gray vest, which was buttoned tightly. "So he's not a real artist, then."

There it was again, the idea that some people were "real artists" and some weren't.

I smiled a little. "I'd say painting is just as valid an art form as . . . whatever it is you do."

Lee laughed. "You would think that, wouldn't you?" His eyes stuck a little too long on my borrowed baseball cap. Snobbish, much?

"I'm a sculptor," Lee told me. That explained the just-washed hands feeling; he probably took as much care of his hands as Case did. "*My* art requires a gentle touch and a firm hand, knowledge of the composition of my materials, a perfect balance of wet and crumbly, hard and soft. It goes far beyond dabbing blots of premixed dye on a blank sheet of paper."

"Actually, it's canvas at this skill level," I muttered. Say what you will about first impressions, but I didn't like Lee.

Ethan pulled out a marker. He put his foot up on the table and started drawing on his shoe.

I watched Ethan go at it as Lee shrugged. "Paper, canvas, doesn't matter. Sculpting has nuances that painting or, worse, photography, could never match. Not that I don't use paint on my sculptures. I'm a well-rounded artist, and the sculpting medium best displays my skills. I'd say I have a sporting chance at winning Best Overall." Lee leaned in, smiling like he knew his chance was better than *sporting*. "You're no artist, so you don't know the difference between someone born with a talent and a hack."

"I think I'm learning."

Ethan snorted. Lee glared at him.

"Sorry, man," Ethan said. "It's just—"

"Shut up," Lee said, and Ethan frowned and added another whorl on his toe.

Wow. What a jerk. I wouldn't feel bad at all about manipulating this guy into a confession.

Not an artist, am I? They don't call people like me *con artists* for nothing. Watch me work my magic.

I looked around the room. Becca had moved on to another girl, one of the contestants who was chatting happily earlier. This one wore a light blue dress and had long, fair hair that reminded me of melted caramel. She looked sort of familiar, though I couldn't place her. From the smile on the girl's face, it looked like not even Becca could sour her attitude. I hoped it stayed that way.

"Is that why you're so confident?" I asked Lee. He looked surprised, and I gestured to all the sick-looking contestants. "You don't think all these painters, with their *brushes and paints*, could *steal* the prize from you?"

Trigger words, emphasized to draw a guilty mind to its guilt, namely, the theft of Heather's supplies. I wanted to see how Lee reacted when he heard them.

Nothing. Just more arrogance. "They don't have a chance. Not against a sculptor. Three-dimensional art will always beat two-dimensional, hands down."

Lee grinned, and I knew that kind of smile: over-confidence from knowing something (or thinking you know something) no one else knows. The hints hadn't worked; I needed a new strategy. If Becca were in my place, she'd be threatening Lee, saying, "I know you did it. Just confess and maybe I won't hit you over the head with your own sculpture!" On second thought, that might be a little violent, even for her. On third thought, whether or not that level of rage was Becca's style, it wasn't anything I wanted to emulate.

So, let's see if I could shake his foundations. I smiled. "You're probably right," I said. "I mean, I'm not an artist, so I wouldn't know. Maybe you can help me. Are the judges the ones with the big gold ribbons stuck to their shirts?"

"Yeah, why?"

I shook my head. "Nothing, I'm sure. I just heard them talking about their favorites, and the name Lee Moffat—that's your name, right?—never came up." I shrugged. "Maybe the judges aren't as into three-D art as you are."

"Once they see my sculpture, they'll have found their Best Overall, and that's for sure. You must have heard wrong," Lee said.

"Maybe I did. After all," I said, "a sculpture must be pretty solid compared to a painting or photograph. Easier to keep in its original form, I mean. Less of a chance of it getting smeared or damaged in some accident."

There. I'd thrown sabotage on the table. See how he likes that.

Lee's fingers twitched.

Ethan smiled, ready to join the conversation again. "Not necessarily. In some cases, sculptures might actually be more vulnerable than other kinds of artwork. If you have any kind of paintwork on your sculpture, that can be smeared just as easily as a painting, and they can also be shattered if dropped."

"Oh," I said to Ethan. "Are you an artist too?"

"Not really. My dad's one of the officials, though."

"Ethan," Lee growled. "No one cares. Seriously. Can't you just shut up for a few minutes?"

Ethan froze. His mouth hardened, and he snapped the lid on the marker and put it away. "Fine. I'll go check out the food." He stood and left.

Lee was quiet and for a moment I thought he'd call his friend back, but he just rolled his eyes and shook his head.

I clenched my jaw to keep it from dropping. Lee *clearly* didn't place a lot of value in Ethan's friendship. I got the feeling Lee didn't value anything but himself. "That was rude."

Lee smirked at me. "Ethan's just a moron sometimes. I try not to hold it against him, but it gets hard."

Right. "Are your parents working here too?"

He shook his head. "I'm the only art aficionado in the family. Which is why I know that what Ethan said is garbage. Sculpture is the more resilient art form. It will always beat painting."

"But paper still beats rock," I said. "Isn't it a funny world?"

This whole conversation proved to me that Lee was up to nothing good. Sure, I disliked the guy, and that could be coloring my perceptions, but come on. That finger twitch? After his motions had been so smooth, so controlled? And snapping at Ethan after being so conversational? Why did talk about sabotage make him suddenly as nervous as the rest of the contestants when he apparently had no worries about doing well in the contest, the thing that had everyone else shaking in their shoes?

And seriously, any innocent person would start to worry about their placement with the judges after I threw doubt their way. A guilty person with a hidden ace would still trust his devious methods to give him the win. I didn't like how much ease I saw in him.

Lee was just like every thief or bully I'd ever retrieved from, glowing with "I got away with it and you can't stop me" light. Even Mark had had it, before Becca and I had taken him down. I didn't have much proof beyond my own instincts, but I *knew* Lee was a crook.

Still, he might not have been the thief who stole the brushes. The trigger words hadn't even fazed him. I had never considered that we might not be looking for a saboteur, but *saboteurs*.

"Do you have any other friends here?" I asked Lee.

"I've got Ethan," he said.

"I mean other than him." I kept my eyes focused on Lee. As I watched, his eyes and then his face turned to the side. I turned too, looking where he had. Lee snapped back, trying to erase what he'd done, what he'd given away, but it was too late. I'd looked, and I'd seen.

Becca and that girl. The girl who had been smiling and laughing when no one else was. Still with Becca, the girl stood with her back straight, arms at her side, feet apart but not too wide. A confident stance, not a shrinking, worried one matched with nervous movements (like touching her hair) or a defensive pose.

Another surprisingly confident person. Could she and Lee be in cahoots? I'd have to talk to her next.

"She's cute," I said, and Lee's face turned spaghetti-sauce red.

"I'm guessing she's a special friend," I added, smiling at Lee.

"Of course she is," Lee said, but for a split second, that grin slipped. Just a moment, but it was enough.

"Is she here to see you?"

Lee scoffed. "She's not here to see rejects like you."

I was done. The wall was back up; I wasn't going to get any more out of talking to Lee. I slapped both hands against the table and used them to push myself to standing as Ethan came back with a plate of lemon bars. "Well, thanks for the conversation. I'd better go." I couldn't take another minute with this punk.

After talking to Lee, I had a feeling the saboteur was a confident person, not a nervous wreck.

Why? Because criminals give themselves away by not acting like everyone else. They're nervous when they should be confident, and vice versa. In this sea of anxiety a lighthouse of confidence stuck out. And that was very, very suspicious.

I headed back to Case and Hack's table. I wanted to report on Lee and ask them some questions about the confident girl Becca was talking to. Maybe they knew something. And, as long as Becca was otherwise engaged, maybe I could get in a couple of games of paper football.

But when I got back, it seemed they'd given my seat away. A girl with freckles and reddish-gold hair was sitting there.

"Nice, guys," I said as I sat down on the other side of the girl. "Real nice."

"What? We thought you'd seen Becca and run off," Case said. "This is Larissa Eccles. Her sister's in the competition." Case gave me a look that said eloquently, *This girl is a dream in the middle of a nightmare. Don't ruin this for me.*

"Then where are my manners?" I turned to the girl and smiled. "You're welcome to take my spot anytime."

Larissa returned my smile.

"And you are?" she asked.

"Jeremy. Friend of a painter."

"Sister of one."

I should have guessed. Larissa looked a year or two younger than me, slightly too young to enter the contest. Also, she was wearing capri pants and a blouse, not the dressier attire of a contestant.

"Which one's your sister?" I asked.

Larissa looked around for a moment and pointed. "That's her. Quinn."

I looked and felt my skin crackle with serendipity. It was the confident girl, the one who'd been talking to Becca. Oh, the fates were smiling on me.

"Whew," I said, getting my game face on. "It's bad enough being the friend of someone caught up in this panic fest. I can't imagine having to deal with an emotionally wrecked sister."

"J, watch it," Case growled as Larissa closed her eyes and shook her head.

"It's not that bad," she said, tracing figure eights on

the table with her finger. "Quinn's handling it well. I mean, I'm sure she's nervous—who wouldn't be with all the pressure—but she keeps saying it's her first year in the contest, so if she doesn't win, she'll have next year. I think she believes it."

"Sure." It didn't seem to be helping the other kids around here.

"Larissa's a painter too," Case blurted out, probably afraid I'd make him look bad again.

"Really? So you and Case should have a lot to talk about." I glanced down at Larissa's hands. Flecks of paint clung to her hangnails.

"She's starting sixth grade this fall," Case added. "At Scottsville."

I turned to Larissa. "So, does that mean your sister is Quinn Eccles?" That explained why I didn't immediately recognize Quinn. I'd heard her name, sure; she was in my grade. Even seen her passing in the halls, though we never shared a class. But the quiet girl in the halls didn't seem like the kind of person who'd stand out as overly confident at an art show. I'd never retrieved either for her or from her. She wasn't the kind of person who made waves.

"I've seen Quinn around," Case said. "She's in my art class. Shy, keeps to herself."

Larissa nodded. "That sounds like Quinn. She's going to be vice president of the Art Club next year, though. Art really is her comfort zone."

Huh. I was starting to wonder if Lee's relationship with Quinn was of the long-distance variety. That seemed about right.

"That's impressive," Case said.

"Two painters, huh?" I said. "Sounds like you and your sister have a lot in common. Maybe we'll see your work in this contest next year."

Larissa blushed. "Oh, no. I don't really like competing. I'll just support Quinn again next year."

"Does she need support?" I twisted the corner of a napkin between my fingers. "I mean, there are a lot of good artists here. Does Quinn have a chance at winning the contest? In your professional opinion, as a painter."

Larissa picked at the paint specks around her nails. "She might. But you're right: there are so many talented artists here. I think it's good that she's not counting on a win. Just a feeling, but I don't think this is her year." She smiled at Case. "It could be yours, though. I saw that beachscape you did; it has class."

"Well, I always try to keep it classy," Case said, leaning back in his chair. There was a creak, a garbled squeak, and then Case crashed to the floor.

Hack and I burst out laughing.

"*Very* classy," I said.

As Hack soothed a mortified Case and I picked up the fallen chair, I mulled over the conversation. Quinn seemed well adjusted and confident, if a little quiet, but her own sister didn't think she was a contender for the top prize. Why would she be so confident if she didn't have a chance of winning?

She would if she knew something we didn't. And Lee *had* looked at her.

The commotion of the falling chair had attracted attention. I scanned the tent to see kids laughing (Mia and Brielle among them) and Case's parents peeking over to make sure their oldest child wasn't hurt before going back to their conversation.

There were Lee and Ethan, talking to Quinn. They glanced over briefly, Lee's face lighting up with smug cheer at Case apparently embarrassing himself. What a *jerk*.

And there was Becca, searching the room. I should have guessed. There had been a crash, a commotion. It would have made a great distraction for some kind of criminal to slip away under her nose, and she knew that. Her eyes were wide and she was starting to redden with anger. Suddenly I realized it was me she was looking for, and she couldn't find me because, without my costume, I wasn't as conspicuous as a circus clown at a high schooler's birthday party. Great.

Again, nice to know the disguises had worked. But I needed to meet up with her soon, or I'd be off the job. And possibly in a lot of pain.

"Nice to meet you, gotta run," I said to Larissa, and waved at Case and Hack.

"Becca?" Hack asked, and I nodded.

"We'll smokescreen," Case said.

"No, you won't. Leave her alone. I've got this." The last thing I needed was my friends taking out their anxiety on Becca.

Hack waved. "Get out of here."

I nodded at him. "Thanks." Then I bolted back to the refreshments table, sliding out of sight.

"Who's Becca?" I heard Larissa ask.

"A nightmare," Case replied.

My stomach twisted as I sorted through the pile of clothes that made up Disguise Number One. I hated deceiving my best friends. Again. But I was doing this *for* them, and they wouldn't understand the details. I had no choice.

No sooner had I replaced the buttons in my shoe and the shoe on my foot than I saw a pair of mismatched feet right in front of my face. Becca.

I waited, again with bated breath (maybe it has something to do with the word *abate*?) as Becca stepped by. Now she was a few feet to my left. Quietly I slipped out from under the table and stood behind her. I grabbed a plate and filled it with a stack of four brownies.

"I'd offer you one, but you strike me as a lemon bar person," I said.

Becca spun around and saw me there, in my poncho, hat, and sunglasses, leaning against the table so close to the lemon bars my snotty costume brushed the plate's edge.

"Me, I'm more of a brownie guy." I took a bite of one of them and grinned, mouth full.

"Where have you been?"

"No need to snap at me. You were the one who ran off." I took another bite.

"I was looking for you. Were you behind that crash? Your crook friends help you?"

"I was right there behind you. Huh. Makes a good metaphor for us. Me there, behind you, the whole time."

"That's creepy."

I thought about it. "Yeah, a little. Anyway, I needed to talk to you."

"About what?"

"Not here. Too many eyes." Four of them belonged to

friends who would know me if they looked too close. They might think I was just messing with Becca, but only for a few minutes. After that, they'd have too many questions.

Becca grabbed my arm and pulled me out of the tent, safely away from my friends.

In and out, safe and undetected, with a few strong suspects, information on the changed prize, and holding a plate of brownies covered in chocolate icing. Not bad for my first interrogation session. I was getting good at this gumshoe stuff.

OUTSIDE THE TENT, I PULLED Becca to a shed that held the park's landscaping and maintenance tools so we could stash our disguises until we needed them again. Sure, Case and Hack *might* see me walking around with my archnemesis, but the odds weren't good, as they would be enjoying the art show or the cool of the tent, and I'd be sneaking around, catching a criminal. Besides, it wasn't worth wearing the poncho in the hot, humid summer's day when I could duck behind a wall for a few seconds. I'd just have to be vigilant.

"Keep an eye out," I told Becca outside the toolshed. "I'll see if it's locked."

If you've been following my adventures, you'll know by now that as far as I'm concerned, no door is locked. But what Becca didn't know couldn't hurt me.

A few minutes later, I tucked away my lockpick set and waved Becca in. "Time for debriefing," she said, tossing her orange hat onto a lawnmower.

"Debriefing? I want out of this costume as much as you do, but that seems a bit extreme," I said, taking off my hat and sunglasses.

"Don't be gross. It means telling each other what we found out," Becca said, giving me a death glare. "Like you explaining to me how you spent your time. Please say you did something productive." She pulled the muumuu off, and I took the opportunity, while she wasn't watching, to stash the plaid shirt and ball cap inside an empty plastic bucket.

As I took off the poncho (finally), Becca grabbed one of my brownies and started nibbling it.

"No, sure, go ahead. What's mine is yours." I tossed the poncho over the bucket, hiding my second disguise from view.

"That's the point, *partner*." Becca winked.

I was torn between telling her never to call me that and playing it up to annoy her, but decided against both. Time to reveal the big information.

"I know why all the contestants are acting like this is a fight to the death instead of an art contest," I said. That made her pay attention.

"And that is?"

"A bigger prize. A *much* bigger prize. The winner of Best Overall gets the picture, art supplies, and display, as well as five hundred dollars plus a scholarship for an art camp at the Harris Art Academy."

Becca looked like she'd swallowed a whole lemon. "That explains a lot."

No kidding. "I think you're right about this sabotage thing. I also think we're looking for more than one thief."

She tilted her head. "Are you sure?"

"I wouldn't say it if I wasn't."

Becca rubbed her chin. "It's possible. The evidence at Heather's was pretty well disturbed by the time I got to the crime scene. Heather had brought friends to her room before discovering the theft, and they'd walked everywhere and touched things. All I could determine is that there was a theft and what specifically was stolen, not how many thieves there were. Two people could have easily done it."

"Or maybe one person stole the brushes and paints and the other acted as lookout," I said.

"What got you started on the two-thief theory?" Becca asked. She stuck the last bite of brownie in her mouth.

I took off my shoe to tip the buttons out. "I talked to this kid, Lee Moffat. He's here with his friend Ethan.

He's also one of the only contestants in the tent who isn't freaking out."

Becca tilted her head as she slid the mismatched shoes off her feet. "The one with the bow tie who hangs around with the guy with the long hair?"

"That's Lee and Ethan."

"And he told you there're two thieves?" Becca asked.

"No, but he was way too confident to be innocent."

"Confidence isn't proof of guilt. If it were, you'd be hiding a million crimes. Oh, wait."

"Before you can take another shot at my *effective* methods for fighting crime in Scottsville, could you let me finish?" Becca folded her arms and waited, so I continued. "Consider the new-and-improved prize. *Now* think about what that much confidence means. I've never seen confidence like that, and I eat lunch with Case on a daily basis."

Becca smiled. "Case didn't seem all that confident to me earlier."

"He pulls this Jekyll-and-Hyde when he's in a contest. On any other day, he'd say he's the best artist in the state."

"I'm guessing Lee would take exception."

"Oh yeah. And he wouldn't break. I tried everything to stir up some real emotion. Prying, trigger words, telling him I heard the judges talking about their favorites and none were him. And you should have heard him talk to Ethan. He was such a jerk."

"A jerk? Oh, call the presses. We have a break in the case."

"It's not nothing," I shot back. "But you're right. It's not much. I couldn't crack that confidence." I laughed. "Confidence? I mean arrogance."

Becca thought about it. "Okay, but none of that's necessarily proof of criminal activity for one person or two. He could just be delusional in his belief that he's the best artist here."

Are you kidding me? That kind of confidence belongs to criminals alone. But Becca didn't know that; she spent most of her time talking to victims and witnesses. Narrowing down a list. For me, the list is always one person: the culprit.

I sighed. "Maybe, if it were just one person. But when you have two people behaving out of the ordinary, you have a problem."

"What do you mean?"

I chewed my lip, considering my situation. "Permission to speak freely?"

"Granted. Are you trying to be exasperating?"

"I just want to make sure that I can bring my expertise

into this without consequence. Remember, I may have asked to join your job—"

"Case."

I stopped. "What about him?"

"No, I mean it's a case, not a job."

"Whatever. But you let me help because I know about thieves better than you do. I just want to be able to draw on the lessons I learned from . . . past experience without you going all Batman on me."

Becca smiled. I think she was imagining herself as Batman. Then she shoved me. "If you have evidence, give it over. Even if it's based on your dark past."

I straightened. "In my past work I've dealt with lots of people who have committed a crime. Some of them act guilty the way you'd expect, sure, hiding and looking over their shoulder. But for some, committing a crime has a certain amount of *fun*."

Becca grinned. "Sounds like someone I know."

"I'll admit I enjoy the occasional jump from a window," I said, smiling at her. I knew from experience she did too. She'd glowed after we'd leaped from Mark's bedroom window.

Becca didn't react, so I continued. "But that's not what I mean. Some criminals love the feeling of knowing something no one else does. Most, though, love it even more if they have someone to share it with. If you know what to look for, you can figure out who your suspect is sharing his crime with."

"And you know what to look for."

I shrugged. "I get jobs where kids give the stolen item to a friend to hold. It's just easier if I can spot the connections and go to the right hiding place first."

Becca paced and nodded, processing my information. "So you think Lee is confident because he knows he will win—"

"Because he is planning to sabotage the favorites."

"But you don't think he's the one who stole the brushes."

I nodded. "Lee is a sculptor. You said the thief had an insider's knowledge on which brushes to steal."

Becca nodded. "Lee would know which brushes to steal if he were in cahoots with a painter."

"Exactly. Or, the painter steals the brushes and Lee stands guard."

"So, brilliant reader of human connections, who do you think his partner in crime is?"

"Again with the sarcasm. When I was questioning Lee, he gave a quick glance at this one girl. Quinn."

Becca stiffened. "Quinn Eccles? The quiet girl from school?"

"How many girls named Quinn could there be in this town?"

"I talked to her. She seemed honest. Not glowing with self-confidence but well adjusted. She told me she was okay not winning this year because she'd try again next year. She seemed sincere. It isn't her."

"Her sister said the same thing. It sounds like a story to me. Nobody is that well adjusted, not when everyone else is falling to pieces. Again, *five hundred dollars* is at stake. And why would Lee look at her when I asked him if he had any friends other than Ethan with him?"

"Maybe he likes her."

"It's possible." More than possible, actually. "But it's more than that. I saw them talking in the tent before we left."

"Maybe they're friends."

"Then why haven't they been hanging out together? If I were free to do as I pleased, I'd be spending the day with my friends."

"She's a girl. Maybe he feels awkward."

"But not too awkward to chat with her in front of everyone?"

"It could be complicated." Becca rubbed her forehead. "Look, I'm not saying Lee's not worth looking into. Just that Quinn is honest. I talked to her, remember? I think I know what a criminal looks like."

"So did I, before the whole Mark incident. Anyone can get played."

Becca raised a hand. "Watch it. I agree that we should look into Lee, if only because we need to start somewhere. But I don't agree with the two-thief idea. It's too complicated."

I was about to protest, but she had a point. One thief made more sense, logically. And hating Lee didn't automatically make him a criminal, no matter how much I wished it did.

But still. "My hunches are usually good. At the very least it's a place to start."

"Agreed," Becca said. "Why would he steal brushes, though? Couldn't he use some other method of sabotage?"

"Maybe he stole brushes to throw the blame onto a painter or as some kind of statement. He really seemed to hate painters, when I talked to him."

Becca nodded. "That could give us motive. But remember, sabotage was a hypothesis, not a proven fact," Becca said. "Maybe Lee is just an unpleasant person. We have to consider all possibilities."

That was technically true; the sabotage angle was just a

guess. If there was no saboteur, though, why was I spending this time with Becca when I could be hanging out with Case and Hack?

I guess Becca noticed my internal conflict, because she raised a finger. "Sabotage isn't out until we've caught the thief, especially when we know how amazing the prize for Best Overall is this year. We have to keep assuming the worst if we want a chance to stop it."

"I'm sick of assuming things. We need evidence."

"My thoughts exactly." Becca pushed a pair of clippers hanging on a rack, making it swing. Then she sighed and sank to the ground.

"What's wrong?" I knelt next to her. "You have a few suspects! It's a good start."

"I'd be happier if I had only one. Preferably carrying the paints and brushes. With a clear motive."

"And twirling an evil black mustache, right? Maybe cackling and muttering a monologue?" I grinned and faked a mustache twirl, and Becca laughed.

"Yeah, something like that. But seriously, how are we going to get the evidence we need to find our culprit? Everyone's away from home, and it's not like they'll have the brushes in their pockets."

"Not their pockets, no." I stood and stretched, exhaling loudly. "We're not going to get a confession by sneakily asking questions. People lie. But objects don't. All the contestants are keeping their things in the locker room of the museum. If I could just go in there and search their belongings, we could have our bad guy in a few minutes."

Becca stood and leaned against the shed doorframe. "I told you, I don't work that way."

"Why not? We'd have the culprit and the evidence. We could confront them and return the stolen goods without even having to worry about cooperation."

"And how would it look to the parents if we showed up with brushes taken from their child's backpack? It doesn't matter that they were stolen; they'd just see two kids who went through private property. Then *we'd* get in trouble. Also, it's wrong. So no. Keep your thieving hands to yourself."

Frustrated, I walked to the door and peered out at the park. Families were wandering the paths, oohing and aahing over every under-fifteen artist's work, completely unaware of the evil lurking in this heart of paradise. If there was a saboteur, we had to catch them before the art show ended. Even if Lee and Quinn or whoever it was chickened out and didn't sabotage anyone, any chance we'd have to catch them would be gone when the prizes had been awarded and the fake walls taken down.

Also, no matter what Becca said, I didn't trust Quinn.

She was too confident, too ready to concede winning a competition that was worth so much and had everyone and their parents sweating bullets. She had a connection to Lee that bothered me. She was hiding something, I could smell it. I'd prove it to Becca somehow.

"We have two strong suspects," I said.

"We have one."

"Two. Lee and Quinn. Humor me, okay? If Quinn's innocent, she has nothing to worry about, right?"

Becca nodded grudgingly, so I continued.

"How about this? I search their things. Search only. I don't remove anything. And I do it, not you. That way you don't get in trouble."

Becca stared at me. For a moment I thought she'd nod or something, but instead she turned away and said, "Sorry. We can't do that."

"You go through my stuff all the time."

"Yeah, but that's because I have reason and I'm too young to get a warrant . . ." She froze, then turned back to me openmouthed.

"Reason," Becca repeated, and I understood.

"You search my things because in *your* mind I'm a thief," I said. "That gives you a reasonable suspicion."

"And we have the same suspicions about Lee."

"And Quinn."

"Fine. And Quinn." Becca grinned. "Perfect."

"Shall we?" I gestured back to the museum we'd left less than an hour before, and we exited the shed, closing the door behind us.

Becca pulled out her cell phone.

"What are you doing?" I asked.

"Calling Heather for a guest list from her pool party when the brushes were stolen. I want to know if *both* of our suspects were there."

"Good plan." I pushed on the door, which didn't seem to want to close again.

"Don't worry about it. The disguises should be safe there, if we need them again," Becca said. She dialed a number on her phone as she walked. I followed. "The shed's better than under a rock or behind someone's art. Lucky we found one that was unlocked."

"I can hardly believe it myself."

Becca narrowed her eyes and watched me. I ignored her. She knew I'd picked the lock on the shed, and I waited for the fight to start. But, out of the corner of my eye, I saw her lips twitch and curl into a smile. Then she raised the phone to her ear, still grinning. I might have been wrong, but I think, in some small way, she appreciated that the best lockpicker in Scottsville Middle had her back.

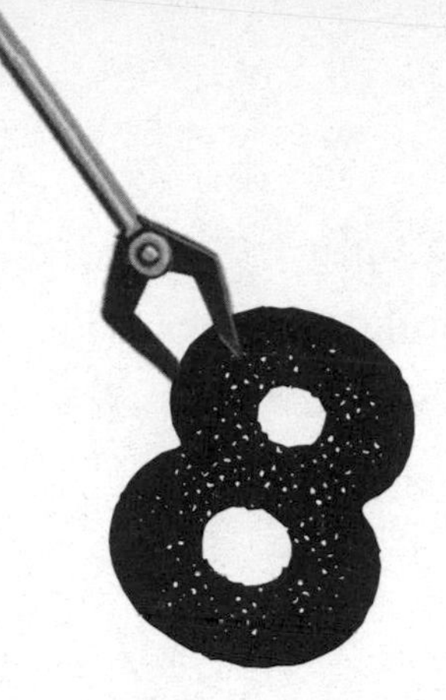

TWO KIDS WALKING INTO THE locker room at the museum didn't arouse any suspicion, but once we got inside, we encountered a couple of problems.

A couple? More like a couple hundred.

"How does a museum this small have so many lockers?" Becca marveled as we walked around the small room, which was complete with a single fluffy chair for sitting and waiting while your friends stashed or grabbed their things.

"To be fair, the lockers are small too." I found a stretch of one-foot-square lockers with stickers on them: RESERVED FOR YOUNG ARTISTS AND THEIR FAMILIES. "Oh, look. They gift-wrap. Beautiful."

But, unfortunately for a poor, hapless retrieval specialist, the museum had forgotten to label each one with the name of the person who rented it.

"By the way," Becca said, holding up her phone. "I got the guest list, and it's disappointing. Heather said she could send me a list of people she invited, but a lot of them didn't show, and those who did come brought friends who weren't invited."

"Are you going to ask for that list?"

"No point if it's not accurate. But Heather did say she remembers seeing Lee, Ethan, *and* the Eccles sisters at the party." She fell silent, biting her lip and frowning.

"So our suspects are still our suspects. Well, better get started." I rested my palm on the combination lock of the first locker in the row.

Becca pulled my hand off the lock. "Hang on. You can't go through all of them."

I sighed. "Fine. I will use my magnificent powers of telepathy to mentally read which locker belongs to which contestant. They all look the same! I need a little more to go on if you're going to be all honest and noble." I looked at her hand holding mine. "Is there something you want to tell me, now that we're alone?"

She let go like my fingernails had started oozing slime. "You're not as smooth as you think you are." Backing away, she said, "Wait here. Try not to look suspicious."

"I have no idea what you're talking about," I said. I left the lockers and flopped down in the puffy chair. "I'm just sitting here, waiting for my mom to stop looking at paintings of ballerinas." That would be my story, if anyone asked.

Becca rolled her eyes and left, shaking her head. I grinned, pleased that I had managed to annoy her. Come on, it was her fault she was annoyed. She was the one taking everything personally.

Maybe I should tone it down, I thought. I didn't want her to throw me off the "team," or whatever we were (symbiotes, maybe?). Either way, she seemed crankier than usual, and I should probably give her a break.

As long as we were working toward a common goal, Becca and I were tied together. I needed to protect my friends, and Becca needed to catch a thief (and possibly a pair of saboteurs). That meant me sitting in a comfy chair while Becca got the numbers of Lee and Quinn's lockers.

Becca came back in, her dark hair tied into two high pigtails. "Cute," I said.

She gave me a look that said, quite clearly, how stupid she thought I was, as she untied the pigtails. "They make me look younger, so the guard was more willing to give me a locker number."

"I know. I still own a shirt with a teddy bear on the stomach for the same reason."

Becca smiled. "You'd probably look about five wearing it, Short Guy."

I smiled back. "Whatever works."

It was odd, and kind of nice, to be on the same page as someone when it came to stopping thieves and other bad guys, even if that person hated my guts. Case and Hack fought crime too, but they did it in their own ways. I never had someone who understood and used my own methods before.

Before Becca and I could have a "moment," I coughed. "The number?"

"Lee's family is number ninety-four. That's the only one I could get. If I'd asked for more, the guard would have gotten suspicious."

"Okay. One safecracking, coming right up." I flexed my fingers and looked up to see Becca grimacing.

"What?"

"Don't call it that."

"Safecracking?"

"Yeah."

"Okay. One act of criminal law-breaking, coming right up." Becca flinched and I added, "You can go outside and wait, if you want."

"And leave you here alone with other people's valuables? Not happening." Becca plopped down in the chair and folded her arms.

I shrugged. "Suit yourself." I knelt down next to Lee's

locker. I placed my hand on the lock's dial and pressed my ear against the door.

Scottsville Middle's lockers can sometimes be opened with a couple of hits or kicks in the right places. Not so at the museum. These were good lockers, new, without the dents that made the school's lockers easily broken into. I'd practiced on the museum lockers before—over the last school year, I realized I needed to hone my safe-cracking skills, and the art museum's isolated locker room was a much better training ground than the school's open halls—so I knew I could open them, but wading through the clicks as contact points spun past, trying to remember each one so I could close in on the combination, took time and patience.

Patience that Becca Mills did not have. "You'd better be quick," she said. "The guard will notice if we don't get out of here soon."

"Shhhh." My eyes were closed, the better to listen with. "There's an art to this, a music. You have to play it softly and listen for the beats."

"Save the flowing metaphors. Just get the locker open."

I smiled and twisted the dial around and around, listening for the next contact point. I found it and made a mental note of it. That was two numbers found, one to go.

A minute later, I had the three numbers of the combination: 5, 8, and 13. How Fibonacci of them. Opening my eyes, I tried the numbers in different combinations. The first three didn't work, but the fourth did: 8, 13, 5. The lock unhitched and the door swung open when I tugged on the handle.

I turned around, ready to counter whatever snide remark Becca might have ready for needing to take four tries to open the door (I'd like to see her do better!), but she didn't have one. She was sitting, eyes glazed but watching me, her head in her hand. A small smile played on her lips. Oh, *that* wasn't worrying at all.

I coughed. "The door," I said, gesturing. "It's open. Shall we see what's inside?"

Becca snapped to attention. "Absolutely." She slid off the chair and pushed me aside. I sprawled dramatically on the carpet.

"I thought we agreed that I'd do this part," I said, pulling myself back up.

"Not letting you anywhere there might be valuables," Becca reminded me.

"That doesn't tempt me and you know it." I sat up and pushed Becca aside. This was *my* part of the job, *my* area of expertise, and I was going to be the one to find the incriminating evidence to prove Lee was a smug, guilty thief.

Huh. I wondered if that was how Becca felt about me, all the time.

Becca was still able to see what was in there, but I was the one who pushed aside a purse and a pair of sunglasses that looked too expensive to belong to a kid to reveal a camera and a notebook.

I reached for the notebook at the same time Becca went for the camera. Our arms tangled.

"Let go."

"You let go."

We got free and retreated to opposite sides of the locker room. I flipped through the pages of the notebook and read a few passages of the darkly inked writing. Yep, this was Lee's, all right. The arrogant voice was the same. I skipped to the last pages. One was torn out, leaving behind a rough edge of paper. Well, that was interesting.

"This guy likes his own face," Becca said, pulling me out of Lee's words. I looked over and she showed me the camera's history—lots of selfies. "I don't know why."

I snorted. "That's not the only weird thing," I said. "Look at this."

Becca took the notebook and handed me the camera. "Torn page? Not too weird. Unless . . ." She ran a finger lightly over the next page after the torn edge. "Indentations," she said. "We can do a rubbing."

"We don't even know if it's anything worth looking at," I said. "Let's try this first."

I took the notebook to a lamp and held it under the light, tilting it until the indentations from the words written on the previous page became clear.

I flipped back to the previous page. "Lee presses hard. We should be able to read it just fine this way."

Becca took the notebook back, keeping it angled under the light.

"'Dear friends and fellow artists,'" she read slowly, "'it gives me great pleasure to accept the award for Best Overall. I have to say, I was surprised to receive it. There are so many fine artists here with us today. . . .'" She looked up. "An acceptance speech?"

I nodded. I held up the camera and scrolled through the pictures. Lee really did like his own face.

"It goes on," Becca said. "He talks about his inspirations, he thanks his parents, and he talks about the future of his craft."

"Does he say anything about tragic events, or sabotage? Like, saying how shocked he is by the turn of events?"

"No. But that might not mean he's innocent. He did, after all, rip this page out and take it with him."

"For practice or to hide the evidence?"

"One of those." Becca laid the notebook on the floor. Then she reached under her skirt and pulled out a piece of paper, a pencil, and her own camera.

"What the—where were you keeping that?"

"Grow up." Becca raised the hem of her skirt. Underneath I could see knee-length cargo shorts with pockets stocked with, well, whatever a gumshoe brings to work.

She set the paper over the indentations and rubbed the pencil lead over it. A faint image of the speech appeared. She snapped a few shots of Lee's acceptance speech before returning the book to the locker. "Evidence," she said, waving the paper and camera at me. "Comes in handy later."

I think that was supposed to be an attack on how I'd once deleted a few of her evidence photos. Case's homemade hall passes were in those shots; I would never feel guilty about erasing them.

As Becca carefully tucked the rubbing away in a plastic bag and then pocketed her evidence, I scrolled through a few more pictures of Lee and Ethan posing with something that looked like Swiss cheese, melted, reshaped, and colored bright primary shades. His artwork, I guessed. In one of the pictures, though, he wasn't with Ethan. A certain caramel-haired girl was standing, smiling, beside him.

"Look," I said, showing Becca. She took the camera and shook her head.

"It doesn't mean Quinn's guilty," she said. "You asked Lee if he had any friends here, and it turns out one is his competitor. So what?"

"So what, she says." I looked at the shot of Quinn and Lee standing side by side with their art, his a weird sculpture, hers a nasty-looking painting of a pack of rodents. It looked familiar. "Quinn goes to our school. Lee doesn't. How do they know each other? And I'm surprised that Lee would be so close with a painter after all the things he said about them." I opened a few more shots. "Here she is again and again. Here they are at the park, and here's the two of them painting someone's kitchen. There are more pictures of Quinn than there are of Ethan." I waved the camera at Becca.

She took it. "Look. In these she's alone. Maybe he's got a crush and is taking pictures from afar."

"Is that what you tell people when they see how many shots of me you have on your camera?" Becca blushed and I continued, "A crush could be part of it. But first Lee gives Quinn away as a friend, then they both have weird levels of confidence, and now this? You have to admit, it warrants further investigation."

Becca nodded. She took pictures of Lee's pictures

and then handed me the camera. I returned it and the notebook to Lee's locker, closing the door quietly.

"Now what?" she asked.

"Another locker, I guess. Do you think you can get another number?"

She frowned. "You want it, you go get it."

I sighed. "I should have brought my teddy bear shirt."

Becca smirked, ready to make another comment about my short stature, but before she could say anything, we heard footsteps coming from the hall.

"Is that—" Becca started.

"Coming our way?" I finished. "Oh yeah."

I thought about sitting down, pretending I was waiting for a parent, but something stopped me: I wasn't alone this time. Becca was with me. What if the person coming wasn't an adult? What if it was a kid from school who knew Becca and me? I couldn't let them see us in the same room, working together!

Becca seemed to be thinking the same thing. She glanced around, looking for a hiding place. "Looking for a closet to hide in? There isn't one," I said. "I've checked."

"We can't get caught here!" Becca hissed. "*I* can't be caught here, especially not with you."

"Serves you right for cracking safes."

Becca's lip curled. Some people can't take a joke. I rolled

my eyes and pushed the chair against the wall. Then I dove under it.

"Really?" Becca bent down to look at me.

"Do you see anywhere else?"

"No." Becca frowned. "So where am I supposed to hide?"

"You don't have to," I said. "As long as they don't see us together."

"People know me, Wilderson. They know I'm a detective. I have no reason to be in this room other than clue hunting. What if it's the saboteur? They'll know we're on to them!"

I hadn't even thought about that. "Hide . . . somewhere?"

Becca snorted. "Move over."

"Not enough room." I thought fast. "Here."

I slid the chair out a little and crouched behind it so I was mostly hidden from view. "Now get under."

The chair shifted as Becca pulled herself under, her face peering out from beneath the seat. We were close; Becca's legs and mine touched as I squatted behind the chair and she pushed herself back as far as she could. Not the world's best hiding spot, but good enough for Becca and me. She wasn't that much taller than me, and I was in no danger of being asked to join the basketball team anytime soon.

"Thanks for leaving me hanging," Becca growled.

"Sorry. I'm just not used to having to protect someone else."

Becca laughed angrily and kicked, hitting me in the shins. I kicked back, and she moved like she was about to turn around and yell at me.

"Shh!" Someone was coming in. A fair-haired girl. Quinn? It was hard to see without making myself obvious behind the chair. Also, Becca kicked me again, and that was a little distracting.

I held my breath as the girl went to a locker on the top row and opened it. I raised myself higher. It was definitely Quinn. As she rummaged around, I got a good view of a couple purses, nothing else. Nothing incriminating. Maybe she wasn't our culprit.

Quinn removed one of the purses. She reached into her dress pocket and pulled something out.

Becca pushed off against me, getting closer to the front of the chair. I bit down on my lip to keep from hissing in pain as her shoes dug into my shins.

I heard a click near me as Quinn tucked the item in the purse, hooked the bag over her shoulder, closed the locker door, and hurried out.

"She gone?" Becca whispered.

I waited a moment. No one came back in. "Yeah."

"Then I'm out of here!"

A few minutes later, we were both sitting on the ground. Becca brushed dust off her clothes. "Freaking thief, leaving me hanging. Almost letting me get caught."

"You didn't get caught, and I said I was sorry."

"Whatever." Becca pulled out her camera and started jabbing buttons like they'd insulted her mother. I shook my head. What was going on with her?

"I got a picture of the thing in her hand," Becca said. "We'll see what she came for—oh."

"What is it?" I peered over Becca's shoulder at the camera's display. She threw an elbow at me, but not before I could see. Pixelated, yes, but very clearly a small bottle of paint.

"Innocent, huh?" I said.

Becca frowned. "It's not one of the paints stolen from Heather."

"You sure?"

"Her paint bottles were bigger."

"I don't think we need to search Quinn's locker anymore. The evidence is gone now."

"If it is, in fact, evidence." Becca chewed her lip. "I'm getting the feeling more is going on here than we thought."

Paint bottles where they shouldn't be, but not related

to the theft? I was getting the same feeling. "Looks like we're done."

"No. I'd like to check one more locker."

I examined the wall of lockers. "You'd better have a number."

"I don't, but you might. We need Casey Kingston's locker."

I stiffened. "No."

"Heather said she saw him at her party. The one *you* said Casey never attended. She was one hundred percent sure. I shouldn't have doubted my intel, but maybe it was a good thing I did. Now I know for a fact that Casey could have stolen the brushes."

What? "That has to be a mistake. I was with him . . ." I trailed off, remembering. We had been playing video games, that was true, but Case had left for lunch and come back hours later. Why would he have gone to the party and not told me?

"Casey would also know which brushes to take," Becca said. "He's a competitor, a nervous one, with something to gain today."

"Case is not a thief."

"You don't tell him everything. Maybe it's time to consider that he has his own secrets."

"I can't."

"You know the locker number, don't you?"

"I didn't exactly have time to get it earlier."

Becca pointed at the door by the security guard. "Then go get it."

"I'm not opening Case's locker."

"Why not? Do you think he has anything to hide?" Becca folded her arms. "If he's innocent, we won't find anything, right? Isn't that what you said about Quinn?"

I gritted my teeth. "This is such a huge breach of trust."

"Do it, and if he's clean, I won't mention it again."

That was appealing. One quick look, and if there wasn't anything suspicious, that would be the end of it. Becca wouldn't pursue Case.

I sighed. "Give me a moment."

Becca sat in the chair as I went out to the lobby to ask the guard for my friend's locker number.

It was easy. I spun a tale about needing to grab Case's inhaler (he doesn't have asthma, but adults question you less when it relates to medical situations) and, because I'm actually Case's friend, it must have rung true. The guard gave me not only the locker number (121) but also the combination.

I went back to the locker room. Becca hung back as I located the locker and began entering the combination, hating myself.

"This is much faster," Becca commented.

"Why don't you break into your best friend's locker, and I'll sit back making snarky comments?" I grumbled.

"I don't think it's 'breaking in' if you already have the combination," Becca said as I opened the locker.

Becca stepped over to see what was inside, but I blocked the door. I needed to get a good look first and make sure there were no forged doctor's notes inside.

A large purse with everything a mom with four kids would carry. And there, at the back . . . oh no.

Becca pushed me aside and looked in. She gasped and pulled out two bottles of tempera paint, one red and one yellow.

"This means nothing," I said. "A painter has paints in his locker. So what? He could have bought them at the gift shop."

"The bottles are old, though, like Heather's. And red and yellow? Tempera? That can't be a coincidence." Becca handed me the yellow paint and examined the red.

She shook her head and pulled out her camera. "I hate to say it, but it seems like your friend is our thief."

"Because this paint looks like the paint Heather had stolen? Let me remind you: Case has plenty of his own paints and brushes. Why steal Heather's?"

"Because they're Heather's, not his. If you're going to

sabotage someone, why not use tools that can't be traced back to you? It would prevent that annoying problem of having to wash the paint out of your own brush before it stains."

"That still doesn't prove Case did it. Tempera is pretty common paint. This could have come from anywhere. It could be for anything."

"Like sabotage?"

"Case would never do that."

"And yet you're holding evidence in your hand. If we found that in Lee's or Quinn's locker, you'd agree that the proof was obvious."

It looked bad. I knew that. But I also knew Case. "If you knew how wrecked Case is right now, you wouldn't suspect him."

"Right. Because criminals never get nervous."

"It isn't Case. This paint is unrelated. It has to be." Although, I didn't know how. Every instinct in me agreed with Becca: this was Heather's paint. Why did he have it? Did Case find it himself and plan to return it to Heather after the contest? When did he have time, and why wouldn't he tell me about it? Could Becca be right? Did Case have secrets I didn't know about?

Annoyed, I returned the yellow paint to Case's locker, slamming the bottle onto the metal floor of the compartment. The bottle's lid snapped open and spurted a glob of paint onto my hand.

Becca laughed. "You and lockers and paint."

"Funny. No, really. Hilarious." I rubbed the paint, friction-drying it to get it off my skin. Tempera paint feels rough and chalky when it dries, and this was no exception. I wondered if I'd have abrasions once the paint was gone. But my skin was fine, if slightly mustard-colored.

I closed the locker door without a word and walked out of the locker room, Becca right beside me. The security guard waved at us as we left the museum and stepped out into the sunlight.

"It's time to go find your friend," Becca said as we reentered the park. Her expression was hard. "I have some things I'd like to say to him."

I turned to Becca, ready to let her know what I really thought about her accusations. But before I could say a word, a scream ripped through the air.

Becca and I looked at each other. "That was from the painting areas," she said.

I tabled my argument and followed Becca, who was already running, to see whatever atrocity had just happened.

WE WEREN'T THE ONLY ONES racing to the source of the scream. Other art show visitors clogged the paths as Becca and I wove our way to the painting gallery's Wall E, where the commotion was raging on.

Becca and I were small for our age, so as the adults stopped to watch, we were able to sneak under and around them. That's when we saw what had happened.

A girl was weeping as her parents tried to console her. I knew her: Diana Legris, a painter who was a rising eighth grader at Scottsville Middle. Her friend had left her wallet on the bus and Diana had hired me to retrieve it. I'd gotten it back in fifteen minutes. Hadn't even missed class. Hold your applause, please.

Becca pointed. "We're too late."

I looked and gasped. Behind the girl hung her painting.

It had to be hers; Diana was a kind girl, but I doubted even the kindest heart would cry that much over the destruction of a competitor's artwork.

The painting was ruined. It was the superhero one I'd seen earlier, when I was scouting out the art show for Case, so realistic that it looked more like photography than painting. But that was before. Now there was a wide zigzag stroke, like a *Z*, covering the work. The *Z* dripped thick, wet, red paint.

"Oh no." Becca's guess, and mine, had been solid. This wasn't just theft. It *was* sabotage, it was real, and it was out of my pay grade. I wasn't equipped to handle sabotage. Good thing I had Becca to help put together the clues and catch our bad guy.

Diana gave another loud sob, and I gritted my teeth. It looked like I'd have to become the kind of person who stopped saboteurs, for Diana's sake, and for Case's. He would *not* be the next one to fall, whether by sabotage or by Becca's overdeveloped sense of justice.

He didn't do it. He couldn't have.

"Come on," Becca said, grabbing my hand and pulling me toward the painting.

What was she thinking? Granted, the painting was distracting, but didn't she see the group of contest officials and park security questioning everyone in sight?

And . . . oh no. Was that Becca's mom, *Detective Mills*, closely examining the painting? Yes, it was. Nope. Nope, nope, nope. I pulled back.

"We can't," I said.

"Come on. My mom doesn't bite."

I wasn't worried about her *biting* me. I was afraid of her in general. I'd met the cub; I had no desire to meet Mama Bear.

"What is she even doing here?" I asked. "Isn't an art show sabotage a little rinky-dink for the head detective?"

"She happened to be here on her day off, and anyway, this is the big Scottsville social event of the summer. Why wouldn't she help out? Now, come *on*."

Becca pulled again and I dragged her back.

She scowled. "We have to go right now!" she said. "Park security is going to take that painting away and we won't get another chance to examine it. They'll store it somewhere safe and that's it. No more case for us."

Case. He must have heard the commotion, and if I knew him . . . I scanned the crowd.

I didn't see them anywhere. Case is tall, and Hack's red hair would be visible from Mars. If they were there, I would have seen them. Good. The last thing I needed would be Becca ripping into Case over what I was sure was just a misunderstanding. Especially with her mom present.

We had to find our culprit soon. Only then would Becca move off Case.

"We have a job to do," I said, pointing at Diana. "And if we want to do it well, we have to split up. Not far. Just so you can examine the painting while I talk to the victim."

"Makes sense. We have a lot of ground to cover and not much time. But I could talk to Diana instead."

"I'll do it. I'm a better people person than you are." I smiled. "Besides, I know her."

Becca narrowed her eyes. "You mean you've done jobs for her before."

"Tomato, tomahto. Ladies first?"

Becca glared at me, one eyebrow raised. I shrugged. "Suit yourself. If you need me, you'll know where to find me." I turned on my heel and edged around the crowd, making my way toward the grieving Diana.

I don't like seeing people upset, and talking to the victim is very much in my line of work. In a way, every client I take on is a victim; I know how to care for them in a way Becca doesn't. I also know how to get information out of a victim without putting her on the defensive.

Diana's wails had subsided into sobs, which stopped when she saw me. "J-Jeremy," she said.

So she remembered me. "Hey, Diana," I said softly. I kept my voice gentle and friendly, sounding compassionate for the sake of the job, which wasn't hard to do. I just imagined Diana, with her hopes high for a prize, finding her painting wrecked after all the hours she'd spent on it. "I'm sorry about your painting," I said. "I wish I could have stopped it."

Diana smiled weakly. "Nobody could have stopped it, and anyway, you catch thieves," she said. "Sabotage isn't your field of work."

"Yeah, well, a bad guy is a bad guy, and I'm going to take this one down." Well, Becca and I would, but that was just details. All I needed was a little more evidence to prove that Lee or Quinn were involved. "Can you tell me what happened?"

Diana shrugged. "I don't know, it all happened so fast! I never expected it."

"People usually don't," I said. I looked over my shoulder at her ruined painting. Becca was there, leaning in close. She wore plastic gloves and was using her hand to measure the paint strokes. Her camera dangled from her wrist. As I looked, the gumshoe caught my eye and glared. I guess she still didn't like me being out of handcuff range.

The red paint was dripping down the canvas like

blood. My heart ached for Diana. She was a sweet girl and didn't deserve this. "I promise, I'm going to catch the person who did this," I said. "You'll see justice."

Justice? Wow, I was starting to sound like Becca. But what else could I promise a girl who hadn't lost a wallet or a keychain but her shot at winning? I couldn't retrieve that.

"Thanks, Jeremy," Diana said. She pulled away and smiled at me. "You're a good guy. How can I repay you?"

"I haven't caught the saboteur yet, and as always, my work is pro bono. Try to enjoy yourself today and remember that you have next year. I saw your painting; it was good."

Diana laughed. "Sure you don't want chocolate cake?"

"If you can find it, I won't say no. But I think all they have here is the brownies in the tent, and it's not the same."

"It sure isn't," said a voice behind me. Case appeared at my elbow, a pen behind his ear. "Brownies are too dense to fully enjoy on the palate." He smiled at Diana.

"Case talks like a foodie when he's nervous," Hack said. His face was turned down, focused on the screen of a phone I was sure wasn't his.

Good thing neither of my friends were looking at me; they would have noticed my face twitch as I had a miniature heart attack. I thought they'd be off at Wall C checking on Case's painting after the sabotage, making sure that his hadn't also been attacked. In fact, I wouldn't have been surprised if Case had decided to stand guard over his baby for the rest of the afternoon.

I glanced at Becca. This time she was facing her mom, and they seemed to be having some kind of argument. Detective Mills waved a hand at the saboteur's paint streaks, and Becca frowned. Then the younger Mills pointed at the crowds.

I didn't know what was going on, but at least neither mother nor daughter was looking my way. Good. As long as Becca was distracted, Case and Hack would be safe.

"Did anyone see anything?" I asked. "When the painting was attacked?"

Hack finally glanced up. "I'm on it. I'm searching through the buzz for witnesses testimonies."

"Whose phone is that?" I asked.

"A friend's," Hack said.

"I can save you the trouble. No one saw anything," Diana said.

Case pulled out a chocolate frosting–stained napkin and took the pen from his ear. "What do you mean by that?"

Diana looked at Case, all ready to take her statement,

and threw me a confused glance. "I'm sorry, is he with you?"

I opened my mouth to speak, but Case got there first. "Always, miss."

"Yep," Hack said distantly.

I swallowed my guilt. Case and Hack always had my back. Surely I could be honest with them about the job and who I was working with—on second thought, no. Becca was already in a bad mood. I didn't need my friends mad at me too.

But I still needed that statement. "So, Diana," I said. "What did you mean when you said no one saw anything?"

Diana twisted her hands. "There was a bit of a . . . disturbance," she said.

Case jotted that down on the napkin. "Uh-huh. What happened?"

Diana took a deep breath. "I had brought my family over to see my painting," she said. "Grandma had just arrived, and she hadn't seen it yet. So we brought her over here. We were just about to go get snow cones when someone shouted, 'Oh my gosh, what is that?' And we all turned to look."

Case and I met each other's eyes and grimaced. It was a simple, stupid trick, shouting for everyone to look at something. But it was simply, stupidly effective. I'd used it several times to get myself out of a sticky situation.

For just a few seconds, you'd have everyone's attention focused elsewhere. It didn't last long, but it worked great if all you needed was a few seconds to escape.

Or to slather paint on someone's art.

"Where did the voice come from?" I asked.

Diana pointed down the path toward her ruined painting. "Not far. And when I turned around, my painting was ruined," she said, sobbing on the last word.

"Did you see any of the other competitors around?"

"No."

"Are you sure?" I rattled off a list of contestants, making sure to include Quinn Eccles and Lee Moffat. "Any of them?"

Diana shook her head. "I'm sure." Well, that was helpful.

Holding back further tears, Diana added, "They told me the judges hadn't had a chance to look at it yet. I'm out of the running. Not just for Best Overall but also for Best Painting. I'm going home with nothing."

"Really?" I said. "That doesn't seem right." The judges must have been out for a while; how could none of them have seen Diana's painting?

Hack coughed. "J," he said in a low voice, "that's kind of the point of sabotage."

"I get that," I said. "But Diana was attacked for a

reason. Don't you think her work was good enough to earn her a prize? Shouldn't the judges give her something as a consolation?"

"You'd think so," Hack said. "But no. They've only prepared enough prize material for the winners of each division and Best Overall. Diana's getting nothing."

My fingers itched. Diana had been robbed, and my specialty was taking back what was stolen. But what could I do when there was nothing to take back for her, no prize promised her that she should have won?

"How do you know that? Maybe the judges will make an exception because of *sabotage*."

Hack raised the phone. "I told you. Buzz. People are talking."

"Because you can trust everything you read on the internet."

"He's right," Diana cut in. "The officials were talking about it after they saw what happened. I'm out."

"For what it's worth," Case said, "you're very talented. I saw your work before. . . ." He waved a hand. "It was exquisite."

Diana blushed. "Thank you. What did you say your name was?"

"I didn't say," Case said. "That way, you can call me whatever you like." He took her hand.

I rolled my eyes at Case's poorly timed romantic overtures and looked back at the painting, checking on Becca. She was still busy arguing with her mom. Next to her a contest official took out his phone. He glanced at the screen, jolted, and hurried away.

I frowned.

Hack, back to looking at his phone, gasped. "Guys."

"Not now," Case murmured.

"Guys, we have a problem." Hack held out the phone. On the screen was a photo of another painting covered with a broad squiggle of red paint.

"There's just been another sabotage. And it's on Wall C."

CASE FROZE, HYPNOTIZED by the tiny picture on the screen. He grabbed the phone from Hack and held it in front of his face. "Is it mine?" he asked. "Is it mine?"

"Hold on, hold on!" Hack yelled. "I need to zoom in."

My blood ran as cold and sour as frozen lemonade. Oh man. Ohhh man. Had Case been hit? Had I been messing around with Becca, playing detective, and let *Case get hit*?

I couldn't think. I didn't wait for Hack to examine the picture and see who'd been attacked. I lunged past my friends and Diana and ran, my feet slapping the sidewalk. I had to get to Wall C. I had to find the ruined painting and see if it was Case's. And if it was, I was . . . I was . . .

I had no idea what I was going to do. But it didn't bode well for the saboteur.

I would rip them in *half*.

"Wait, J!" Hack was shouting.

"Wilderson! Get back here!" Becca had spotted me.

I ignored both of them and ran. I'm good at it, and it felt wonderful to be able to do something right in the middle of this whole mess. So I ran harder, pushing through crowds and dodging bystanders who hadn't heard the news yet.

It's not Case's, I thought. *It can't be. I'm going to turn this corner and see it and it won't be Case's.*

I turned the corner, saw the painting, and felt my knees turn to jelly.

It wasn't Case's painting. His color-dabbed seascape hung on the wall, untouched, as I sagged with relief. The painting two spots over, however, dripped red. People swarmed around the damaged art. Two men in park security uniforms were carefully lowering the painting off the wall as a boy watched, ashen-faced.

I let out my breath in a rush. I turned back to the painting, now in transit. It wasn't Case's, but the next one could be, unless I did something to stop the saboteur before he (and/or she) struck again.

Forget Becca and her protocols. *I had to get a closer look at that painting.*

I darted at the two park security officials. Or, more specifically, the painting between them.

"Wait!" I reached for the painting. I missed; my hand dragged across the canvas, smearing through the wet paint.

"Kid! What's wrong with you?" One guard yanked me away from the painting.

I retracted my stained hand, balling it into a fist and holding it close to my chest. "I'm sorry," I said. "Is it my friend's? Did someone ruin his painting?" I let the fear from when I thought Case might have been the victim slide into my voice.

"Yeah, and we might not know who did it now that you put your fingers all over it." He waved at the canvas. My fingers had painted four lines through the broad strokes. "See?"

I looked at the paint on my hand and rubbed two stained fingers together. I checked out the ruined painting. Under the red paint, I caught images of neon shapes against a black background. I thought I would have liked it if I'd seen it earlier.

But the sabotage strokes themselves were what interested me. Where my hand hadn't smeared it, there weren't any bristle marks, like I'd expect to see if the saboteur were using a stolen brush. However, the paint was thicker in small, round spots, and on the edges, I saw holes in the paint spread. Like maybe this paint was smeared on with a sponge.

Huh.

The guards whisked the painting away. "You'd better hope you didn't leave fingerprints," one said. "Then people might think you're the saboteur."

"I'm sorry," I said. "I didn't mean to touch the paint."

I *hadn't* meant to touch it. Honestly. I just wanted a better look at the painting itself, and the saboteur's stroke marks. But as the guards hurried away before any other kids could turn the evidence into a Touch-and-Feel exhibit, I looked again at the paint on my hands.

I rubbed my fingers together and watched as the paint dried into rubbery strings. Heather had reported tempera paint stolen. Tempera paint, as I had discovered earlier in Case's locker, dried with a gritty, chalky feel. Not smooth and rubbery.

I smiled. I knew it wasn't Case, and now I had proof.

Hack appeared next to me. "It was Justin's painting," he said. "Not Case's."

"Yeah, I figured that out." I raised my hand and looked closely at the paint. It wasn't a match for the paint in Case's locker, I was sure of it. I hadn't realized how worried I'd been until the relief swept through me.

Hack groaned when he saw the paint on my hand. "Please tell me you didn't leave fingerprints."

"You know me," I said. "I don't have fingerprints. I had

them laser-removed when I dedicated my life to retrieving." Hack hit me in the shoulder, almost making me get the paint on my face. "Or the guards saw me touch the painting, so they know where those fingerprints came from," I said. "Your pick."

"Good thing for you there were witnesses," Hack said.

"Good thing," I said. "Where's Case?"

Hack jabbed a thumb over his shoulder. "Making out with his painting. For a guy so concerned with manners, he's really rubbing that kid's face in it."

I looked back to see Case hugging his painting, face almost pressed against it. The white-faced kid whose painting had been ruined watched enviously from the comforting embrace of his mother.

"Should we call him, or should we let them have their privacy?" I asked Hack, grinning. He smiled back.

"Let's give them a little longer. That's the most loving Case has gotten since Erin Gimley jumped him after school on Valentine's Day."

"She was very enthusiastic for a first grader." Hack's lips twitched, and we both busted up laughing. I don't know if it was the sight of Case's extreme gratitude for his painting's safety, or the release of tension after fearing that Case had been attacked, but Hack and I laughed so hard his glasses were spattered with tears.

"I-I'll go get him," I wheezed. "I need to ask him about—"

"Jeremy. Wilderson."

I stiffened. When I turned around, Becca was about fifty feet away, stalking closer and closer. That's right. I'd run from her. I'd left her to go chasing after the new sabotage—the one she didn't know had happened! And now I had red paint on my hand and I was here with Hack and she was coming at me with murder in her eyes.

Hack shoved me. "Go," he said. "Case and I can handle this. You just get out of here."

I nodded. "Thank you."

"Get out of here before the psycho catches up. Meet up with us later, and we'll work the job together. All three of us."

Ouch. "I don't know if I can."

Hack nodded, but he seemed hurt. "Then we'll see you when we see you."

"Till then," I said. I turned to run and then spun back to see Hack deliberately getting in Becca's way. He wouldn't hold her for long; she was on the track-and-field team, like me. She'd dodge him and come after me.

Good. I'd survive whatever threats she'd level at me. It wasn't like I hadn't dealt with worse. And as I ran,

I looked at my hand. We had a lot to discuss and the sooner the better.

Sooner it was: Becca ambushed me as I rounded a corner. "Gotcha. You know, you always take a right turn first when you're running."

"Really? How reliable of me."

"I can count on you for a lot of things," Becca said, scowling. "Unfortunately, one of those things seems to be *running off in the middle of an investigation.*"

"It's not like I didn't have a good reason."

Becca started to advance on me, so I backed away. All the while, Becca took me to task. "I don't care what your reason was. How dare you run off after I told you to stay where I could see you? Because of you, I had to abandon the crime scene before I'd thoroughly examined it—*what is on your hand?*"

I looked down at the smeared paint and swallowed. "Red-handed, once again," I said weakly.

Becca grabbed my wrist and raised my stained hand so she could see it. Her eyes blazed. "This is from the other painting, isn't it? You tampered with a crime scene. You tampered with evidence! You really can't help yourself, can you?"

"It's not like *I* did it."

"That's not the point," Becca said.

"Then what is?"

Becca twisted my wrist, forcing me forward. I could almost hear my arm groaning under the stress. Any harder and it'd fracture, I was sure.

"S-stop," I gasped.

Becca leaned down, her hair brushing my face. "You listen to me, Wilderson," she hissed in my ear. "When this is over, I won't hesitate to gather intel on your illicit summer activities so I can bring you to justice when we're back in school. But for right now, we're working together. On my case. That means it's my reputation on the line, not yours. Any of your monkey business will be connected back to me. So, for once, you will do what I tell you, and you will do this *by the book*. If you tamper with evidence or break the law, so help me, I will use your head as a shot put. Do I make myself clear?"

I nodded and Becca released me. "Taking off my head doesn't seem very just," I said, rubbing my wrist. Good thing she hadn't twisted my clean arm.

"After everything you've put me through, you're lucky I don't have you hanged, drawn, and quartered." Becca folded her arms and watched me.

I winced. Have you ever looked up what being hanged,

drawn, and quartered is? I have. Even as an (I was pretty sure) empty threat, it wasn't one I liked leveled at me. "I'm sorry, but is something up?"

"Oh, like now you care." Becca turned away from me.

"I care. I mean it."

Becca snorted. "Right. If you cared, you'd have been around when I needed you. If you cared, I would have been able to count on you."

"Is this about me racing off to see if my friend's painting was sabotage number two? If so, I'm sorry," I said, trying to calm her down, but still feeling annoyed because I hadn't done anything wrong. "And I'm sorry I got a very valuable piece of evidence smeared across my hand, especially since you had to leave your own crime scene to come chasing after me."

She still seemed upset. I stepped closer to her. "What else is up?"

"Nothing you need to worry about."

"Tell me."

Becca sighed. She pulled out her camera and took a few photos of my hand.

"It's my mom," she finally said.

"What about your mom?" I asked. "Wouldn't she be helping us?"

Becca scowled. "You'd think. But Mom is convinced

our saboteur is an adult, so she's running her own investigation."

"An adult?"

Becca gestured at the dried paint staining my hand. "It's this paint. The sabotage on Diana's painting was done with the same kind, or something that looks a lot like it. Mom didn't tell me what kind of paint she thinks it is because she wants to hear back from the lab. But she thinks a kid wouldn't have access to this kind of paint."

"I don't know," I said. "It's an art show. Kids here have a lot of different kinds of paint."

"Maybe the kind of paint Mom suspects isn't typically something used in art," Becca said. She shook her head. "There's more. The park is so crowded—someone must have seen *something*. But no one seems to have noticed anything amiss. Mom and I both think this suggests a level of trust in the saboteur. Mom thinks a kid wouldn't carry that kind of trust, but an adult leaning close to a painting would seem like a judge or just a parent admiring their child's work."

"Fair point," I said. "So why are you upset?"

"Because I still think it's a kid doing this!" Becca squeezed her camera.

"Okay," I said. "Clearly we have a lot to discuss. But not here. Not where anyone can hear us."

Becca nodded. "The shed where we stored our disguises," she said. "You go. I'll follow after a few minutes."

"So savvy. That's why I like you."

Becca smirked. "Save your so-called charm for your fan club."

"I don't have a fan club."

"Exactly. Now go."

I hurried to the shed, let myself in, and waited for Becca to come back. Being alone in a stuffy shed that smells like gasoline and cut grass tends to make your thoughts circle faster, if only to keep you company. At first I thought about how it was around noon, and the tent would be serving lunch, and I was hungry and should go back for a sandwich, but soon my thoughts turned to more serious matters.

The police thought the saboteur was an adult. What if they were right? Then we should just let them handle it and enjoy ourselves. But then again, Becca knew her business well enough that I couldn't dismiss her theories, whatever they were, and honestly, how much could I enjoy myself when a couple of saboteurs were running around?

The saboteurs had taken out two paintings quickly, one after another. For all I knew, they were attacking another painting as I sat waiting. What if there were more than two saboteurs, systematically taking out everyone else's art?

No, I couldn't think like that. I had no proof that there were more than two saboteurs, or even that there were two. At most, there was one to distract and one to do the deed. That's all I had. I needed to think through what I knew.

Interesting, how only paintings had been struck so far. Did that mean one of the two possible saboteurs was a painter? That was a point in my favor for Quinn being saboteur number two. What about Heather's stolen supplies? How did they factor in? Why was that paint in Case's locker?

"Don't think too hard. You'll hurt yourself." I looked up to see Becca standing over me with a snow cone in each hand. She smiled. "Green or red?"

"Green."

"Huh. Would've figured you for red, given your history with the color." I made a face and she laughed. "Here. Tell me what you found out."

"How much do I owe you?"

"The cones were free. I discovered damage in the snow-cone machine's cooling system. Nothing big, just spotted some leaking hoses on my way past. It seriously took me a minute. But the guy gave me a couple freebies as a thank-you." She sat on a stack of neatly arranged paint cans.

I took the snow cone in my clean hand and sipped up the drippy parts. "Discovered damage. You really can't turn it off, can you?"

"Neither can you. Now talk."

"You first. Why do you think our saboteurs are kids if your mom thinks it's an adult?'

Becca shrugged. "More to lose, first of all. Parents may want their kids to win, but it's the kids on the chopping block. They're the ones who are trying to succeed, and they're the ones who are freaking out in the Contestants' Tent. But also, people wouldn't notice a kid standing by the paintings. Adults tend to forget about kids. They trust us, maybe more than they should."

I nodded. I'd used that particular trust a lot in my work. One innocent, wide-eyed kid, coming right up. Did the job every time.

"It just doesn't make sense to me that the saboteur is an adult. A kid could get this paint, whatever it is," Becca added.

"What do you think it is?" I asked.

"Not sure. It's red, like the paint in Case's locker—"

"But it's not the same kind." I rubbed my painted

fingers together quickly, making the dried red paint twist into rubbery strings. "Look."

Becca caught them as they fell. "That's interesting."

"Remember the yellow tempera paint I got on my hands?" I said. "When that dried, it had a dull, chalky look. It fell off in flakes. But look at this." I showed her the paint that was still on my skin. "See how it's thin and glossy? It's not the same paint as the paint we found in Case's locker. He's not the saboteur."

"He might still be the thief," Becca said, pulling out a bag and dropping the strings of paint inside. "The bottles in his locker match Heather's. Give me your hand. I need a bigger sample."

I did as she asked. "Case doesn't steal," I said as she used a torn piece of paper to scrape the wettest spots of paint from my skin.

"You have a blind spot when it comes to your friends, you know." Becca tucked the bag away.

"Not this time. Why would Case hide stolen paint in a family locker where his sisters and parents could see it? You're going to have to look elsewhere for your culprit."

"I think you're right." Becca nodded and gazed at the ceiling for a moment. "Should we turn our attention to Lee, then?"

"And Quinn." I sighed and gave back her snow cone.

"I know you don't think it's Quinn, but we did see her grab that paint. It could be whatever this is."

Becca groaned. "Stop jumping to conclusions."

"Stop staying put on yours."

She looked at me sternly. "Think about it, Wilderson. Quinn grabbed a small tube of paint, and the saboteur clearly has paint to spare. Also, like Case, Quinn shares a locker with her family. Why would *she* leave materials for sabotage where her family could find them?"

As much as I hated Becca turning my own argument against me, she'd made some good points. Quinn didn't have enough paint in that little tube to commit the sabotages, and she wouldn't hide evidence where her parents could find it.

"She did have that purse, though," I said. "She could hide the paint in there."

"Still not enough for sabotage." Becca sipped some syrup off the edge of her cone. "Anyway, the fact that the paint used for sabotage doesn't match the paint we found in Case's locker doesn't rule Case out. We were in that locker room for a long time, waiting forever for you to finish opening that lock—"

"Hey."

"And we only saw Quinn come in. Your friend could have kept the sabotage paint somewhere else, or had it with him when we were in that locker room. We still don't really know the timing of the attacks."

"It wasn't him!"

"Find me some better proof and I'll consider it. But he has Heather's paint," Becca said, counting on her fingers.

"We don't know it's hers."

"We don't? Really?" When I didn't answer, Becca continued, "And he's panicked about the contest. Sounds like motive."

"Without means or opportunity. He doesn't have the right kind of paint."

"Do you know that?" Becca asked. "Do you know where he was when Diana's painting was attacked?"

I fell silent. I didn't know. "Not committing sabotage."

Becca scoffed. "Please tell me you got something useful before running off on me."

"How about the victim's story?" I filled Becca in on my chat with Diana.

"So, she saw her painting, and it was fine, and then someone shouted to look away and she did, and then when she turned back, the painting was ruined?" Becca frowned. "I agree with my mom that someone is doing this sneakily, and that it has to be someone who is overlooked. *Like a kid.* Not an adult, like she thinks!" Her eyes gleamed.

"Yeah, and there's more. I don't know about the first

painting, but the second was done sloppily with a sponge or rag or something. There weren't any fiber lines in the paint, so not a brush."

Becca drained the last of the juice from her cone and held up one hand. "That makes sense. The saboteur could have soaked a sponge in paint and placed it in the palm, here. It would just take a rubber band to secure it, and it would only take a second to brush it on the painting."

"So we're looking for a red-handed saboteur?"

"Not if the sponger used a glove. But it supports your theory that there are two saboteurs," Becca said.

"How so?"

"Because Diana's painting was attacked with a brush."

"No way."

She nodded. "It's one of the reasons Mom thinks we have an adult saboteur. It was a large, coarse brush, the kind they sell at hardware stores. Thick fiber lines, broad strokes."

"So, not one of Heather's brushes either." I shook my head. "The sponge and brush work were so sloppy. I'm getting the feeling the saboteurs aren't painters themselves. At least, not necessarily."

"Well, sabotage isn't precision work, and paintings are being attacked first, which makes me question motive, but I see your point. We can't rule anyone out. But at least we know there are two saboteurs. One to distract everyone and one to sabotage the painting. One to use a brush, one to use a sponge."

"No kidding." I drained my own cone.

"Two people. Much like, let's say, Case and Hack."

I glared at her. "Or like Lee and Quinn."

"Quinn is innocent."

"So is Case."

She shrugged but didn't press the issue, so I didn't either. The truth would come out eventually. She'd see.

"At least your friend has this going for him," Becca said. "I'm convinced Heather's thief is unrelated to the sabotage. Since the sabotage is the bigger threat right now, if Case stole Heather's paints, I'll have to deal with him later."

"Case didn't steal anything—"

Becca held up a hand. She passed me her camera, reached over, and pressed a button. A single shot filled the screen. "Later. Right now, look that over. I examined the painting, but a second opinion is always useful. Tell me if you notice anything with your trained thief eyes."

"Retrieval specialist eyes," I grumbled, but I looked closer at a photo that was annoying me for some reason. It seemed different from the version of Diana's painting that I'd seen pre-sabotage. I zoomed in and realized why. "This painting was marked."

Becca snorted. "I thought the red *Z* would have made it obvious."

"Not that. I mean, it was marked before the saboteur hit it. Look." I showed her the picture, zoomed in. "See that in the corner? Doesn't it look like—"

"A little black dot." Becca took the camera and saved the zoomed-in picture as a new file. "I would have noticed that," she said, "if I had more time." She scowled at me, but it didn't carry any real power.

"Right." I had a thought. "Is it marker or paint?"

"Can't tell," Becca said, peering at her picture. "Marker would be easier, but paint would blend in on a painting. Only the saboteurs would know what to look for."

My skin prickled. "Quinn. Her small tube of paint."

"Drop it."

"But a small tube would be perfect for marking paintings." Why was she ignoring the evidence? Quinn was guilty!

"So would a marker, and anyone could have one of those."

"Lee's friend had one," I said, remembering. "He was creating his own masterpiece on his shoe with it. It would have been easy for Lee to borrow and mark a few competitors."

"Too much speculation. Let's focus on what we actually know." Becca straightened her back. "The victims were Diana Legris and Justin Baker. Both painters, but Diana just finished seventh grade and Justin is our age. Both good artists, but why them?"

"What does the saboteur know that we don't?"

"Good question. Throw it on the pile." Becca looked at the camera in her hands and sighed. "There's too much, Wilderson. We don't know what kind of paint you got a sample of. We don't know how many saboteurs we have or who they are."

"We have an idea of who they are. You just won't admit it."

Becca shot a look at me but continued. "We don't know if the black mark in the corner there is paint or marker or what that would mean. We also don't know how the saboteurs are choosing their victims."

She groaned and stood up, making the paint cans rattle. One almost fell. Becca caught it and sighed. "Too many questions. We need to get some answers before the saboteur strikes again." She closed her eyes and was silent for so long I thought she'd fallen asleep.

"We need to split up," she said suddenly.

"What?"

Her eyes snapped open. "I'll say it again. We have to split up."

"How can we do that when we haven't even been on a

date?" I said. "Unless this is one, in which case, I am way underdressed. Where's that trilby?" I searched through the heaps of our discarded disguises.

"Not funny. I don't like this. Who knows what you'll do if I leave you unsupervised?"

"Maybe what I came here to do. Hang out with Case and look at art until my brain shatters. Unless you can think of a better use of my time?"

Becca closed her eyes and rubbed her head. She looked like she'd been trampled by the soccer team. "Diana's painting. I'm pretty sure the paint used to sabotage it was the same as the kind used on Justin's, but we have to be sure. We also need to identify what kind was used. You need to get a sample."

"Um, okay. No problem. Where's the painting now?"

Becca winced. "My mom has it."

What? "Hang on. It sounded like you just told me to go track down a painting that is currently under guard. By your *mom*."

"You heard me," Becca said through gritted teeth.

"Do you realize what you're asking? I'm not sure you do."

"Trust me, I'm aware," Becca said bitterly. "But Mom's not the only one with access to a lab. If I can prove the paint is something a kid might use, and even that some competitor here has used it, then I can get her to consider other options." Becca handed me a plastic bag and a piece of paper. "Put the sample here. Just get the sample. That's all. Whatever you do, don't get caught."

I grinned. "Hey, it's like you don't even know me."

"You'll be sneaking into a place full of adults. Cops. My mom."

"Why can't you get the paint? Just go up and ask your mom."

"Mom's running her own investigation and she doesn't need my input. So she's blocking me out of this one unless I can find some substantial evidence that the saboteur is a kid."

"Great." Holy cow, she was doing it. Using me and my skills to help her solve a crime. This wasn't like the Mark job, where I was in control and she operated on a "don't ask, don't tell" policy (for the most part) when it came to me sneaking around. This was Becca Mills straight-up asking me to find and break into wherever park security was keeping Diana's painting. Sneaking past actual law enforcement, somewhere I wasn't supposed to go. Becca had crossed a line. I could get in real trouble if I got caught, and this was on her orders.

From the defeated look on her face, I knew it wasn't a setup. She was sacrificing her high ideals to stop the saboteur, and it made me like her more. Thrilled but valuing my life enough not to comment, I tucked the bag and paper in my pocket. "I have ins in the art crowd, so I can find out why anyone would target Diana and Justin. I can also scan the crime scenes for clues."

"Perfect," Becca said. "I'll look for art marked with black. I can also interview bystanders to find out if they saw anything. A lot of the contest officials are art teachers. They might also have some insights on why Diana and Justin were attacked first, but teachers can miss things kids notice, so you'll need to talk to your friends. We should also check alibis for when the sabotages happened."

Becca still looked green, and I'd been the one with the apple snow cone. Her guilt must be weighing on her. Maybe letting her hire me for an actual retrieval job wasn't a good idea. "You sure you want to split up?" I said. "I don't have to go . . . do my thing."

Becca sagged with relief when I didn't say *breaking and entering*. She gave me a small smile. "Thanks. But I'm sure. There are too many bad guys out there, and they're hurting people. We have to make them do the time for their depraved actions."

I wanted to say, *You say that I hurt people and I need to do the time at every opportunity, and now you're telling me to go steal from your mom.* But saying that would have meant I had a death wish, which I don't, regardless of what my actions sometimes imply. So I just said, "I'm off, then."

"Great. Just remember, I'm counting on you. Okay?" Becca gave me a serious look. "Get the evidence and get back here. Don't get in trouble. We need this."

It was weird seeing her so solemn. "What's the matter?"

"Nothing."

"You sure? You seem . . . uptight."

"Never mind me," Becca snapped. She took a deep breath. "Let me worry about my own job. Keep your head clear for yours. You know what you need to do, right?"

"Yeah, I got it. Get the paint, get the info, get out. Meet you at the snow-cone stand in an hour? So that's . . ." I looked at my phone. "A little after one p.m. Is that enough time? I mean, I could have the paint sample, the saboteurs' names, *and* Heather's stolen stuff by then, but you might need more time."

I wasn't trying to kick Becca when she was down. The opposite, actually. She looked so upset at herself for telling me to do shady things that I thought annoying her, challenging her, would spark her back up.

It did. Her eyes blazed as she said, "I'll have the case solved by then. And I'll have figured out how to stick you with every crime you committed during sixth grade and summer vacation. Don't talk to me about time."

"Fine, then." I raced out of the shed before Becca could realize that I'd tried to cheer her up on purpose. Becca Mills endorsing the shadowy techniques of Jeremy Wilderson, retrieval specialist? A new, shining age had begun.

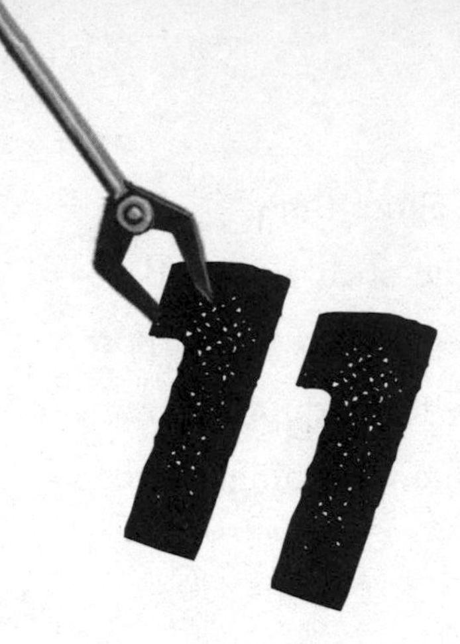

I SLOWED DOWN AS I reentered the swirling masses of the art show visitors. I needed a plan. What did I have to do? Get the paint sample from Diana's painting, look for general clues, and find out why Diana and Justin were targeted. On top of that, I had to find some evidence to make Becca reconsider Quinn as a saboteur suspect.

Quinn may have fooled the gumshoe, but I'm a bit more cynical. I've met my fair share of crooks, and one thing I've learned is that no one is truly innocent. Once upon a time, I would have added "except Becca," but now she was contracting my less-than-legal help on her case. I half expected her to put herself under arrest.

So much to do and only an hour to do it. Where to start?

The smartest idea would be to get the information

about Diana and Justin first. All I'd have to do would be to talk to Case and Hack.

I also didn't want to rush into getting the paint sample. I needed time to think up a plan for obtaining it. If I was caught messing around with Diana's painting, who do you think the cops would suspect first?

Messing with the cops at all wasn't a smart move, but I'm known for being sneaky, not smart. It was time to show it. Time to find my friends, and then later I'd find Diana's painting and get the sample without anyone spotting me.

First things first: time to go into disguise again. I circled back to the shed and put on the baseball cap and plaid shirt. I didn't want Becca spotting me later when I looked for evidence on Quinn. I'd burned the disguise on Case and Hack, but as I'd have to go talk to them eventually, this wasn't a bad thing.

Becca's voice floated back to me. *Maybe it's time to consider that Case has his own secrets.* I shivered and dismissed the thought. Case was not our saboteur. He was probably off enjoying the sun and catching a saboteur, a job he should have stayed far, far away from. I had to trust he'd be smart enough to stay away from Becca.

That might make it hard for me to find him and Hack. Hmm. Maybe I could multitask: look for Diana's painting (but not get near it) and scan for clues while I look for my friends. That way I could use my time more wisely.

Despite my worries about Case, when I returned to the crowds nearest the Contestants' Tent, I felt like a new, more gung-ho person. I have to admit it was exciting. As I hurried past displays and through crowds of people, looking for my friends and a hint as to where security was keeping those paintings (high number of guards, a general aura of "don't come here, buster"), I enjoyed a tingling on my neck I hadn't felt since, well, since taking down Mark. I felt alive, but in more ways than just a physical adrenaline rush. The mystery, all those fragments of a solution, made my head fizz with a different kind of exhilaration.

As I searched for Case and Hack, I located the place where I'd had my run-in with the guards, over by Case's landscape (which was still safe). A quick but thorough search of the area turned up no new clues.

Let's see. Last time I was here, the guards yelled at me for touching the wet paint and then they carried Justin's painting off . . . to the right. So I turned right as well. Before too long I noticed I was heading toward the help office. Not to be confused with the help kiosk, located near the museum, that handed out maps and sold umbrellas on rainy days. No, this office was near the entrance to the park and was for reporting missing kids, renting out sports equipment, and handling medical emergencies. It was a larger, more stable structure, and there were too many people around it, even for a busy day in the park. The sabotaged paintings had to be inside.

I leaned casually against a tree and cased the building from the outside. A tan brick structure, with double the number of guards they usually had on duty milling around the building's front door. A woman was talking on a cell phone outside. I squinted; it was Becca's mom. Wouldn't it have been easier to put up a sign: SABOTAGED GOODS INSIDE, GOING HOT?

On the other hand, who would be stupid enough to try to break into a place while Detective Mills was around? Oh, right. Me.

Well, clearly my usual plan—walking through the front door with a grin and enough charm to drown a whale—probably wasn't going to work. Next thing on the list: check for alternate entrances. Where could I get into the building without Becca's mom or any other adult seeing me?

I pushed away from the tree, planning to go around back and look for a window or a door I could use later. At that moment, Quinn and Larissa came up the path. They moved slowly and stopped to look at a painting of a ballerina on a high wire. Quinn's purse was dangling loosely from her hand.

I thought back to that black spot on Diana's painting. The whole procedure appeared in front of me like a vision: Quinn, wandering the park, quietly marking the competition, and leaving her partner in crime, Lee, to come by later with the red paint.

I had to search that bag. But how to get it? I could wait until she put it down, and go through it like I usually did when I was on a job.

Still, what would it prove? If there was a tube of black paint in there, all it would reveal is that Quinn, a painter, had a tube of black paint. She could have borrowed it from a friend, or bought it at the museum gift shop. I could almost hear Becca chewing me out: *innocent until proven guilty*. How much proof would it take to convince her?

A lot. I needed more than the paint. I needed Quinn to make a mistake. I'd dealt with Lee, and he was a snotty little nut but a tough nut. He wouldn't break; he was too full of himself for that. But if Becca saw innocence in Quinn, maybe I could break her. Then she'd make a mistake, do something she shouldn't, and I would be there.

It took some quick thinking, but I came up with a plan. I waited until the girls were turned away from me, and then I ran.

I hurtled full-speed toward them like a six-year-old on his first two-wheeler. "Stop!" I shouted. "Stop!"

People froze as I raced past them. I paid no attention. The Eccles girls glanced back at me, and I looked at them, though I pretended to focus on a target past them. As I passed the girls, I raised one arm, like I was reaching for someone.

My arm just *happened* to hook Quinn's purse, tearing it out of her grip as I ran past.

"Hey! Wait!" Quinn yelled.

"Come back!" I called at nobody. When I heard the sound of footsteps racing after me, it became hard not to smile.

A glance over my shoulder informed me that Quinn and her sister were both in pursuit. My gambit had worked. Now to end this charade before too many people got interested.

I detoured, veering into a grassy area of the park. No art, and therefore fewer people. "Stop!" I called again weakly, and then slowed. Placing my hands on my knees, I visibly caught my breath.

"Hey! You!" The girls reached me. Larissa's eyes widened with recognition when she saw my face, but Quinn just looked angry. "That's my bag."

"What?" I looked at the purse hanging from my arm

like I'd just noticed it was there. "I'm sorry. I didn't even notice. Here."

I slid the purse from my arm and held it out to Quinn. She reached for it, but just before her fingers made contact, I dropped it, letting it fall top-down onto the grass. The bag had been open, and several items spilled out.

"My bad," I said. I squatted, as did Quinn, and we started picking up the stuff. I grabbed the purse itself, letting everything else fall out. I shook my head. "I'm sorry. I'm just flustered. It's been a . . . long day."

Quinn sighed. "I guess I understand." We turned back to the items on the ground.

There it was, among the grass. A little tube of black paint. I picked it up and looked at it. Quinn snatched it from my hand and stuffed it into her bag with all her other gear.

"Paint, huh? Going to be working on a new project while you're here?" I asked.

Smiling at me, Quinn said, "It's actually for a friend."

Sure it was. If people are going to constantly lie to me, why can't they be more creative about it?

But Becca would buy that story, because Quinn exuded "innocence." I could see how Scottsville Middle's best detective could be fooled; Quinn had a wholesome look and bright eyes. She didn't seem guarded or shady. I needed more. Good thing I had a plan.

Conning is a complex business when you put it into practice, but at its heart, it's all about either offering the mark something they want more than anything, or threatening them with something they'll do anything to avoid. The most effective cons do both, making the mark hand over what you want because they think it's in their best interest. I wanted Quinn to make a mistake. She would do that if she was overly confident, or if she was scared. Since confident criminals weren't messing up today, I decided to go for scared.

"You're Casey's friend," Larissa said as Quinn and I stood up. "Jeremy, right?"

"That's me."

I was still breathing heavily, even though I had long since caught my breath. Why? I couldn't just volunteer what I was "doing." I needed them to *ask*.

Quinn's smile morphed into something more quizzical. "I know you."

I hate it when someone I don't know says that. It's usually followed with "You're that thief."

"You're that thief Becca Mills is always chasing."

What did I tell you? "Retrieval specialist, actually," I said, holding out a hand. "Jeremy Wilderson."

Quinn slipped her purse strap over her shoulder and shook my hand. "Quinn Eccles. And I don't know, you seem more like a thief to me."

The words didn't sound angry, but Larissa touched Quinn's arm. "Leave him alone. It was an accident. I'm sure he didn't mean to grab your bag."

"I didn't," I said. "I was just in a hurry to catch the saboteur."

Quinn tilted her head. "You're trying to catch the saboteur?"

That's right. Walk into my trap.

"See? He's one of the good guys. Like Robin Hood." Larissa smiled at me. I grinned back. Robin Hood, huh? I could get used to that.

"Yep. Normally I wouldn't get involved in a case like this, but my friend is a competitor. I'm sure you know how it is; I get very protective of my friends." I smiled, watching Quinn. She nodded and smiled gently, giving nothing away. Larissa nodded too.

"Think you're getting close to catching this person?" Quinn said.

Time to up the ante, whatever that means. "Very close. I think I have a suspect."

Both Quinn's and Larissa's eyebrows shot up. "Really?" Quinn said.

"I noticed a guy hanging around the site of the second sabotage. I couldn't see his face, but he was short, with light hair. Wearing a gray vest." If Quinn was working with Lee, her mind would instantly jump to the guilty party. "Anyway, I just saw him again," I continued, "so I called out and went after him. He ran off. I was in such a hurry to catch him, I didn't realize I'd grabbed your purse. It was an accident."

Quinn straightened her purse strap. "Way to go. I guess you are as heroic as Larissa says." She gave me a sunny smile as I tried on the word "heroic" for size. It fit well.

Larissa frowned. "Your description sounds like Lee."

Quinn shook her head. "Can't be. We were just with him."

"*I* wasn't," Larissa said.

"Right." Quinn nodded. "That must have been when you ran into your friend from soccer camp. Lee came by and we talked."

This was interesting. "Who's Lee, and how long ago was this?" I asked.

"Lee's our neighbor," Quinn said. "He goes to Burdick Charter. But I don't think your suspect could have been the same person. I saw him about half an hour ago, maybe less, and he said he was going back to the tent."

About the same time as Diana's sabotage. That wasn't the only thing that smelled funny about Quinn's words. It was also a little too convenient that Larissa had happened to miss seeing Lee, almost like Quinn was providing an alibi for Lee, the way a partner in crime might.

My plan wasn't working like I needed it to. I had to layer on a little more threat. "Can I trust you two?" I said in a low voice.

The Eccles sisters nodded, and I leaned in close. "I may need your help. If you see Lee, let me know. I want to ask him some questions. Here's my number." I rattled off Mom's cell number. "And if you see him talking to anyone in a suspicious way, let me know. You see"—I looked around, as though worried someone would hear me—"I think we're dealing with two saboteurs."

"No!" Quinn looked horrified while Larissa's eyes just widened. Well, that was telling. Way to give me the reaction I was looking for, Quinn Eccles. Thank you, sincerely, for looking scared.

"Yes. Two saboteurs, working together. If I can get one, I can get the other." I leaned back and put my hands in my pockets.

Quinn had risen to my bait but not enough. I needed to give her a sense of urgency, a reason to do something stupid. I looked back and saw the roof of the help office beyond the crowd. Perfect.

"Of course," I said, "I might not need to do anything."

"Why not?" Larissa asked.

I pointed. "Right over there is the help office, where Scottsville's best detective is going over both paintings with a fine-bristled brush, so to speak. Yep, Becca Mills's mother is here. Not to mention that the park security is so thick, any evidence, and I mean *any* evidence, in that building will be found." I smiled and shrugged. "It's just a matter of time. Who knows what will turn up in the sweep?"

Quinn nodded. "We'll definitely let you know if we see anything. Count on us." Larissa was quiet, looking at the building, but she caught my eye and nodded, wearing a bright smile.

"Great. And I'll try not to scoop up your property again."

"Come on," Larissa said, pulling on Quinn's arm. "Let's go get one of those snow cones."

"Ooh! I hope they have orange. Blue raspberry stains my teeth." Quinn flashed me a smile. Was it possible she was smiling too much?

I smiled back and watched as the sisters left. Well, that was interesting. My seed had been planted; now I had to wait and watch for Quinn to make a mistake. Maybe she'd talk to Lee, tell him that there were too many people involved now and they should stop. Or maybe she'd try to salvage the job by trying to take evidence from under the cops' noses. That wouldn't go well for her.

She'd do something now; I could feel it. But I had to get back to the help office and figure out a way inside, and at some point I'd have to find Case and Hack—

"J! Back in the lumberjack costume? I guess that means you managed to ditch the snitch?"

Or they could find me. I spun around. Case and Hack approached me, snow cones in hand. My stomach lurched. Now was my chance to get information, but I didn't know how to keep them from suspecting my involvement with the job.

"Hey, guys. Not hungry for that," I said, pointing to their snow cones. They were about to ask. But I would have to stop by the tent and get some real lunch soon. No good trying to be sneaky when your stomach is rumbling. Also, I might be able to find out if Lee really had gone back to the tent. That would be good evidence for Becca.

"Snow cones are less food and more of a drink," Hack said. His lips were stained green. It looked odd under his red hair. Kind of like a reverse carrot.

"Then why do I get even thirstier when I have one?"

Case said. He sounded more cheerful. The warm summer air and a little high-fructose corn syrup did him good. That, and the job he thought we all had. "Becca leave you alone, or did you escape?"

"I think she's got other things to deal with besides me." I caught myself changing my weight from foot to foot, and stopped. As much as I would have loved to track the saboteurs down with my friends, I couldn't. Becca was waiting for me to find, break into, and retrieve from a building guarded by park security and her mother, and I still had no idea how I was going to do that.

But you know me. I like a challenge.

"Oh, right. The sabotage. Of course she'd start tracking that scent." Case looked into his snow cone like it was a crystal ball. I guess it was, being a ball of ice, but you know what I mean.

He looked uncomfortable, and as Hack shook his head at me, I regretted bringing the subject up. But since it was, I felt freer to talk about it.

"Look, about this saboteur thing—"

Case raised a hand. "Stop. It's okay; we know you can't give this job your full attention. You're too busy running from Becca."

"But don't worry. We've got it!" Hack aid.

"Why else would we skip lunch?" Case asked. "We'll

take care of the big stuff, and you can help out when you can."

"If you get involved, Becca might think you two are the saboteurs," I warned them. "Maybe you should back off and let her handle it. She's good at what she does."

Case folded his arms. "What, you don't think we can handle this?"

It was like the Mark job all over again. "Of course I think you can."

"Besides," Hack said, "if she's so good at her job, why is she still chasing you? She doesn't actually believe you did it, does she?"

I shrugged. "I don't think so. She thinks I'm a thief and don't have the ambition for sabotage."

"Which you do."

"The ambition, sure. But sabotage isn't my style."

"Then why is she still chasing you?"

I smiled. "Fish gotta swim, birds gotta fly. Anyway, you guys keep telling me I'm insane for working in Becca's jurisdiction. I'm just thinking that it might be safer for all of us if we all concentrate on protecting Case's painting and staying out of Becca's way."

"That's what we're trying to do," Case said. He walked over to a tree and leaned against it. It was like my words were sapping the strength Hack must have worked hard to bring back. "Protect my art and the art of everyone else here. You can help us, or you can sit in the tent, hiding from Becca. What sounds like more fun?"

Dang it. They were really serious about this, and to be fair, they had a good reason to be. Case could be the next to fall. Maybe if they were busy tracking down the saboteurs, they'd be out of Becca's way.

Besides, I did want to spend time with them. Playing both sides might be the only way to please everyone.

I was going to regret this later, I just knew it.

"Okay, I'll help. But like you said, I can't commit a lot of time to this job," I said. "Not when I have to run at any moment."

Case nodded. "We know. But we'd like to hear your thoughts."

"Well, I got a smear of the paint. It's weird." I explained how the paint was stretchy and rubbery.

Case bit his thumb. "I know a few paints like that. What I wouldn't give for a sample. . . ."

"Detective Mills Senior is on the case."

Hack paled and Case stomped a foot. "Way to ruin my day, J."

"I'll try to make it up to you," I said. "But I have a question. Why would the saboteur target Diana and Justin first?"

Case nodded again. "That was our first question too. Turns out Diana and Justin were favorites to win Best Overall. Whoever's doing this is targeting the judges' favorites."

"How'd you know Diana and Justin were favorites?"

"Hack told me."

"And how'd he know?"

After a few seconds of calculating silence, we both turned to Hack. He waved his almost-empty paper cone, flinging green drops at us. "What? Is it my fault if the judges e-mail their opinions back and forth on an unsecured network?"

"I thought you gave that phone back to its owner," Case said.

I had a different kind of confusion. "Since when can you hack e-mails from a mobile device?"

"Case, the owner of this phone was so freaked that he could be the next to get sabotaged that he graciously told me I can keep the phone as long as I need it. I'll give it back. And J, school is a wonderful, educational time. Especially when you're banned from the computer lab for a month."

I raised my hands in surrender. "Okay, you've leveled up. Congratulations, and watch out for the boss fight."

Hack shrugged. "I got those down. Always aim for

the eye. J, want the number for this phone? You might need it later if Becca keeps chasing you."

"Sure," I said, and a moment later Mom's phone buzzed with a new text. "Thanks. But still. Diana told me that the judges hadn't seen her painting yet. How could she be a favorite if they hadn't judged her work?"

"The judges have pictures of the art," Hack said. "Like a guidebook. Just small photos the contestants sent in with their submissions. Enough to give an impression but not enough to fully judge. They're basing their favorites on those. You should hear the chatter about which ones they're most excited to see."

I turned to Case. "Who are the other favorites? Are you one of them?"

Case laughed. "No."

"Really?" Relief washed through me.

He shrugged. "I'm not surprised. I mean, it's my first year. I'm not that good yet, and the judges tend to choose older kids who've done this a few times. Giving me Best Overall would be as weird as, well, you spending quality time with Becca Mills."

Right. Weird. I swallowed and said, "I'm not convinced you're not a favorite. You're sure you're not on the list?"

"Not according to Hack."

"Let's see," Hack said, cutting in. "Diana was a favorite for the paintings, as was Justin. Some kid named Henry is a favorite for photography—"

"What about sculpture?" I asked.

"Top pick is Sandra Lynn. You should see her work. Case was in awe."

Sandra Lynn. The girl who made that intricate wax statue. "I saw it earlier." Perfect. I had a hit list, and neither Quinn nor Lee was on it. This was motive. I was thinking like Becca.

Man, I hoped that wasn't permanent.

"Who are the second placers?" No one at the back of the pack would risk sabotage when it wouldn't get them the win anyway. From my experience, the scariest people are those who are half a point away from the coveted A grade. People in second or third place were more likely to be our crooks.

"That twerp Lee Moffat. I can't think of anyone who deserves it less," Hack said. "Have you seen how he talks to his friend?"

"Oh yeah." But Lee was a sculptor. "What about the painters? The paintings were attacked first."

"We wondered about that too," Case said. "Why the paintings first?"

"Easy targets?" I asked.

Hack played with his glasses. "The judges have a lot of favorites in paintings. Maybe the saboteur thought his greatest competition would come from there."

Maybe. Or maybe at least one of the saboteurs is a painter. But is it Quinn or someone else? "The judges are talking a lot about the paintings, but you don't know who the next heads on the chopping block might be?"

Hack shrugged. "They haven't said yet."

But I didn't miss his eyes and his meaningful glance at Case, who had gotten syrup on his glove and was trying to lick it off. *It's Case,* I could almost hear Hack saying. *Case is one of the top picks. But if you value your sanity, don't tell him.*

Case. Case was up there, behind Diana and Justin. I didn't know how high, but high enough for Hack to worry. Now, before you go all Becca Mills on me, *Case would never sabotage anyone.* I know my best friend. He would rather die than win on anything other than pure merit. If he's not the best artist, he'll take the second place and try again. He'll forge and cheat when it's for other people, but when it's for himself, Case is the epitome of integrity. Which is probably why every teacher at Scottsville loves him so much.

But this meant Case was possibly the next to fall.

"Who else could know this?" I asked. "We have to assume the saboteur has access to these e-mails too."

"Not necessarily," Case said. He had managed to clean his glove and was straightening it. "Everyone knows who the front-runners are. I mean, Justin was a bit of a surprise, but everyone thought Diana would be walking home with the prize. Before this happened, of course."

"What about Henry and Sandra?"

"Sandra is a shoe-in. Henry, though, I wasn't sure about."

"How could the saboteurs be sure, then?"

"Maybe they hacked the system," Case said. "Or maybe they know one of the judges."

"Who are the judges?"

"Let's see. There's our school's art teacher, Ms. Grant, and a couple art teachers from other schools in the area," Case said. "And one museum docent. Remember Larissa?"

Her again? "What about her?"

"The docent judge is her mom."

Oh, that was interesting. Larissa and Quinn's mother was a judge. Talk about conflict of interest, but I guess they wouldn't put her on the judging committee if it were a problem to have a daughter in the competition. Either way, it wouldn't take much for Quinn to get the list of favorites out of her own mother, by careful questioning or by a more Hack-esque method.

Also, as the vice president of the Art Club, maybe

Quinn had other methods of getting that information. Maybe she knew Ms. Grant's e-mail password. It's not like teachers were good at hiding them.

And then there was Lee. Ethan's dad was a judge; if Lee bullied Ethan enough, he might get access to the list of the judges' favorites. I smiled. It would feel fantastic to bring that creep down.

The judges hadn't seen Diana's painting before the sabotage. I'd be willing to bet they hadn't seen Justin's, either. Something didn't add up. The sabotage would have been meaningless if they hadn't seen the art yet. That meant . . .

"When did the judges start their rounds?" I asked.

"About ten thirty," Case said. "They talked to us, told us what the prize for Best Overall was this year, and left."

"Where did they go?"

My friends glanced at each other. "To judge the art, I guess."

"So, neither of you knows where each judge goes first? No buzz online, no texts or e-mails from the judges?"

Hack shook his head, and Case said, "Why would the judges talk about it? They already know where they're supposed to go. It's for the best. If the contestants knew, they might hang around when the judges were looking at their work."

If the contestants knew, they might know when to attack

a painting before the judges get a chance to see it.

"I have to go," I said.

Hack ducked. "Is Becca around?"

Case waved. "Go. We'll call you with any new developments."

I ran off, my thoughts swirling. The saboteurs knew the judges' schedules. They knew where they'd be, when they'd be there. They had knowledge they shouldn't have.

The saboteurs have inside knowledge.

I HAD TO FIND BECCA AND tell her what I knew. She wouldn't like that I hadn't gotten the paint sample yet. But she needed to know who might be attacked next, and she *really* needed to know that the saboteurs had inside knowledge.

My first thought was to call her, but even though we'd worked together before, I'd only ever called her on her family's home phone, and for so long the idea of having Becca's personal number was like begging my parents to hang out with me at school: totally unimaginable. I had to physically look for her. But where would she be?

First I stopped by the tent. Becca might be there, interviewing contestants or looking for contest officials.

But I found nothing but lunch. Well, it made no sense to work on an empty stomach. As I got a turkey sandwich and a bag of chips, I asked a parent volunteer, "Hey, I'm looking for a friend of mine named Lee Moffat. Light hair, bow tie, gray vest. Have you seen him?"

The dad leaned back and gazed up as I waited to hear if Quinn's alibi for Lee was true.

"You know what," he said, "I do remember him. He came through for lunch not long ago, but he's gone now."

"That's okay. I'll find him. When was he here, though?"

"He came in about half an hour ago. I remember because he tried to take two sandwiches. Said one of them was for his friend. I said no. Then he sat over there"—the man pointed to a table—"and ate his lunch. He probably left about ten or fifteen minutes ago."

My heart sank. Quinn's word was true; Lee was here when the sabotage happened. He might have been out near Diana's painting during her sabotage, but Diana hadn't seen him there, and for sure he wouldn't have been around for Justin's. It had happened during that window of time the man said Lee had been at this tent. Not at one location nor at the other. That meant he couldn't have been either one of our saboteurs.

I had *so* wanted it to be Lee.

"Thanks," I said to the dad. I ate my sandwich and chips so fast the dad looked like he was mentally prepping to give me the Heimlich maneuver.

After that, I speed-walked through the maze of walls,

searching for Becca. Once I found her, I'd stow the disguise somewhere nearby. I halted near the place at Wall B where Becca had found me earlier that day, back when she still thought I'd been the thief who'd stolen Heather's painting supplies. I could still remember the fear and annoyance I'd felt when I'd seen her coming toward me, her eyes blazing with the desire to put me in a headlock and read me my rights.

Or throw me to the wall, right between the painting of the hamster army—wait.

The painting of the evil hamsters was gone. Well, not *gone*, as in nothing but a blank spot left on the wall. I mean gone, as in the painting now showed a flame-colored monster with fiery eyes. But earlier it had been a bunch of mangy rat-things, I was sure of it.

I thought back, remembering the unsettling feeling the painting had given me. Yep. Hamsters, not a monster. And the hamster painting had been better. Maybe not the best painting in the contest (Diana's was amazing, and I was loyal to Case), but solid. This one wasn't bad, but it lacked a certain finesse, a level of skill and technique. Okay, maybe I do listen when Case talks about art. Though I couldn't name the father of Cubism either.

Why switch the paintings? Who would have done it? Had yet another painting been sabotaged and carried off, and had the park officials hung another one in its place?

No. With Diana and Justin, the guards had taken the ruined paintings and left a blank space behind, like a memorial to the fallen. Every artist had a designated space. It wouldn't make sense to just slot someone else in.

But why would anyone switch the painting for one that was worse? To sabotage their chances? That was the only motive that made any sense, but we already had a saboteur running around, and this didn't fit the pattern. It was too well planned, too complicated. The saboteur would have to plan this out in advance, prepare the alternate painting. Why do that for this one painting but slather red all over the others?

The tag beside the painting read, "*Terror* by Quinn Eccles." Oh, this just got better and better.

More questions to answer. Why would Quinn switch out her own painting, if she was the saboteur? That would only make sense if—

If she and her partner had a falling-out. If Quinn, worried that her partner (whoever it was—Becca and I would have to figure that out) would sabotage her in his drive to win Best Overall, prepared a dummy painting to take the heat if he chose to attack her. With the inside knowledge from her mother about when the judges would be near her painting, she could easily switch it back for the judging after the threat was gone.

Suddenly it all made sense! No wonder she wasn't scared of losing or of the saboteur! Quinn had it all planned out.

I had to tell Becca. Now, if only I could find her.

"Back off!" My head spun to the sound, and the rest of me followed. Down the next path, I found quite a scene.

Becca's arms were folded, her feet spread in a firm stance. Across from her, leaning forward with gloved hands clenched, was Case. Hack hung back a few paces.

Oh no. Oh no, no, no.

I slid behind a stationary family and watched the scene. What else could I do? Getting involved would only make things worse.

Becca was grinning. Of course she was. Angry and forceful was exactly the state in which she liked to live, work, and attend Fourth of July parades.

I scanned the crowd, and my skin prickled. Not far from Becca and Case were the Sisters Eccles, Quinn and Larissa. They were watching Becca, and they looked kind of freaked out. Larissa was so pale that the blue raspberry syrup from her snow cone looked black on her lips, and Quinn, I was pleased to see, kept fidgeting with her bag.

Yeah, you should be worried. I've got your number.

"I bet you'd want me to back off," Becca said to Case

as Quinn and Larissa and me and, now, a whole bunch of other kids watched. "Leave you to commit your ugly sabotage."

Gasps and murmuring at Becca's accusation.

"You think I'm the saboteur? Not very bright for a detective, are you?"

Becca reddened. "It's not my fault if it all adds up. You're a competitor, you're panicking—"

"So is everyone."

"Wouldn't it be great if you didn't have to worry anymore? If you knew you would win?"

Case scowled. "Winning is no good if you don't have any competition."

Becca rolled her eyes. "Don't try to act all noble. I talked to judges and contest officials, and guess what I found out?"

Case's nerve flickered. "What?" Despite his anger, he was still afraid of Becca. I could see Hack's eyes widen and he shook his head.

"These sabotages are moving you up the leader board. Pretty far up, from what I understand. Only paintings have been attacked, and now you're a favorite. That sounds like motive to me."

Case was shaking at the news that he was a favorite. He glanced back at Hack with a pleading look, but

Hack had already put his face in his hand. That was all the answer Case needed. "That's a coincidence," he said to Becca, but his voice had lost its strength.

It didn't look good; it looked like Case was cracking. I had to get in there and help, but what could I do that wouldn't aggravate the situation? I couldn't step out there, or both Becca and Case would turn on me, then back on each other with renewed venom.

It wasn't fair of Becca to do this. She had less evidence that Case was the saboteur than I did that Quinn was. She had accused Case because she hated me, and that was coloring her perceptions. And to do it publically like this . . . it was ugly.

"A coincidence?" Becca said. "Really? You still believe in those. I thought you and your crook friends believed in taking matters into your own hands. It wouldn't be hard for you, right? Your computer guy finds out who the front-runners are, and then you get busy. Everyone knows how . . . *creative* you can be with a brush, Casey."

"Hey!" Hack rushed forward, but Case pushed him back.

"I've done nothing wrong. We're finished here." Case turned to leave.

"Oh, nothing wrong? So, what you're saying is that if

I looked in your locker, I wouldn't find paints that look just like Heather's stolen tempera paints?"

Case stiffened and turned back around. "Those aren't Heather's. They're a friend's."

"*That* sounds believable."

"How do you know what's in my locker?"

Becca ignored the question. "Can anyone account for your actions at Heather's party?"

Hack looked at Case. "You went to Heather's party?"

"I made an appearance. I was coming back from lunch, and I saw people there, so I went in and said hi. Five minutes, tops." Case glared at Becca. "Ask Heather."

"Sure. You were there for a few minutes, but that's all it takes, right? I can see how it happened. You took Heather's paints and brushes so you could commit sabotage without getting caught. But when you got here, you realized you didn't have enough paint to adequately destroy all the great art you found here, so you stowed the stolen temperas and found yourself another kind of paint to use. Where did you get it?"

But then Case stepped toward Becca. "Listen, you self-righteous, stuck-up, little snot—"

Becca raised her hands. "Back off."

"Why don't you make me?" Case got closer and Becca backed away. It looked like *Case* was the one menacing *Becca.*

"You don't *ever* insinuate that my friends or I would do something as cruel and horrible as sabotage someone else's art," Case said. "Never again. Do you hear me? Or we're going to have problems."

"I think we already have problems. I know what you do. I know what Wilderson does. You can't get away with it forever."

"With what? We didn't do anything."

"Oh? So where were you when Diana's painting was sabotaged?"

"With my parents. You can ask them. We heard the screams and ran over. And, before you get any ideas, I was talking to Diana when Justin's art was attacked. You can ask her, too. You see? I have an alibi."

Becca frowned. "You're up to something and I will find out what."

"Is it painful, having that much suspicion running through you all the time? No wonder you don't have any friends."

Her lips tightened. "*My* friends don't lie to me."

Whoa. This wasn't going to end well. I started to move forward, ready to break up the fight and deal with the fallout later.

But before I could, a contest official stepped between them. "That's enough," he said.

Case and Becca glared at each other. I could almost see flames flying between them.

"This isn't over," Becca said.

"Yeah, it is. Just as soon as you check my alibi. Then you'll feel stupid, won't you?"

"I said, that's enough," the official said. A second man led Case and Hack away, and the first took Becca aside.

I was still breathing hard. Oh man. That wasn't good. There was a reason I never wanted Case and Becca to get too close. I knew *that* would happen. Accusations on one side and anger on the other. Good thing the grown-up had stepped in to stop it.

But why had he taken Case and Hack away?

Quietly I followed my friends to a calm area of the park and hid behind a tree. Now was not the time to get involved, not when the contest official was with them. As I watched, the man talked quietly with Case, who still looked mad.

". . . You understand, with everything that was said, we need to check," the man was saying. "I need you to give me your parents' phone number so we can ask them where you were when the sabotage happened."

Case fumed. "I didn't sabotage anyone. Becca just has it out for me."

"I believe you, but sabotage is serious. It will be better for you if we can clear this up now."

Hack nudged Case, and Case, still steaming, gave the man his mom's number. The man called Mrs. Kingston, had a short conversation with her, and then smiled at Case. "Your mom says you were with her when you heard the scream. You both were."

"Darn right we were," Case muttered as I leaned against the tree, relieved.

"Go cool down," the man said. "I'll make sure everyone knows you're not the saboteur."

And I'll go make sure Becca knows. I turned and crept back to the scene of the ruckus.

As I was walking, a voice called out, "Hey! Gibson, right?"

Oh, right. That was my name. I stopped and saw Aaron kneeling on the ground with a paintbrush in his left hand and a sandwich in his right. He was wearing a bright orange vest over his shirt. A box full to the brim with paints, brushes, and markers of all kinds was next to him, and a half-completed poster with the word "SNOW" painted in green lay in front.

I smiled. "Hey."

"Good thing you're wearing the same shoes. It took me a moment to recognize you without the poncho."

Gotta love an artist's eye. I'd have to be more careful with creating disguises in the future. "Yeah, I had to ditch it. It was getting hot. But," I said, remembering my character, "that doesn't mean I'm giving up! I won't rest until I get the same rights as every artist here."

Aaron grinned. "Good. Someone needs to stick up for the little man."

I looked at the poster and the vest. "You're a contest volunteer?"

Aaron shrugged. "I like art. Thought I'd participate this year in a different way."

"Huh." Aaron was a volunteer, not a contestant. That explained how he was able to get Becca and me into the tent.

That's when Lee and Ethan came around the path. Lee must have also decided extra layers weren't comfortable; he'd ditched his vest.

Lee saw Aaron and his face lit up. "Hey, Aaron," he said. "Good to see you using a brush."

Aaron sighed, still painting. "Go away, Lee. I'm working here."

Interesting how Lee and Aaron seemed to know each other.

"I can see that," Lee said. "I'm so happy that even after everything that happened, they still let you use the extent of your talents." He nodded at me. "Nice to see you hanging out with your artistic equals."

Aaron clenched the brush tightly and looked up, scowling at Lee. Lee just laughed. "Come on, it's not like you're a real artist." He looked at me. "This is what I mean by an artist who can't cut it. This kid here? He's a finger painter. Like a kindergartner."

"No one ever said you had to paint with a brush," Aaron said in an even tone. "And as far as I understand, my painting was good enough to please the judges." He glared at Lee.

Lee crouched beside Aaron. "Maybe for a little while, but even they couldn't deny that everyone was right: finger painting is not real art, and you are not a real artist. You're just a joke."

So Aaron was laughed out of last year's contest because he finger painted his entry? And Lee, being Lee, didn't seem ready to let him forget it.

I looked at Ethan. His face twisted with discomfort. "Come on, man. Leave him alone."

"Yeah, Lee," Aaron said. "You should go. Let me work."

"Sure. But maybe I should take the brush. It's not like you need it."

I couldn't take it anymore. I had to do something.

"Shouldn't you go check on your sculpture? With the saboteur still out there, your sculpture might be next."

Aaron grinned. "Yeah. And wouldn't that be a tragedy. All that clay, or cement, and then you paint the sculptures? Must cost a lot."

Lee's composure cracked. "Not as much as you might think. I recycle things."

"So you make your art out of garbage?" Aaron said, and I decided I liked him.

Lee turned red. "It's not garbage. It's my art."

"So is mine. I deserve just as much respect as you. And with all I'm learning, I'm going to get that respect."

Ethan pulled on Lee's arm. "We really should check. You don't want your sculpture attacked."

"The saboteur wouldn't dare attack my sculpture," Lee said. He glared at Aaron but let Ethan tug him away.

I wasn't sure what to make of what I'd just seen, except that Lee was a jerk. I really wished he was the saboteur, but no. He had an alibi. That was no fun.

"Sorry about that," Aaron said.

"Not your fault. How do you know that guy, anyway?"

Aaron shook his head. "Friend of a friend. I do one favor for the guy and he thinks he owns me."

A spiky-haired guy about Aaron's age appeared, wearing the same orange vest as him and carrying a bunch of finished posters under his arm. "Aaron, you done?"

"Not yet." Aaron looked at me. "I should get back to work. See you around."

"See you around." I left Aaron to his work and returned to where Becca and Case had had their meltdown.

On the way, I ran into Quinn Eccles. She was alone; Larissa must have left. Quinn seemed flustered. I wondered what effect Becca's public accusation had had on her.

"Hey," I said.

Quinn jumped. She hadn't noticed I was there. "Oh, hey," she said. "Still on the case?"

"Looks like I'm not the only one. Becca's intense, huh?" Let no one say I don't know how to use what I'm given. "I'd hate to be the saboteur, with *her* on the trail. So, got anything to tell me?"

Quinn shook her head. "No, nothing. I'll . . . keep you posted." Then she merged with a passing clump of people and was gone.

So, after removing my disguise and tucking it behind a garbage can, I approached Becca, my current employer (ha!). She was still where she had come to verbal blows with Case, talking to an adult, probably laying out my best friend's guilt. So I didn't feel bad at all pulling her away.

"Hey, I was just—" she began.

"I know what you were doing. Case is innocent."

"I know." Becca sighed. "His alibi checks out. That man just told me Case's mom confirmed that he was with her when it happened. He's not the saboteur, him or Hack."

"Well, good." I licked my lips. "What's going on with you?"

"Nothing."

"Nothing? You were harsh with Case, even by your standards."

She rolled her eyes. "You have to admit, it looked suspicious. I'm still not convinced he's not Heather's thief."

"He's not."

"Of course you would say that. So, how'd the job go? Did you get the sample?"

"Uh, not yet."

"Wilderson! What did I specifically ask you to do?"

"Getting around your mom is going to take a little more time and planning. I'll get the sample. I promise."

"I need more than empty promises. I need evidence." Becca's cheeks blazed red.

"We'll get it."

"Another promise. I can't go to my mom with promises." Becca looked furious for a moment, then threw her hands in the air. "Don't you get it? Mom is chasing the wrong people. She's cutting me out of the investigation because she thinks I don't know what I'm talking about. If we don't find some evidence, if we don't catch *someone,* my mom's not going to take me seriously and the saboteurs are going to get away."

Becca looked about one unwise comment away from snapping. Wow, there was a lot more riding on this case for Becca than I thought. It kind of explained her attack on Case; she needed a win.

"Good thing I didn't come back empty handed," I said.

"Yeah?" Becca looked annoyed but no longer stressed.

"I know who the next potential targets are. According to my sources, Diana and Justin were the judge's favorites for the painting division. Maybe could have won Best Overall. The others are a boy named Henry, in photography, and—"

"Wait." Becca pulled out her notebook. "Okay, keep going."

"Henry," I repeated. "And a sculptor named—"

"Sandra Lynn," Becca and I said at the same time. Becca looked at me. "I found small black marks on their work. Not enough to show Mom, but enough to worry me. We're running out of time."

"Case?" I asked, my heart racing.

"Nothing on his. It's one of the reasons I thought he might be, you know . . . I'm sorry."

"Not as sorry as the saboteurs will be if they do anything to his painting," I said. "But get this. Lee Moffat is one of the second-stringers, just under Sandra in the sculpture division."

"Hmm," Becca said, perking up. "His sculpture wasn't marked, I don't think. But there were so many colors that I might have missed something. I'll go check it again."

"Don't bother. Lee has an alibi. He wasn't around when Diana was sabotaged, and I confirmed he was at the tent during Justin's sabotage. He wasn't the one with the sponge *or* the brush."

Becca deflated. "So Lee's not a saboteur."

"Doesn't look like it."

"Do we have any other suspects?"

"We still have one."

Becca's gaze grew steely. "I thought we decided to drop this subject."

"Lee doesn't have enough evidence or motive supporting him as our saboteur. He's a jerk, yes, but that's all we can get him on. You've proved Case is innocent. It's time to start seriously considering Quinn as a suspect."

"Not yet."

"You need to listen to me. The saboteurs know the judges' routes. They know when the judges will look at the art, and they're attacking them before the judges can see them. This is *inside information.*"

Becca didn't look impressed, so I continued. "The favorites might not be a secret, but this is. Only the judges and the contest officials know which art gets viewed when. Did you know Quinn's mom is a contest judge? Add to that the fact that Quinn's VP of the Art Club and you have a girl with information she shouldn't have."

"Any contest employee could know the judges' routes. It's not Quinn."

I grabbed at my hair. "Why do you keep insisting that she's innocent?"

"Why do you keep insisting she's guilty?" Becca rammed a fist into her hip. "I've been around the block too, Wilderson. I know guilt when *I* see it too. Quinn is not guilty."

I hated to shatter whatever illusions she had, but truth was truth. "Quinn's painting has changed. It's not what it was before. The proof is on Lee's camera. Remember that picture of them with their contest entries? Go look at Quinn's painting now. It's not the same. Something very weird is going on. It's time to seriously investigate her."

Becca was silent for a while. "Go get the paint sample."

"But I can show you. We can go look at Quinn's painting now."

"I'm the detective. You're the thief." Becca's voice was low and hoarse. "You will go get the sample of paint, and you will not get caught. *I* will investigate Quinn. *I* will find out who had access to the judges' routes. You're right. It is time." With that, Becca whirled around and hurried off.

Great. I knew I was right. It was time for Becca to wake up and see all the strangeness surrounding Quinn. Becca needed a win, and investigating Quinn would give her that win—I knew it.

We had to get evidence. Time was running out, and I had a paint sample to retrieve.

NORMALLY WHEN I START a job, I like to know where I'm looking. Normally this isn't a problem. *Normally* the client tells me, "Ms. Browning put my cell phone in her desk drawer," or "My money's in Mitch's pocket." That takes care of half the problem and I can set my mind to figuring out when Ms. Browning's at lunch or how to rig a milk explosion at the perfect time to send Mitch for a change of clothes. Normally, after that the job is easy, just a quick grab and go.

But let's be honest. What part of this day was normal?

I stood outside the park help office, back in my plaid disguise, licking a red-white-and-blue snow cone that was more prop than anything. Outside the help office, men and women in park uniforms were buzzing around like anxious bees. No police blue yet, but somewhere in there was Becca's mother, suddenly on duty. Did knights feel this way standing outside the dragon's cave?

How was I going to pull this off? I couldn't be seen, but there were too many people around to just sneak in and out. If I got caught, it wouldn't just be a slap on the wrist. Best-case scenario, I'd be tossed out without a chance of getting what I needed. Worst case, they'd think I was the criminal and question me, maybe punish me.

But I had to do something, and soon. Becca was waiting for me to deliver the paint sample. Then I had to help her stop the saboteur before he attacked again. Or, rather, *she* struck again.

Hmm. I tossed my sticky cone, half-full of ice, in a trash bin. I didn't see Detective Mills anywhere. This could be a good thing. Maybe I wouldn't need to sneak. Maybe I could use the adults' busyness to my advantage.

I shrugged my shoulders twice, clenched and unclenched my hands, and started walking to the office. *Stand tall*, I told myself. *You're supposed to be here. Believe it and they will too.*

I chose my path carefully, weaving behind one guard standing outside the office and to the side of another, just out of their line of sight. Another, posted next to the door, was on the phone. I slid by easily.

Stay quiet, I reminded myself. *Don't draw attention*

to yourself. The door creaked as I opened it, making me wince, but no one glanced at me as I entered the office. It was a small building; the main room was just a counter with a table behind it. Adults sat at the table, talking. Some leaned against the counter, on phones or looking over papers, or both. No other kids were present, not even possible suspects. No one to blend in with.

I felt like a piece of broccoli on a chocolate cake platter.

Straightening my back, I walked with purpose, like I was supposed to be there. A couple guards glanced at me and frowned. But when I smiled at them, they returned to what they were doing. You'd be amazed how much you can get away with if you act like you're supposed to be doing it.

My confidence protected me like a shield. Just as long as I looked like I was supposed to belong, I could go unnoticed by the guards. The effect wouldn't last long, but I didn't need it to. I just needed to find Diana's painting and get out with the sample.

I strode past the desk. There were no paintings on the table, or on any counter I could see. What if Detective Mills had already sent the paintings away to the police station?

I glanced around the room. There were two doors.

One of them was open and led to an eating area. I couldn't tell if the paintings were in there. Still, it was a good place to try. I headed for the door.

"Who are you looking for, kid?"

I flinched. Crap. Just like that, my invisibility was broken. I turned to see a man in a brown park uniform.

"No one," I answered. Not my greatest moment, but I had to say something.

"Then what are you doing here?" The man tilted his head. He was built like a walrus, large of body and bushy of face.

My mind raced. I had to give the impression that I had a reason to be there, one that wouldn't win me unnecessary attention.

"I was told to come here and grab some mops. Someone spilled a lot of snow-cone syrup. Where can I find them?"

The guard smiled. "Probably in the storage room where we keep all the recreational equipment," he said. "You can't get to it from here. You'll need to go around."

"Thanks, sir." But that wasn't going to help me. I needed a reason to stay inside. In a flash of brilliance, I changed tactics. Widening my eyes, I said, "What's going on here? There are so many cops." I let my jaw drop, as if in realization. "This is because of the sabotage, isn't it?"

"Terrible thing to happen on such a nice day," the guard said. He took out a ring of keys and added, "Let's go get you those mops."

Oh, that wouldn't do. If I was taken to the mops, that was it. Disguise or no disguise, they'd know my face. I wouldn't get a second try. I grabbed the man's arm. "Can I see the ruined paintings?"

The guard stopped and gave me a look that made me let go, quickly. "I won't be any trouble," I said. "I just wanna get a look at them!" I smiled, looking as innocent and eager as I could manage. "My friends would never believe me."

The man sagged, hesitating. Just a little more, just another push. I toyed with my baseball cap, ready to lace my enthusiasm with promises to behave, with hints that this was part of boyhood hijinks (grown-ups love that), with all the signs that this would just make my day, and it wasn't like anyone had to know—

The closed door opened, revealing a back office with a desk and computer. Out stepped a short woman with dark hair. She smiled at me from behind the guard, and my eager grin slipped. I knew that smile. Like mother, like daughter.

The woman approached us. "Hello, James. Who is this?"

The guard gestured at me. "This kid came here looking for mops, Detective."

No wonder I hadn't seen her from my post; she'd been in the back office. This is why it's important to be thorough when you case a building.

Detective Madeleine Mills looked like her daughter: same small frame, same firm jaw, same raised eyebrow when she looked at me. I met the detective's eyes and looked away. They were dark brown, almost black, and felt like a pair of black holes trying to pull my secrets from my skin.

I understood why Scottsville's adults committed so little crime.

"I believe the mops are kept in the restroom closets," Detective Mills said. She looked at me, lips pressed tightly together, and I felt a shiver race down my spine. "It's all right, James, I can take it from here."

The guard, James, shrugged and left me with the Fear of God herself. She folded her arms. "You're the boy who lives across the street, am I right? The Wilderson kid."

I swallowed and nodded, mentally pleading that she knew my name because she knew the neighborhood, not because she had heard Becca talking about me.

If Detective Mills had heard stories about me, she didn't comment. She just nodded and said, "Did your friends dare you to come here?"

"No, I just need . . ." My words died on my lips as Detective Mills's mouth curved into the family smile. There was no point. She knew I wasn't as innocent as I looked.

The smart thing to do would be to leave. Apologize, and scarper (great word, right? It means "escape"). But next thing I knew, my mouth was running. "My friend's in the competition. I don't want him to be attacked next. Maybe if I see the paintings, I could help."

Detective Mills grabbed my shoulder with a grip like iron. Any tighter and it would hurt.

"We have it well in hand," she said, "as long as we are not distracted from our work by children who mean well. Go be a kid and let us do our jobs. If you come back here, I will have to call your parents and tell them to keep an eye on you. They wouldn't like that."

No, I was sure they wouldn't. Especially since they were visiting colleges with Rick.

"And while I'm talking to your parents," Detective Mills said, "I might mention some rumors I've heard about your extracurricular activities that have nothing to do with your position on the track team."

It was like someone had slipped an ice cube down my shirt. I looked at Becca's mom and she gave me the cold, calculating family smile.

No. She didn't know about that. Becca had never told her. Detective Mills was bluffing. If she knew about my retrieving, I would have already gotten in trouble, right?

Detective Mills gave me a little shove and I was back on the path. "Please escort this young man to the restroom," she said to a nearby officer. "He's looking for mops."

I left with the officer, feeling like I'd just come off a super-scrambler ride at an amusement park. Becca was scary, but she was nothing next to her mother, who was quieter, calmer, but somehow so much worse. I was glad I'd gotten out alive.

The officer escorted me to a bathroom, where he watched as I grabbed a mop and bucket. Playing my role, I carried them deeper into the park, toward the snow-cone stand closest to the Contestants' Tent (and the farthest from the help office).

Just forget the sample, I thought as I walked, arms full. *It can't possibly be worth going back and getting caught by Detective Mills a second time.*

But then I thought about Becca, who needed that sample to identify the kind of paint used in the sabotage. It could be the key to solving the whole mystery! It could save Sandra and Henry and all the other artists who deserved to at least be able to take their work home so their parents could show it off.

It could save Case.

So I circled back to the restroom, made sure the officer was gone, and returned the mop and bucket. Then I went for a second look at the help office. A storage room, Guard James had said? Well, it wasn't ideal, but it sounded like a great place to start.

I headed around to the storage room. I'd seen it right before I'd run into Quinn and Larissa. It was annoying that the storage room wouldn't connect to the main building, but at least no one would be watching while I got inside and figured out Plan B.

Making sure no one, especially not Detective Mills, was watching, I headed to the door around the back of the office. It was a heavy metal door, solid and efficient. I tugged on the handle. Locked.

Well, that wasn't a problem. I may not have brought all my tools—my grappling hook, basic disguises, snacks and water bottle, and bandanna—but I was never without my lockpick set.

I looked around again. No watchers. Then I crouched and got ready to work.

Huh. I leaned closer, tilting my head back and forth to change the view. From every angle, it was the same. Little dents dotted the edges of the key slot. I knew these kinds of scratches, but I hadn't seen them in months.

When I first started picking locks, I got in trouble because I did some serious damage to our garage door's lock. I'd left it scratched and dented, exactly in this way. These were the marks of an amateur lock picker. No one fumbling with a key makes marks just like this.

Someone had gotten inside before, and I didn't think they were looking for volleyball nets. I pressed my finger on the lock and it came away glittering with tiny flakes of metal. This was recent, maybe even today. Who did it? Why did they care about this storage room? And how did no one notice them at work? Lockpicking is tough when you're just learning. It can take hours.

My gaze landed on a patch of yellow-and-white grass, the kind that hasn't seen the sun in a long time, just next to the door. Something had been there and been moved. I didn't have to look far to find it; a plastic storage crate had been pushed a few feet aside until it sat directly under a window.

I peered up. The window, one of those small, rectangular kinds that flip open, was open as wide as it could go. It wasn't very high, but it would be a hard climb without the crate.

My fingers tingled. Unless I was wrong, the person who had tried to pick the lock had failed and tried a window. They might have even still been inside.

Instincts took over. I stepped back and ran at the wall. In a move I'd practiced many times in past jobs, I vaulted off the crate and up the wall. My hands gripped the edge of the window, I kicked up off the wall, and I hauled myself, headfirst, through the window.

As I fell, I twisted in the air. The last thing I wanted was to fall face-first onto the concrete floor. I fell on my back on a pile of soccer nets. All the air in my lungs "oofed" out of me, and something blunt jabbed my back.

I heard a gasp and sat up to see Larissa Eccles staring at me with wide eyes. In her hands she was holding a painting.

"YOU?" I WHISPERED. THAT flight through the window, while kind of awesome, had taken a lot out of me. Also, the police might have been able to hear through the wall, even if this room didn't have a door connecting it to the main building.

Larissa. Quinn wasn't the only one with a parent for a judge, and Larissa was a painter as well. She would have known enough to commit sabotage. It had been Larissa the whole time.

I rose to my feet. "It was you."

Larissa didn't say anything. Her eyes darted around the room and then she threw the painting at me.

I grabbed for it, snagging my foot in a net as I lunged. We fell, the painting and me. As I landed, I held the painting by its frame, keeping it off the ground. The saboteur's paint, *Larissa's* paint, might still be wet.

I couldn't let it touch the floor and get contaminated.

Success. The painting survived. I turned the canvas around to see what I'd won.

A small army of rabid hamsters glared at me. Quinn's original painting. Huh.

"This is . . . how did it . . . ?" I looked up from where I lay sprawled, ready to make Larissa tell me everything.

She had climbed on top of a rentable grill and was facing the wall. "What're you doing?" I asked. I tugged at my foot, still caught in the net.

Larissa didn't glance back. She tossed something aside: a screwdriver. Metal crashed on concrete as Larissa took the loosened air-vent grate off the wall and threw it to the ground. I winced as the sound echoed around the room.

Horror filled me as I realized what she was about to do. "No, stop!" I called, yanking my foot free. I reached for her, catching only air as she dove into the air vent.

I climbed the grill, put my face into the grate, and hissed, "Come back! Please!" The air duct behind the vent echoed with the sound of Larissa wriggling through it.

I muttered every unpleasant word I could think of, from those Rick said when playing Call of Duty with his friends to words like "crevice" and "moist." Then I tossed my baseball cap aside, pulled my borrowed plaid shirt up over my nose and mouth, and crawled in after her.

Here's the thing about air ducts: they're horrible. That may sound surprising coming from someone like me, who once jumped out of a second-story window using a homemade grappling hook.

Ha ha. No. Air ducts are not like they are in the movies, all large and quiet and shiny and clean and well lit. Air ducts—this air duct included—are dark and cramped and covered in layers, plural, of dust, pulverized building material, and more dust. Dead insects are scattered everywhere. My shorts and borrowed shirt were getting covered with the gray-and-white filth in the duct. The shirt I could ditch later, but the pants I'd have to hand-wash before my mom picked me up at five.

As for how people seem to move silently and undetected in air ducts, well, that's a myth, too. Air ducts echo. They emphasize every whisper and turn it into a roar. You can tell if there's something moving in the ducts. I'd figured out a way to minimize sound, but it had taken me a while and it still wasn't perfect.

Larissa, the amateur who only knew what Hollywood told her, was discovering the joys of air duct travel. I could hear her coughing ahead as she (loudly) turned a corner.

As bad as the dust and dirt were, or as loud as the echoes were, they weren't mine or Larissa's biggest problem. Navigation was.

The first time I'd traveled by air duct, I'd taken a wrong turn and almost ended up in the boiler room. If it hadn't been for Case tracking my progress through the wall, I could have fried. After that, I'd gotten stuck, wedged headfirst, when the duct narrowed. Hack had had to come after me, hooked into his climbing gear, and pull me out by my feet. Since then, I'd made sure to look up a building's layout and map the ducts before I ever tried climbing through them for any reason.

But Larissa didn't know any of that. She hurried ahead, and all I could do was follow her and hope to catch up before she got both of us caught or seriously hurt.

And getting caught was becoming a real possibility. The girl was not quiet, and the naturally echoing metal ducts didn't help. Even though the storage room wasn't connected to the main office through an internal door, they were still part of the same building. Soon anyone would be able to hear us.

Keeping my body, legs and all, flat, I pulled myself forward as fast as I could. Larissa might be trying to get away, but I knew how to move in a duct. I had practice. She didn't. Soon I was close enough to reach out and grab her ankle.

Larissa stiffened at my touch and kicked. I held on tighter and hissed, "Stop that!"

She aimed the next kick at my head. I ducked and tightened my grip. "They'll hear you," I said, and Larissa calmed down.

"Okay," I said, whispering. The duct made my voice echo. I hoped she could understand me; I couldn't afford to be louder. "It's not safe in here. We have to get out. Listen to me; I've been in ducts before. You have to spread out your weight. Flatten out. Use your legs to take some of it."

Larissa hesitated, apparently decided that I knew what I was talking about, and did as I told her. "Great," I said. "You can't turn around. Back out. Use your hands to push."

Air ducts are cramped. That's why it's so important to know where to go, so you can get back out in reverse if you have to. I learned that the hard way.

"What are you going to do when we get out?" Larissa asked, her voice barely audible over the echoes.

"Probably run." This whole job had shattered. After dealing with Detective Mills Senior and getting dragged into this air duct mess, I didn't know how I was going to get that paint sample for Becca. There wasn't much more I could do with a building full of cops and so little time to make a good plan.

Maybe it wouldn't matter, if I could get Larissa's confession. But Larissa didn't need to know that I wanted to interrogate her. Not yet.

Larissa was still for a moment, and then her foot slid back toward me. Her whole body started to come my way and I backed up to make room. "That's it," I said. "Very good. Let's get out of here."

I pushed myself backward. Now that Larissa and I were quiet, I could hear the voices of the cops through the walls. I could also hear the air blowing through the ducts.

That was good—the sound of the air might help mask our echoes. But it came with another problem: flying dust. The air kicked the dust up into my nose, despite the shirt in the way.

Larissa sneezed. We both froze. "Sorry," she whispered. I didn't say anything; I just listened. When it didn't sound like anyone was coming for us, I tapped her leg and we kept sliding back.

My feet clanged on metal. We both flinched at the sound. I twisted slowly and looked back. We'd hit a fork.

That's right; Larissa had turned a corner. But was it right or left? In the dark and the hurry to catch her, I hadn't paid attention. I thought it might be right, but that meant I had to turn left to get out, right? I mean, correct?

The lefts and rights spun in my mind. I decided on left. I angled myself that way, slid out, and pulled on Larissa's foot to show her where to go.

It seemed like forever, inching back out to the shed.

I kept thinking we should have gotten there, that it couldn't be too much farther. We passed duct openings, two of them. How had I not noticed them before?

Clang. My feet hit another wall and my blood ran cold. Another wall. We had gone the wrong way again.

I breathed deeply, trying to calm the panic. *It's fine*, I thought. *We just crawl forward now. It will take us right out.* I was about to signal to Larissa what to do, when I realized I wasn't sure if it would. What if I'd miscounted and Larissa had turned two corners? What if we'd backed into the wrong duct?

The panic came back, hard. I was lost in air ducts with a girl who had no idea what to do.

15

"UHH," LARISSA WHISPERED. She wants to know what the hold-up is, I thought. But you can't tell the truth.

Panic wouldn't get us anywhere. I thought hard. Okay, emergency procedures. Got it. "Stay there," I said. "Don't move." I picked the left again, and slid backward down the new duct.

It got a little tight around my legs. At least I'd found out this side wasn't the right way. I looked straight ahead; the duct on the other side narrowed too, but parallel to mine.

"Okay," I whispered to Larissa. "Come on, but turn right."

She did, slowly easing herself down the opposite duct. We lay there, facing each other. Larissa was breathing hard. Dirt was sticking to the sweat on her face. Her nose was crusted black. But her eyes were bright and scared.

"Am I in trouble?" she asked.

I raised a finger to my lips. I looked back down the duct we'd come through. At the end of one of the ducts, I could see light.

Turning back to Larissa, I whispered, "I'm going to go down there. Stay here. I'll find the way out and come get you."

Larissa grabbed my arm. "How do I know you'll come back?"

"I will." I pulled free, tugged my shirt higher over my nose, and crawled down the duct. To her credit, Larissa didn't follow.

A light meant a vent, which meant it opened into a room. If I could see the room, I could reconstruct the building in my mind and map out which way the storage room was. I could see where the boiler room would be and know how to avoid it.

I turned and pulled myself through a widening duct to the grated intake vent cover. Down below I saw a desk with a computer and a—*wait*.

I moved closer, my face almost touching the grate. Then I took such a deep breath that some of the dust got past my makeshift mask. As I smothered my coughs, I checked again. Yes. Lying on top of the desk, just below me, was Diana's painting!

No way. I might be able to pull off my original job. But there was no time to lose. I pushed on the grate. It didn't budge.

Of course it didn't. These things are screwed on from the outside, because it makes sense and because nobody crawls around in air ducts when there are doors. But maybe if I just tried a little harder. . . .

Just as I placed my hands on the grate, the door opened. Detective Mills walked in and sat down at the desk. From where I was, I could see her twine her fingers together and peer over the sabotaged painting.

This was the office, the room Detective Mills was using as a base. There she was, right below me. I stayed still and made my breathing absolutely silent.

What was I going to do? She wasn't moving around, talking to people, or listening to music. If I moved, she'd hear me. Getting caught skulking in an air duct by a cop is a good way to get yourself sent to military school.

I'd had a window, a chance to get the paint sample, and now it was gone. I would have to wait until Detective Mills left before I could even move to slip away. I could be here for hours, waiting, while Becca tapped her foot outside, the saboteurs continued their scheme, and Larissa waited for me to come back.

But I couldn't do anything but hang tight and watch

Detective Mills examine the painting. She didn't move at all. She just looked at the painting, not touching it. What was she thinking about?

There was a knock at the door. "Come in," Detective Mills said.

A park security guard opened the door. "There's a phone call on the office line for you. Says it's urgent."

"Be right there," Detective Mills said. She stood to leave, then leaned over the painting one more time. "It really would be a strange paint choice for a child," she muttered, then hurried out the door.

Finally! With the detective gone, maybe I had a chance to get the sample and escape. I was trying to figure out how to get past the grate when the window to the office opened from the outside.

I stopped (wouldn't you?) and watched as Case fell through the window, sat up, and looked around.

No, you moron! Get out of here!

But I couldn't shout it, of course. I couldn't do anything but watch helplessly as Case bent over the painting. "Weird paint," he said to himself.

Case pulled a couple of plastic gloves out of his pocket. They looked like the kind of gloves the catering staff used to put brownies on the platters in the Contestants' Tent. They probably were.

Using the finger of a gloved (well, doubly gloved, in Case's situation) hand, Case scooped up a puddle of the drying paint. He then pulled a Post-it from the office desk and carefully dabbed the paint on the paper.

Case set the sample aside. I couldn't take my eyes off it. All I would have to do would be to whisper his name, and he'd give me the sample. I'd get what I came for.

After I explained to Case why I was hiding in an air duct: on an errand for Becca. I'd seen a preview of how well *that* would go over. Plus, our voices coming from an empty office wouldn't raise *any* suspicion.

But the sample lay there, tempting me. What if I could snag it? *I* couldn't go through the grate, but a small piece of paper sure could.

Steal the sample from my friend? Could I even do that? I lay there, breathing in the dust, fighting myself. I couldn't, wouldn't, steal from my friend. But if I didn't, Larissa would be waiting on me for nothing, and Becca wouldn't get the sample she needed to solve this.

Case leaned closer; he'd seen the mark in the corner. He leaned in close, scratched the mark with his fingernail, and leaned back.

What was he doing? Wait, couldn't get distracted. To steal or not to steal?

This would be stealing, not retrieving. It wasn't mine

to take. But if I didn't, how many people would be hurt by the saboteurs?

Maybe Case and Hack could solve this on their own. I didn't have to do anything except use this opportunity to escape.

But that wasn't going to happen. Case and Hack weren't detectives; they might find clues, but they couldn't piece together what those clues meant. I needed Becca for that.

Besides, Becca was counting on me. She had taken responsibility for me, for my actions, on her job (or case, whatever), and I needed to return the favor by giving her the evidence she needed. She was my partner, like it or not.

"I'm sorry," I mouthed as I twisted slowly, reaching for my shoes. Not easy to do in a cramped duct, but I have experience with crawlspaces. With some maneuvering, I slid them off and undid the knotted laces. I pulled the laces of both shoes out of the holes and put the loose shoes back on my feet.

Then I slid a piece of gum out of my pocket and chewed it hard as I tied my shoelaces together.

A tap on the window made us both jump and look over. Hack was there. "Are you done yet?" he asked as he climbed through, rather more gracefully than Case had.

Case turned to face Hack. "Give me a minute," he whispered. "Genius like this takes time."

I wrapped the chewed gum around one end of my tied-together laces and carefully poked it through the grate. Slowly I let it out over the sample Case had taken.

"We don't have a minute," Hack said. "I sent Mama Demon to the other side of the park on a bad lead, but she's not going to be fooled for long. Get what you need and get out of here."

My blood ran cold. Hack . . . called . . . Detective Mills—the *grown-up* Detective Mills—and . . . gave . . . her . . . a . . . bogus . . . tip? He was going to get skinned alive! Who knew what kind of dirt she had on him, a well-known kid hacker? I suppressed the urge to scream at both of them.

"Look at this," Case said. He picked up the painting and brought it over to Hack, leaving the sample behind him on the desk. Hack rolled his eyes and sat on the windowsill. Case pointed at the corner. "That's marker."

Aha! It was marker, not paint! Good clue.

But Hack scoffed. "You brought me in here to show me that?"

The lace reached the desk. By wiggling the end, I could make it touch the sample.

"Yeah, and this," Case said. "Look at the paint marks. This was made with a coarse brush."

They were focused on the painting, so I swept the lace across the sample. Miss.

"So? How does that help us?"

"It could narrow our suspect list."

"How? Am I supposed to scan social media for reports of someone shady carrying a big, red brush?"

I landed the lace's sticky tip on the paper and pulled. The paper didn't come with it. I gritted my teeth.

"You just faked a phone number *and* your voice to get Scottsville's head detective out of the office," Case hissed. "You can do something."

"Maybe, once we *get out of here*!"

"Shh!"

I drew the lace back and went for the sample again. This time, I swung the lace, letting the gum-wrapped tip land on its side on the paper. I pulled, and the sample came up.

I froze, but only for a moment. Someone was going to notice the floating paper if I didn't move.

As carefully as I dared, I drew the sample up. One mistake, one shaky hand, and I could lose it.

Two more feet, one more . . . got it. A corner of the paper came through the grate, and I pinched it tight and pulled it in. A careful twist later, I had Becca's plastic evidence bag. I put the sample inside and tucked the laces in my pocket. I'd deal with them later. Then I reached for something else.

After a minute, Hack's borrowed phone went off. Loudly.

"Turn it off!" Case hissed.

"I'm trying!" Hack said, mashing buttons until the music stopped. "They'll have heard that. We have to go."

Case rushed to the desk to put the painting back. He looked around. "Where's the sample?"

Hack was already out the window. "The what?"

"I took a sample of paint. It's gone."

Hack rushed back over and grabbed Case's shirt. "We're gone." He dragged Case out to the window, and they vanished. Just before James the guard came in, looked around, and mumbled something about technology.

I exhaled and put my mom's phone away. I was shaking; I'd thought Hack's borrowed phone was set to vibrate! Most kids' phones are, because they don't want them going off in school. I just wanted Case and Hack spooked enough to wrap it up and get out. I couldn't let my friends stick around.

I had what I needed: the paint sample, and a mental map of the ducts. I slid backward and returned to where Larissa was waiting for me.

"What took you so long?" she whispered as I dragged myself to face her.

I just pointed down the way we came. "*Follow me*," I mouthed. Then I headed away to freedom.

Larissa followed me. I needed to take a right, up ahead, and then a left. Then we'd both be out. It was almost over. But I needed to stay quiet until then. We could still get caught.

After the right turn the unthinkable happened.

The air ducts erupted with the sound of Mom's ringtone, a generic chime. It echoed, getting louder and louder.

I'd called Hack. Like a good friend, he was calling me back. I wasn't used to carrying a phone on a job, but I should have known enough to set Mom's phone to vibrate when I'd called Hack. Stupid, amateur move!

I tried to grab the phone but couldn't reach, not in this much narrower duct. Not without twisting and taking a million years to do it. Larissa grabbed my leg. She knew, too, that everyone near a vent would have heard us.

Stealth was gone. Time for speed. "Let's go!" I crawled through the ducts as fast as I could, Larissa on my heels. The music played, the duct got lighter, and then we were back in the storage room.

As soon as I pulled free of the ducts, I silenced the

phone. Then I hopped down off the grill and pressed my ear against the wall closest to the main building. Cops were moving on the other side. Yep, they heard that.

Larissa climbed down beside me. I picked up my borrowed baseball cap and put it on. Then I grabbed Larissa's hand. "Time to go," I said, pulling her to the door.

As solid as a locked door is from the outside, it's less secure from the inside. Within minutes, Larissa and I had escaped into the crowded park.

I PULLED LARISSA THROUGH the park, making sure to stay far away from the crowded areas. Larissa looked like she'd been swimming in a full vacuum cleaner bag and I knew I was no better. A cloud of dust fell off us with every step. We kind of stood out.

We didn't stop until we reached the public bathrooms on the other side of the park. Larissa headed toward the girls' room, but I tugged her behind the small brick building. Back there, we found exactly what I expected: a spigot.

"Right here," I said. "I'll go first and you watch. You're going to have to do this on your own." Then I took off my shirt.

It was really bad. The blue shirt I had on underneath was clean, except for some dust on the hem and collar, but the plaid was hidden under white-and-gray smears. Near the hem on the front, I found a greasy black stain that was going to take forever to get out, if I could get it out at all. Glancing down, I saw a thick layer of grime on my pants. Now *that* would be a problem.

Larissa looked uncomfortable as I took my shirt off. It has that effect on girls. "I'm wearing another one," I said, stating the obvious.

"Why? Who does that?"

I smiled. "Someone who knows how to be prepared."

I turned the shirt over, glanced at the back (not as bad, but I still might not be able to return it to the Lost and Found), and nodded at Larissa. "Watch closely. The first thing you have to do is beat it hard. The walls in the bathrooms work well for this. You need to get as much dust off as you can before you even get it wet." I showed her, and a cloud of dust kicked up.

"Why are you doing this?"

"Because I don't want my mom or yours or *anyone's* to know we were in the air ducts."

"No." Larissa shook her head, dislodging dust. "Why are you helping me? You could have left me in the air ducts. But you didn't. Why? Why do you care if I get caught?"

"The air ducts are dangerous. I wouldn't leave anybody alone up there. I knew what to do, and you didn't.

So I helped. And maybe in return, you'll help me." I watched Larissa, never breaking eye contact, as I continued to beat the dust off my shirt. When she didn't say anything, I added, "Like by explaining why you were in that storage room to begin with."

Larissa squeezed her lips tight and looked away. I examined my shirt and decided that was as good as it was going to get. So I went to the spigot and turned on a thin stream of water.

"Don't use too much water. You need to keep it controlled so the wet spots can dry out later. You'll have access to soap in the bathroom, so you should use it."

She kept ignoring me, so I flicked a few drops of water at her. "Pay attention. Otherwise everyone will know you were up to no good."

"I wasn't up to no good!" Larissa bit her lip, looking embarrassed.

"You were up to *something*." I brought the worst of the stains under the water and worked the fabric gently between my fingers. Yep, that wasn't coming out. I hoped the stains would come out of the pants more easily.

Larissa trudged over and watched me work. She hadn't run away yet. That was a good sign.

"I saw the marks of a failed lockpick on the door to the storage room," I said conversationally. Larissa stiffened, but I kept going. "The crate was moved and the window was open. I knew someone had tried, and succeeded, at getting inside. I also knew that person was looking for something a lot more interesting than mops."

"Mops?"

"Never mind. Anyway, I had to see what was going on."

She grinned. "That's when you did your Peter Pan impression through the window."

"I bet it looked awesome."

"Until you fell on your butt."

"My back, not my butt. I know because I can feel it bruising." I beat a little more dust out of the shirt, looked it over, and plunged it into the water. It needed more than a spot treatment.

I looked at Larissa. "So?"

"So what?"

"So are you going to tell me what you were doing sneaking into a locked storage room next to a building full of park security?"

Larissa sat down. "You're a thief, not a detective."

"Retrieval specialist, and it's a good thing I am. A detective wouldn't have followed you into those air ducts. What were you thinking? What is worth endangering yourself like that?"

Larissa raised her chin defensively. "It wasn't that dangerous."

"Oh yeah? You could have gotten stuck in a narrowing duct with no way to back out or turn around. You could have slid down a steep incline into the boiler, or fallen down a shaft and broken an arm or leg or something worse. It can happen. It almost happened to me my first few runs."

Larissa's eyes bugged as she realized the danger she was in, and I was glad. While I didn't want her panicking up in the ducts, down here a little fear would keep her safe. She'd never try that again without serious thought and preparation.

"I didn't know it was dangerous," she said. "They do it all the time on TV."

"They also crack safes in seconds on TV. That doesn't work as well in real life either."

"Really?" Larissa looked at me, her blue eyes wide. "How does it work, then?"

"Well, first you have to spin the dial, and you have to listen really closely for clicks. If you miss one, then you have to go around again—wait. This is about you."

When Larissa didn't talk, I threw more water at her. A lot more water.

As she sputtered, I said, "Listen! I know this business.

You don't. You could have left serious evidence inside the storage room. Now there's a saboteur around and a lot of people, scary people, want to catch him *or her* before they strike again. What do you think will happen if they realize you were in the ducts near the ruined paintings? What conclusions do you think they'll draw?"

Larissa paled. I lowered my voice and continued, "I've been on the wrong side of a false accusation before." And a lot of true ones, but that was beside the point. "I know the painting you had was your sister's. I just don't know why it was in that room instead of hanging on a wall. I can't help you if you don't talk."

The shirt was as clean as it was going to get, so I laid it on the grass to dry. I took off my hat and started beating the dust out of my hair.

Larissa was quiet. She nodded, then took her sandals off and stuck her dirty legs and feet in the stream of water. I took off my unlaced shoes and did the same.

As I peeled gum off my laces and wove them back into my shoes, Larissa talked. "It started when Quinn entered the competition," she said. "At first I was excited for her, but then she showed me her painting. Okay . . . you won't tell anyone what I'm about to say, right?"

"It's safe with me."

Larissa shook her head. "When Quinn was three,

Mom and Dad went out for the day. I think they were shopping for furniture or something. They left us at this lady's house. This lady had a lot of hamsters."

"I'm starting to see where this is going."

Larissa shrugged. "I don't remember what happened, but Quinn does. She was playing with one of them, and she must have left the cage door open, because next thing she knew, more of them were crawling all over her. They weren't going to hurt her, but after one crawled up her shirt and scratched her, she thought there was this army of hamsters out to get her."

I nodded. "Scarred for life?"

"Scarred for life. To this day, hamsters give her the creeps."

"Okay, so now I understand the painting, but why switch it? Why go through all that trouble?"

Larissa laughed. "Maybe I shouldn't have. But my sister is, well, she's nice. She's kind of innocent. When she showed me her finished painting, all I could think about is how much of her soul she was putting on display, how vulnerable she was making herself. You know what this contest can be like."

I thought of the two guys who had brawled over a slight comment and the guy last year who had gotten laughed out of the contest. "I do."

"Then you know why I had to do it. This deep fear, out on display for everyone to see. All the kids from school would be here. They would see her nightmare, and attack her for it, and she wouldn't even see it coming. It would be like Aaron Baxter all over again. I had to protect her."

"Why?"

"She's my sister and my best friend. Why else?"

I thought of Case and Hack. Oh hello, guilt. I missed you. "So what happened next?"

"Well, clearly I couldn't let that painting be seen. I came up with this idea to replace the painting. People would pay attention if there were a gap where Quinn's painting was. But I couldn't use Quinn's art supplies, because she'd notice. I couldn't paint it at school, because people would know it was mine. I needed to use paints and brushes that wouldn't be connected to me."

Ideas flashed in my head, one right after another, like a string of firecrackers. "Heather Caballero. You *both* were invited to her party. You're the one who took her paints and brushes."

"Not all of them. I took what I needed to create a painting. Six brushes and a couple of bottles of paint in primary colors. I could work with those. The party was so busy, no one paid attention to me. I thought Heather wouldn't realize they were missing and I could come back and return them later."

"She noticed." *And hired Becca Mills to find them.* This wasn't good. Larissa wasn't a bad person, but she'd made a mistake and had Detective Mills Junior chasing her.

"So you replaced the painting. Earlier today, right? You'd want your family to see Quinn's, but after that you swapped them before the park got too crowded."

"How do you know that?"

I kept letting the mental firecrackers burst. "The storage room was open then. You walked right in and left the painting where you thought no one would notice it."

Larissa nodded. "Behind the replacement bases. The judges would see my painting. I'm not the artist Quinn is; they wouldn't pick mine to win. Quinn might be disappointed, but she'd never know the truth. I spent all day today helping her feel comfortable with not winning."

"How?"

"First, I found out from Mom who the favorites were. Quinn wasn't one of them, but that was to be expected after my switch. Then I told Quinn so she could prepare. After that, I kept her away from her painting. I talked about how undesirable the prizes are this year, and how next year's would be better. I told her we'd make a fun day of it anyway, and I pointed out paintings I thought were really good. I used the words 'next year' a lot."

"So you discouraged her in the nicest way possible." A con artist's trick, selling what you want the mark to want, and downplaying what they think they want. Also, repeating "next year" would get Quinn thinking about the next year's competition and not this one. That, with her sister supporting her all day, could explain why Quinn wasn't as freaked out as the other contestants.

Besides, the marks on Diana's painting were marker, not paint. Quinn didn't have a marker with her.

My most incriminating evidence against Quinn had gone up in a puff of air duct dust. She didn't seem like a viable suspect anymore.

"Was that too mean?" Larissa looked at me, worried. "Should I have just left Quinn's painting alone?"

"No, it was brilliant!" I grinned at Larissa. "I mean it. You've got a talent for this kind of work. But you need to practice. Lockpicking doesn't just come in the moment."

Larissa blushed. "I didn't have time to wait. After you kept talking about the saboteur and the cops and guards and that detective, I was so scared someone might search the storage room and find my painting. They might think Quinn was a saboteur."

Like I did. My net had caught a fish, just not the one I expected. "So you went in to take the painting."

She nodded. "But I didn't get it. What if they find it?"

"That's not your biggest problem. Becca, the detective, was hired to find Heather's paints and brushes."

Larissa jerked so suddenly she splashed me with water. "She was?" She glanced at the park, toward the paintings where Becca had had her showdown with Case, and paled as she remembered what being on Becca's bad side looked like. "That means she's coming after me."

"Yeah. And trust me, that's not a good thing. With one exception, she always catches her thief. Good thing the paints are at your house. She might not come after you in public."

Larissa turned white, and I tilted my head. "They are at home, right?"

"I didn't have as much time as I thought to finish my decoy. I was working on it up through this morning. I hung it still wet!"

"Larissa, where's Heather's paint?"

"I gave it to Casey to hold on to. I didn't want it in my family locker, and he was so nice at the tent."

I pinched the bridge of my nose and exhaled. Great. Just great. "All this time, Becca thought Case was the thief when it was really you."

"I'm not a thief. I'm—" Larissa sighed. "I'm a thief."

I thought hard. Larissa was guilty. She'd put Case in a bad situation. By all rights, I should help Becca catch her and bring her to justice. But Becca was under pressure, and I'd seen what uptight Becca did to people she thought were guilty. Even after everything, Larissa didn't deserve that. She was just trying to help her sister.

I had to make all the hard decisions!

"As soon as you can, get those paints from Case and give the paints *and* brushes back to Heather," I said. "You might stay out of trouble if you end this."

Larissa nodded. She stood up. "What about Becca?"

I stood up, feeling heavy and sore. "I'll talk to her. See what I can do to get her to drop the case."

"Thank you!" Larissa threw her arms around me. Then she pulled away, looking at the water on her arms and the dust smears on my nice blue shirt. "Sorry. I'll give everything back. I was going to do it anyway. I'm going to go get cleaned up."

She stood and I raised a hand. "Wait." Something had been bothering me. "You said if Quinn's real painting were revealed, it would be like 'Aaron Baxter all over again.' What do you mean by that?"

"You don't know?"

"I know he got laughed out of the contest last year

because he's a finger painter, and I get why you wouldn't want that for your sister, but it doesn't seem worth stealing art supplies over."

Larissa gaped at me. "You don't know, then? What happened next?"

I shook my head and she continued, "Aaron's art was pretty good, and the judges liked it. But then word got around that it was finger painted, and other painters started talking about how finger painting wasn't real art, that it was just like what you do in kindergarten. Kids laughed, and the judges weren't supposed to listen to that kind of thing, but they heard what the painters said and it might have affected their judgment. Aaron didn't win the Best Painting prize because of the reputation he got for being a finger painter. But that wasn't the worst of it."

"Then what was?"

"Nobody let it go, not really. Aaron doesn't get invited to parties with other painters anymore. He wasn't at Heather's party, and that's nothing new. He goes to Burdick, but even I've heard things. Other painters snickering when he walks into a room, not sitting with him at lunch. Someone even put preschool toys in his backpack when he wasn't looking."

My skin tingled. Aaron had been robbed of the prize last year, embarrassed by his method of art. He'd become a pariah in the art community, all thanks to other painters mocking his unique painting style.

I remembered the box of art supplies sitting next to Aaron, full of paints and markers of all kinds. Aaron was also an employee and might know the judges' routes, and a finger painter would be practiced enough to swipe a sponge-laden hand across a painting before anyone could notice it.

What had Aaron said to Lee? *I deserve just as much respect as you. And with all I'm learning, I'm going to get that respect.*

Motive . . . means . . . opportunity. It all fit. Could it be that he was targeting the artists now, especially the painters, to get revenge?

Larissa waited a moment as I thought, then smiled, waved, and left for the bathroom. I groaned and brushed at the new dust she'd left behind. I needed to clean up too. And, while I was at it, I needed to figure out what to say to Becca to convince her to drop Heather's case without implicating Larissa. I figured my new information about Aaron might be distracting enough.

AFTER BEATING AND RINSING everything I could out of my pants in the bathroom, then hiding the wet plaid shirt and the ball cap behind the bathroom trash can, I left to find Becca. Did I have any idea what to do or say? Kind of. I couldn't wait to tell her about how *Aaron* was our guy. I didn't look forward to discussing how I was wrong about Quinn, especially since there really was a guilty Eccles sister the evidence could point to.

I liked Larissa. Something about her reminded me of myself when I was just starting out.

I couldn't find Becca anywhere. I returned to the scenes of both sabotages: nothing. I wandered the park as fast as I could, looking for her. Still no Becca. I even visited the Contestants' Tent in case she was questioning people. I considered looking for Aaron, but honestly, finding Becca would be easier, and with her help, finding Aaron would be a cakewalk.

Where is she? I thought, skulking near the help office. I had gone there in case Becca was visiting her mother, but I didn't see Becca. Granted, she could be in disguise, but give me some credit: I'd spotted her following me after a particularly bizarre job involving a pep rally and five cans of spray cheese, and the halls had been crowded then. Worse than the paths today. Besides, would she really disguise herself when talking to her mom? Maybe. I didn't know what kind of weird family habits had spawned the creature known as Becca Mills.

As I was imagining Detective Mills Senior reading bedtime case files to a preschool-aged Becca, I saw her. Becca, I mean. She emerged from the help office, but not from the front where I was watching. She came around from the back. *Oh, crap.*

When Becca saw me, she waved me over. I threw a glance at the building to make sure Becca's mom wasn't watching, and then I ran over.

"What happened to you?" Becca asked as I followed her around back to the storage room. She sounded better, more like her old self. She must have found some evidence.

"What do you mean?"

She gestured at my soaked shorts. "I'd comment, but it's too easy. I don't know if I should start on the stains or the water."

"Definitely the stains. That's where my mom's going to start." I sighed. "There were complications."

Becca smiled but didn't say anything.

"Aren't you going to ask what kind of complications?"

"So you can brag about your exploits? No way. Besides, I just talked to my mom. She had *such* interesting things to say."

"Oh. Was this a friendly visit, or did you find evidence for her?"

Becca rested one hand against the brick wall and grinned at me. "Friendly, at first. But then she told me the neighbor kid came strolling into the office to see the sabotaged paintings. Had the worst possible excuse for being there too."

Ouch. "I'm sure the excuse wasn't that terrible."

"And if that weren't enough, Mom got sent on a false tip and then, right as she got back to the office, the air ducts started to play music. They didn't find anyone; they think someone put a phone too close to a vent and no one wants to own up. But Mom thought it was interesting, and so do I. No evidence, but I know someone who is very good at not leaving anything behind."

I rolled my eyes. "Before you bring out the handcuffs and pepper spray, please remember who hired me for this particular job."

"Yes." Becca's eyes turned steely. "While I'm glad you listened to me and didn't get caught, after all that trouble, you'd better have gotten what I asked you for."

"Relax." I pulled the bag out, complete with its sample of paint. "I got it."

"Don't wave that around!" Becca snatched the bag from me and, hunching over it, examined it. "Excellent. I'll give it to Liesl to analyze."

"Who's Liesl?"

"A friend. The one who likes to hang around in the science rooms."

"Who?"

Becca stared at me. "How is it I know all about your friends and you know nothing about mine?"

"I don't follow you around."

Becca rolled her eyes and went back to examining the paint.

"You seem a lot happier than earlier," I said. "I take it that means there haven't been any new sabotages?"

"Nothing. I think they saw the police working on the case and got scared. But that's not the only reason I'm smiling."

"You made a break in the case?"

"You could say that. Come with me."

Becca pulled open the door to the back storage room. Feeling like ants were crawling under my clothes, I followed Becca into the room—the same one I had just vacated with Larissa. The grate from the air vent was still off, and the painting Larissa had thrown at me was where I'd set it, leaning against the wall. The hamsters looked up at me with evil eyes, like they were saying, "*I know you stole that sample, thief.*" I didn't think they would accept the term "retrieval specialist."

Becca glanced at the grate, grinned at me, and tossed me a screwdriver. I caught it and then climbed the grill again. Within moments, the grate was relatively well fastened to the wall. Then I jumped down. "Tell me you didn't bring me in here just to do that."

"You're the one who takes pride in not leaving evidence."

"*That* wasn't me. It was—like that when I got here." At the last minute, I decided I didn't want to bring Larissa up. Not yet.

Becca looked up at the grate. "Huh. Then why'd you go fix it?"

"Because whether I did it or not, it looks suspicious." I am as smooth as freshly made chocolate milk.

"Uh-huh. Anyway, I came back here to make sure *someone* wasn't in any trouble, and I found something. You were right; something isn't quite aboveground with Quinn Eccles."

Beaming, Becca picked up Quinn's painting and brought it over to me.

"After you told me Quinn's painting was weird, I went and checked it out. The painting hanging there wasn't the same one I saw there earlier when I first ran into you."

"Oh, is that what you're calling it these days?"

Becca glared at me over the painting, then broke into a smile. "So I went searching for it. This storage room is so close to where Quinn's painting was supposed to be, and it was unlocked. Odd on a day when the park has something more interesting to offer than a cookout or a volleyball game. Imagine my surprise when I found *this* just waiting for me. Now, why would a painting be here?"

"I'm sure there's a reasonable explanation."

"Sure," Becca said, flipping the painting around to look at it. "And I'm a six-foot grizzly bear who likes tabletop role-playing games. This is it, Wilderson. This is the evidence I need. Why would an adult trade out a child's painting, especially when the saboteur's method is to slather it with paint? A kid, like Quinn, would have a different reason. Here's what I think: she decided she wanted insurance against her partner sabotaging her painting, given that she was a painter and they were targeting painters, so she swapped it for the one that's out there now. When the judges come by—and she'll know when, thanks to her mom—she'll put this one back."

That was exactly what I had thought before Larissa had told me the truth. It didn't mean Quinn wasn't guilty of something, but now, after hearing the other side of the story, I doubted it. "I don't think that's what happened."

Becca tucked the painting under an arm and tilted her head at me. "Right. Like that wasn't what you were getting at every time you said Quinn was our culprit. Do you think it happened another way?"

"I don't think it happened at all. I don't think it's Quinn anymore."

"Even seeing this?" She rolled her eyes. "Stop messing with me. I get it; you were right. Too confident to be innocent. I can't believe I didn't spot it before."

Becca tapped my shoulder. "Guess I should have trusted my partner more, huh?"

Oh, this was bad. As much as I wanted to support Becca in her ideas, I didn't want to send her on the warpath to an innocent artist. Even if Becca didn't attack Quinn like she had Case, Quinn could be out of the running, shamed by the officials, possibly banned from competing in next year's or any other year's contest. Not to mention, the real saboteur would still be out there.

I took the painting from Becca and put it back against the wall. "This isn't the evidence you need," I said. "I'm sorry."

Becca's smile fell into a scowl. "What do you mean? Look at it. It's incriminating. When matched with Quinn's proximity to a judge and her confidence despite the large prize, it tells a pretty clear story."

"Not as clear as you might think."

Her eyes flashed. "What did you do?"

"Nothing! I swear, I just did what you asked me to. And I also found something better than a painting in a closet. I have the identity of one of the saboteurs."

"I do too. Quinn Eccles."

Weird the way things change. Now Becca was trying to convince me of the same thing I'd worked so hard to convince her of not that long ago. Her mood was souring; I needed to give her something good. I plunged ahead. "It's Aaron Baxter. He's one of our saboteurs."

Becca frowned. "The guy who got us into the tent?"

"Yep. Last year he entered a finger-painted work into the contest. Everyone laughed at him and said he wasn't a real artist, and it cost him the Best Painting win. During the past year, the other painters at his school kept teasing him about it. It got bad. Now, this summer, Aaron is working as a volunteer at the contest. Perks for employees? Access to the tent, which we saw firsthand, inside information on where the judges will be during the day, and a supply of paints and markers that could be used for making snow-cone signs or, I don't know, sabotaging paintings."

Becca nodded. "It's a good theory. Aaron would have motive and means to sabotage the art. And only paintings have been attacked so far. That would suggest a grudge. But we don't know where he was when Diana's painting was attacked."

"Doesn't matter. We know the two paintings were attacked by two different people. If Aaron got Justin's piece, his partner must have attacked Diana's."

"Then we have our suspects," Becca said, stone-faced. "*Both* of them. We'll go talk to Aaron and then we'll bring Quinn in too."

I shook my head. "You were right earlier. Quinn is innocent. We should focus our attention on Aaron."

"Aaron isn't working alone. Lee isn't his partner, because he has an alibi, so that leaves us with Quinn."

I tried to find some proof that kept Quinn clear of

accusation. "No one reported seeing Quinn at Diana's sabotage. I asked."

"You asked *one* person. Just because Diana didn't see Quinn, doesn't mean she wasn't there."

"The marks on the paintings are marker, not paint. Quinn didn't have a marker."

"But Aaron does, if he has access to all the contest's art supplies. I think he'd be willing to lend it to his partner, don't you?"

I started to pace the small room. "There must have been someone else there."

"The evidence is piling up against Quinn," Becca said. "I think it's time to bring her down for this." "The way you tried to bring down Case?" I glared at her. "I saw it. There was no mercy there."

"The only reason you care about 'mercy' is because Case is your friend. You were just as happy to tear down Mark as I was."

That touched a nerve. "Mark was different. He took *joy* in being a terrible person. He stole because he wanted to be a thief. He deserved to go down for his actions. Quinn doesn't."

Becca squared her shoulders. "Quinn is a saboteur. In the end, she's no better than Mark."

"You're kidding yourself."

"And for a minute there, I thought we were all on the same page," Becca spat. "Would it kill you, just once, to support my ideas?"

"I do support your ideas."

"Sure. No matter what I say, you say I'm wrong. Quinn is evil, Quinn is good. Make up your mind. And now I can't even stop a criminal without you criticizing me."

That annoyed me. "I'm sorry to shatter your world-view, but I've had experience dealing with criminals, maybe as much as you have. Have you ever thought about why I never turn in the names of the thieves I retrieve from?"

That got her attention. She leaned against a child-size soccer goal, wearing an "impress me" expression.

Feeling suddenly very exposed, I said quietly, "I've seen things, even before I became a retrieval specialist. Not everyone who makes a bad decision is a bad person. Not everyone who does something wrong deserves to be treated like a criminal."

Becca straightened up. "This is personal for you, right? *You* don't want to be seen as a criminal. I got that, with all the stupid 'retrieval specialist' talk. Too bad you *are* a criminal and 'retrieval specialist' is just a fancy term for thief—"

"This isn't about me!" I took a deep breath. "And let's not pretend this isn't personal for you, too."

She stiffened. "I want to stop a saboteur—two of them, actually—before they hurt someone else. How is that personal?"

"So none of this is about you proving to your mom that you were right?"

Becca looked livid. "This is about helping people."

"Is it? If Quinn broke the rules," I said, "and I'm not saying she did, we have to consider that she did it with a good reason. Five hundred plus a scholarship? She's stressed and doing what she thinks she has to. How are you going to *help* her?"

Becca's mouth dropped open. "You're judging me."

I felt knocked back. "Of course not."

"Yes, you are. Really? *Me?* When Quinn is clearly the bad guy?"

Oh boy. "Do we know that? Do we even know if Quinn did anything wrong?"

Becca laughed. "Understandable. Right. No doubt right now you're taking Quinn's side because she's one of you. A criminal. I shouldn't have trusted you with this case."

That hurt after I'd chosen her over my friends earlier in the air duct. "I have been nothing but trustworthy all day."

She shrugged. "You did what I asked, but you didn't do it for me. You did it because you enjoy being a thief."

"Not true, and also, *retrieval specialist*."

"Don't quibble. A thief is a thief."

"Except when they're not." I threw my head back and groaned to the dusty ceiling. "You don't get it. You've *never* gotten it. In your mind, every criminal is a totally depraved bad egg. A mustache-twirling, black-hat villain. Look at me. See a mustache?" I stuck my face up in hers and enjoyed her uncomfortable expression as I violated her personal bubble.

She pushed me away. "Not true. I thought you were worth saving, for a while."

"I'm not the only one. I retrieve so many stolen objects. Some of them are taken by people just to be mean. But sometimes good people make bad decisions with the best intentions. Sometimes doing right means doing wrong."

Becca was red-faced but calm. "Like when?"

"Let's see," I said. "How about when a kid steals a wallet because he left his money at home and is hungry? Or a girl steals makeup, thinking her friend won't mind and meaning to return it, but she likes it so much she never gives it back. Someone breaks an iPod and steals it to hide the damage." I stared at her. "A detective hires a known *thief*, or so she thinks, to get hard-to-reach evidence."

I watched the rage creep up her face as my meaning sunk in. Then, when it reached her hairline, she shoved me. Hard. Becca's strong; her push sent me sprawling into the pile of nets. The blunt object jabbed me in the back again. I think it was part of a goal frame. Joy.

"How dare you?" Becca hissed as I checked for broken bones. "I'm not like Aaron or Quinn or any of the thieves you should take down but don't. And I'm certainly not like you."

I stood up and dusted off my shirt and pants as best I could, despite the wet cloth. "Got that right. If you were like me, people wouldn't be so scared of you. Talk to Quinn. Fine. But do it in private. Not in a big drag-out fight like you had with Case."

Becca grew quiet. She studied me. "You're protecting someone."

"No, I'm not."

She nodded, smiling. "Yes, you are. Just like you were protecting someone when you deleted those photos of Mark's stash."

How'd she know that?

"Have you had a stick up your butt about that all day?" I asked. "That was a long time ago. We got the guy. What does it matter?"

"What does it matter?" Becca's eyes were wild. "You really don't get it?"

I shook my head and Becca kicked a bag of baseball bats, making them clank and my nerves fire.

"You really are the worst, Wilderson. All day. Taking me up to that overlook on a fool's errand, leaving me out in the open when Quinn came into the locker room, and I know you've been running gambits behind my back. That's so like you. I should have expected this ever since you deleted those pictures off my camera. Are we partners or not?"

"We are!"

"Really? Then why aren't you helping me? Why are you taking the best evidence I found away from me?" Becca picked up Quinn's painting and then threw it back against the wall. "Why are you blocking me and protecting other people? Where are you when I need you?"

I didn't know how to respond. I was working with Becca, but I couldn't do everything her way. I had to protect people from her. Working with the law, or against it, it didn't matter. I always lost.

"I'm here," I said. "I'm your partner. I'll help you catch the saboteurs. I promise."

"I doubt that," Becca said, advancing on me. I hurried backward, stumbling on the nets again. "If you were with me, you'd support me. You'd come with me to show my mom this." She picked up Quinn's painting.

"You can't show her that! It's circumstantial evidence at best. There's no proof that it's related to the sabotages at all."

Becca frowned. "You're right. You know what would be better? A confession. I think it's time to talk to Quinn."

I froze. If Becca put the heat to an innocent Quinn, Quinn would only be hurt. But that wasn't the worst of it. If Larissa was anywhere near her sister, and I bet she was, Larissa would probably give herself up just to protect Quinn. And Becca would fry Larissa. She was already upset, but after this fight, Becca would be even angrier. It would be worse than what happened to Case.

I couldn't let this happen. "Let me go with you. Someone needs to save people from your medieval methods."

That was probably the wrong thing to say. Becca stood taller, stiffer, and she smiled in a way that brought a new brand of terrifying into my life.

"No," she said gently. "You'll stay here. Consider this a taste for how the rest of your criminal life will be."

So fast, before I could blink, Becca pushed the painting at me, slamming it into my chest. It wasn't painful, but it had force. I landed in the nets again. I struggled to toss the painting aside and sit up.

"Maybe you're right. Maybe it is personal," Becca said. "But I'd terrify a hundred suspects if it would give me the proof I need to stop the sabotage."

She slipped out, slamming the door behind her.

"Becca!" I stood and grabbed at the handle. I pushed. Locked.

No matter. The lock was on the inside. I undid it and pushed again.

Thud. The door stopped against something hard and heavy.

"Oh no you didn't." I clambered up a stack of crates and peered out the window. The crate Larissa and I had used to get inside the storage room had been moved so it blocked the door.

Over to the right, running away through the park, was a very angry, very scary private eye.

I fell back. This was my fault. I'd brought back all of Becca's bad feelings, plus interest, and she had trapped me inside the storage room. Now she was off to take her feelings out on her prime suspect, a girl so sensitive that her own sister had replaced her painting to protect her. Becca had no idea of the damage she was about to inflict on two girls who deserved so much better than a public trial and punishment.

I GRIPPED THE DUSTY WINDOW-sill, stunned. If I hadn't pushed so hard that Quinn was guilty, if I hadn't discovered and then tried to defend Larissa, if I hadn't gone and riled up Becca, none of this would have happened. Becca wouldn't have gone back and checked on Quinn's painting, wouldn't have gone looking for the real one, and wouldn't have found it in the storage room.

If I had backed up Becca with her belief in Quinn's innocence, this wouldn't have happened. If I had acted like a good partner earlier, this wouldn't have happened. Is that irony? I get confused.

But come on. Becca's whole thing was that breaking the rules hurts people. That's why she guns for me so hard. How can she not see that what she does hurts people too? Justice isn't kind, not always, but it should be.

Especially for the people who are stuck in a bad situation. I don't care what kind of pressure you're under; you don't take it out on other people.

And her attack of the Eccles sisters was going to have other, worse consequences. I was sure Becca was right: the only reason the saboteurs hadn't been attacking more victims was because the heat was on. The freaking cops were here, looking for a culprit. If Becca went in, guns blazing, and hauled Quinn and Larissa off for sabotage, sure, the adults would consider a kid criminal. But in the meantime, Aaron would still be free to act while the adults wasted time with the wrong suspects. That would prove the Eccles sisters were innocent, but some comfort that would be for whomever got hit next.

I needed to do something. Now. I needed to fix this so that everyone walked away safe. And I needed to prove to Becca that I was there to help her, not hold her back.

I looked down at the crate blocking the door. Becca had locked me up, imprisoned me in the storage room. *Consider this a taste for how the rest of your criminal life will be,* she had said. Sick sense of humor on that one. At least I'd be able to play some baseball.

Good thing she hadn't been thinking straight. I flipped the window up and let myself out feetfirst. It was a bit of a drop, but I've had way worse. Come on; I broke into the room. Did Becca really think I couldn't break out? But she had slowed me down. Which, now that I think about it, might have been her intention. She was on her way to confront the Eccles sisters, and she had time on me. I had to find them before she did. I broke into a run.

And then what? Say I managed to find the sisters before Becca did. What then? Becca would still show up, mad at me, and ream out the girls like she had with Case. Worse than with Case. I kept thinking of Aaron, laughed at for finger painting, and still mocked for it a year later. It didn't matter that the accusations were wrong. What would happen to the sisters if they were publicly accused, in front of other kids, of sabotage?

They'd get eaten alive, and the saboteurs would be free to act again.

The idea hit me so hard I actually stumbled as I neared the sculpture garden. Huh. If the girls were publically accused and arrested, the real saboteurs would feel like they were getting away with it. But was that so bad?

Looking around the park, I picked up the pace. My mind raced with my feet. A good con either threatens the mark with something they can't live with, or offers them exactly what they want. Usually that thing is security, safety, in some way. If someone else got caught for the saboteurs' crimes, and they knew it, they'd feel safe.

I couldn't threaten them, because I didn't know for sure who they were. But if they felt safe, they'd come out of hiding. And we'd be ready for Aaron *and* his real partner if they took one wayward step toward anyone's art.

Also, if my plan worked out, Becca might trust me again. I really did want to help her catch the real saboteurs. I still thought our best bet to do that was by working together.

I stopped the run as soon as the crowds thickened, and then I wandered the paths without any kind of direction. That's the best way to find something quickly, pure wandering. Hopefully I'd reach the Eccles sisters before Becca did.

Oh man. This new plan was *not* going to be easy. There was a good chance it wouldn't work and the saboteurs would attack before we could catch them. I would have caused someone else to lose their artwork. There was also a good chance that Becca would kill me for ruining an investigation, or get her mother to arrest me and have me tried as an adult. Not to mention what it could do to Larissa . . . but I had no choice. This was my strongest option. At least if I were doing the accusing, I could control it. I couldn't do that if Becca were in charge.

And a good retrieval specialist knows how to stow a

few aces up his sleeve. I pulled out my mom's phone and called Hack.

"Hey, J," he said. "Was earlier a bad time?"

"Huh?" I remembered getting the call while I was in the air ducts. Amazing how stress can make you live in the *now*. "Oh yeah. A little bit. How's the investigation going?"

"Not great. Case lost . . . something that mattered to the job, and now he's bummed. He did get some interesting information before you called me. Talk about bad timing, man."

Oh yeah, let's talk about bad timing. I'd been in an *air duct*. But I said, "I'm sorry about that. What were you two up to?" I had to act the part, after all.

"Never mind. So, what were you calling about?"

There was my opening. "I had an idea for you guys. You still have the list of possible targets?"

"Dude. It's me. I have backups of my backups."

"How's Case? Is he still worried?" While I talked, I walked and craned my neck, looking for the Eccles sisters.

"Yeah. Finding out he's a favorite wasn't a good moment for him."

"What if you kept watch over his art? Post a guard?"

Hack was quiet for a moment. "Not a bad idea, but who would investigate?"

"One of you could stay stationed at the painting. The other could keep looking for clues."

"That could work. Yo, Case!" The sound became muffled as, I knew, Hack and Case debated the idea. I waited for them to come back as I kept walking and looking for the sisters. Where were they? With a chill, I wondered if Becca had managed to slow me down enough to find them before I could. What if she already had them down with her mom at the help office?

I hurried faster, wishing I could run. But the crowds and my need to be thorough in my search prevented that. I took a left, and a right, and saw nothing. I pulled the phone a little away from my head. My ears needed to be free to listen for the sisters.

Another corner, and the next. Case and Hack weren't done debating yet. I walked farther, then spun around on a whim and headed back to the sculpture garden. There they were. Quinn and Larissa, talking and looking at Sandra Lynn's sculpture, the one expected to win the whole thing. Oh, if Becca saw them there, next to a favorite's statue, nothing I could do would save them.

They weren't alone. Lee and his buddy Ethan were with them. They'd see what I was about to do. Judging by how many pictures of Quinn Lee had on his camera, he would not be pleased with me. So what—it's not like I cared what that jerk thought.

Aaron wasn't there, though. If it turned out that Lee was the accomplice, my life would be easier; he could take the message to Aaron. But I couldn't explain away Lee's alibi. He hadn't been around when Diana's painting was attacked, and he'd been in the tent during Justin's. We knew there were two different attackers, and he couldn't have been either of them.

I hated myself for what I was about to do. But it was better this way. I wasn't Becca; I didn't have her credentials. If I played this right, people would later think I was just some angry kid hurling wild accusations.

But right now the saboteurs, and the Eccles sisters, wouldn't think that.

I took a deep breath, straightened my shirt, and walked over to the sisters. Larissa saw me coming. Her eyes flashed with fear, then with warmth. "Hey, Jeremy," she said. "How's it going?"

Quinn smiled at me. "Want to join us? We're just admiring the art."

"Yeah, I bet you were," I said, keeping my voice cold and bitter. Quinn's smile slipped.

"Jeremy, what's going on?" Larissa's voice was guarded.

I looked at her and cleared my throat. "I know you

two are the saboteurs. I'm going to bring you in," I said, as loudly as I could without yelling.

Larissa's jaw dropped. Quinn looked like she'd been turned to stone. I wished I could explain my plan, but that could compromise their reactions. I needed it to look real.

Lee and Ethan turned to watch the proceedings. "You?" Lee said when he recognized me. "You're no cop. You're a hayseed."

"I'm a detective," I said, lowering my voice. The rest of the crowd didn't need to know this part, but Loudmouth Lee might make the perfect messenger for my trick, even if he wasn't the other saboteur. "Undercover. I've been working to stop crime at the art show today. It's not my fault if you were so easily tricked."

While Lee fed on that, I turned to the sisters and laughed without any joy. "I thought I could trust you, Larissa," I said. "But it turns out I was wrong."

"I—I don't get it," Quinn said. "You think I'm the one sabotaging the other art?"

"She wouldn't do that," Lee said. His face was serious. When I met his eyes, he looked away. I imagined myself as Becca, vicious and glowing with Justice. *Don't show weakness*, I told myself. *Be the angry gumshoe. Take them down. Play your part in this con.*

"I'm afraid she did," I told Lee. "It was only a matter

of time before we found out the truth." Then I turned back to Quinn. "Why are you so calm today, Quinn? Everyone around you is losing their minds, but not you. What do you know that they don't? We found small dots of black in corners of the sabotaged art. Black, like the tube of paint you have in your purse. Do you think it will be a match, Miss Eccles?"

"But I—I didn't do anything." Quinn looked on the verge of tears. She was holding her left hand in her right, her fingers curled up like a dying flower. She wouldn't meet my eyes.

Now that I knew the story from Larissa, it was easier to see the signs of Quinn's innocence. Attacking her like this felt like a punch to the gut.

I hated myself. But I kept going. This part, though, I said loudly. "Who has been attacked so far? Painters, Quinn. Your biggest competition. Do you really think I'd think that's a coincidence?"

Bad logic. Easily picked apart later. But it made a good show.

"Back. Off." Larissa advanced on me. So I took a step toward her and pushed my face close to hers, like Becca always did to me.

"Don't get me started on you," I hissed. "There was a theft of paint, among that was *red* paint, and brushes, from Heather Caballero during a pool party that both of you attended. Care to enlighten us about that one, Larissa?"

She glowered at me but didn't say anything. Good girl. Never give anything away until you know there's no point to keeping the secret. But that glare twisted the knife I felt was bent under my ribs. I was doing the exact thing I'd promised to protect her from.

"We also know the sabotage was done by two people," I said. I wished Aaron had been there for that part. Carry that one away, Lee.

"Sisters, like you, must be close," I said. "Must share everything. Let me lay out how this went down. Quinn enters the contest, and this morning learns about the special new prize the judges added to the pot. Greedy and scared, she comes to her trusted sister for help. Together you hatch a plan to better Quinn's odds."

Lee grabbed my shirt. "She didn't do anything."

I pried his fingers off. "Can you prove that? Have you been with her all day? Can you give me an alibi?"

Lee's face reddened. "No. But I know Quinn."

"Not as well as you thought, apparently."

"She didn't do it!"

"How are you so sure? Maybe you know who did it. If so, now would be an excellent time to speak up."

Ethan touched Lee's shoulder. "He's right. If you know something, you should say it."

Lee rounded on him. "Shut. Up. Man, you're so annoying."

Red-faced and stiff, Ethan stared at Lee. Then he shook his head and walked away.

Lee scowled at me, then turned and melted into the crowd.

I turned my attention back to the sisters. "Well?"

"No, that's not . . . I mean, I wouldn't . . ." Quinn was sobbing now, tears leaking down her face.

I held up a hand. "Not here. We have a lot to talk about, and I'm sick of being stared at." Then I reached out to both girls. "Come with me, now."

No, seriously, come on. Before the adults get here and start asking questions.

Larissa jerked back, murdering me with her eyes. Gritting my teeth, I reached out and grabbed both girls' arms. I pulled them to either side of me. "Let's go somewhere else, and you can explain everything to me."

I turned around, ready to lead the girls toward the help office, where everyone knew the police were. As soon as we turned around, I saw Becca staring at me from the crowd. It gave me a weird feeling of déjà vu. She broke away to join me and the sisters.

"Hey," I said to her as she fell into step beside me.

"Hey," she said. I couldn't read her face exactly, but I didn't see any anger there. "You got them?"

"He got the wrong people," Larissa barked. "Let us go."

Quinn just looked at me, emotions in her eyes I couldn't identify. I wasn't sure I wanted to.

"Yeah, I got them," I said to Becca.

That weird, not-angry, not-smug look on Becca's face hung there for a moment. Then she banished it and nodded once. "Let's take them to my mom."

"No," I said. That would ruin *everything*. "Let's talk to them in private. Let's make sure. I'm not as good a detective as you are."

"You're not a detective at all," Quinn said. "You're a thief."

I smiled and tugged on the girls. Hard. "This way."

They followed. Becca came up beside me and took Quinn's arm. As she did, we passed a sculpture that looked like a melting Rubik's Cube, only with holes through the center. I'd seen it before; but where? It was painted all kind of colors. The paint was interesting, kind of shiny.

But I had a show to finish putting on. Becca and I led the Eccles sisters away.

"Thanks," Becca said to me in a low voice. "Look, everything I said before—"

"Don't worry about it," I replied.

Becca walked silently next to me. "It just . . . I was watching from the side. It all looks different from that angle."

I thought of my experience watching Becca attack Case. "It does."

"I guess . . . partners should say something when the other one crosses a line."

"I've always thought so. And hey, you've done it for me."

She sighed. "I'm sorry. How I've been today. It's just . . . this is important. I want to do well."

"I get it. And we're one step closer to getting the proof you need for your mom."

"Right. So how do you want to play this?" Becca asked. "I can take good cop, since you've already set up bad cop."

In other words, Becca wanted to work together again. It felt surprisingly pleasant to be on her side again.

It was also weird, thinking of Becca as the good cop. I guess I'd put her in that position earlier, at the tent, but here she was, volunteering for the role.

"I've got a plan," I said. "Let's get away from the crowds first."

I steered the group to the help office's storage room door.

"What, are you trying to make some kind of point?"

Larissa spat at me when she saw where I'd brought them.

"Sure am," I said as I let her go. "But not for you."

All three girls gave me confused looks. Becca raised an eyebrow. I sighed and faced Quinn, who still wouldn't meet my eyes.

"I'm sorry for all this," I said. "I know you're innocent. If nothing else, your reaction to the accusation proved it."

"So all of that was for show?" Larissa said. Quinn put her face in her hands.

I nodded. "I'm sorry I couldn't explain ahead of time, but your reactions needed to be real. Everyone watching needed to buy that you two were the saboteurs, at least for a little while."

Larissa's eyes blazed. She stepped up and slapped me hard across the face. I reeled, and Becca burst out laughing.

"Oh, I like her!" she said between howls of laughter.

"Great, I'm glad," I mumbled through a swelling face. "Can you find my nose? I think it landed over there somewhere."

Quinn had recovered, apparently. She was looking at me with a grin on her face. I was happy that my face getting torn off was good for something.

"How dare you?" Larissa yelled. "How dare you humiliate Quinn in front of all those people? After all I did to protect her, you—" She stopped, realizing what she had just said.

Becca, who had been leaning against the wall, chuckling, stood up. "What exactly did you do?"

I waved at Becca. "You may as well tell her," I said to Larissa. "If she didn't hear it when I was doing my accusation, Quinn probably did. It's time to come clean."

Larissa paled, but then she took a breath and started to explain the theft of Heather's art supplies.

"I didn't mean to hurt anyone," she finished. "I just wanted to protect Quinn."

Quinn was frowning. "Larissa. Do you realize what you did?"

Larissa nodded. "I made it so you can't win the contest. I'm sorry. I thought I was doing the right thing."

"Not to mention leaving incriminating evidence with an *innocent* person," I said, looking at Becca. "Who knows what that would have looked like?"

"Shut up, Wilderson," Becca said. "Case is in the clear on all counts. We get it."

Quinn wasn't done with Larissa. "If anyone had found the painting you hid, they would have thought I was involved."

"They wouldn't," Larissa said.

"They might," Becca said, looking at me. I shrugged.

Then Becca turned back to Larissa, her arms folded. The younger Eccles sister visibly shivered.

"This is what you're going to do," Becca said. "You are going to return all those stolen art supplies to Heather. Personally. You are going to look her in the eye and say you're sorry. She can decide what she wants to do, but if it's unfair, you come to me."

Larissa nodded. "Anything else?"

"This business with the painting was discovered too late to bring to the judges' attention," Becca said. "Either your dummy painting wins something or Quinn walks away with nothing. You two need to decide how you will handle this." Larissa didn't move, and Becca flipped her hand at her. "Like, now."

Quinn grabbed Larissa's shoulder. "She's right. We need to talk about this."

As the sisters made things right (it sounded like Larissa would have to do Quinn's chores for the rest of the summer as penance, and return the stolen painting), Becca came over to me. "That was gentle of you," I said.

Becca grinned. "It's summer. Not my jurisdiction." Then she punched me hard in the arm. "But don't think for one moment that I'm going to go easy on you once we get back to school in the fall."

First Larissa, now Becca. I was everyone's favorite

punching bag that day. "I really don't know what I did to merit this level of physical abuse."

"Well, you did make us look like criminals in front of everyone," Quinn said as she and Larissa came back over. "Can't say I appreciated that."

"Again, I'm sorry. But we had to do it."

Quinn raised her chin and glared at me. "Seriously? Everyone would have seen that. All our friends, their parents . . ."

"The saboteurs," I added. That got everyone's attention. "Yeah," I said. "Word of my fake accusation will probably get around. Now that they saw you get taken down, they'll feel safe."

"Safe enough to try again," Becca said, catching on. She beamed. "We know one of our saboteurs, but not the other. They'll make their move, and when they do—"

"We'll be there, waiting. For both of them," I said. Oh, the cleverness of me. It's wonderful when other people see it.

"Not sorry I hit you," Larissa said. "But that's a good plan."

Quinn's glare had changed to a soft warmth. "Not bad, thief."

I smiled and bowed.

"Who's your suspect?" Larissa asked.

“Aaron Baxter,” Becca said.

“The finger painter from Burdick?” Quinn asked, frowning. “Well, he would definitely have motive.”

“He has means, too,” I added. “Lots of access to paints and judge notes. He was also nearby when Diana’s painting was attacked.”

“So if Aaron’s one saboteur, who’s the other?” Larissa asked.

“That’s what we’re trying to figure out,” Becca said. “By the way, I’m still not convinced Quinn is completely innocent. I understand about the painting switch, but there are still some things that I need cleared up.” Her phone rang, and she looked at the screen. “It’s Liesl,” she said. “I bet these are the paint sample’s results. I better take this. Wilderson, would you?”

“Yeah, I got this.” I turned to Quinn. “Why do you have that black paint on you?”

Quinn shrugged. “I bought it at the gift shop. A friend from the Art Club needs a little for shading, and it was on sale.”

I nodded. Over to the side, I could see Becca talking but also glancing over at us, paying attention to what we said. “Why not just leave it in your locker?” I asked. “That’s where Lee kept his weird notebook and camera.”

"How did you know about Lee's things?" Quinn asked.

"I—uh." There was no good way to answer that.

I expected another glare, but instead Quinn burst out laughing. "Wow. I heard you were the best, but this is unbelievable. Did you really safecrack Lee's locker?"

"That's nothing," Larissa said. "You should hear what happened in the help building—"

Oh man. Becca was looking over and she had that steely look in her eyes. "Tell her about it later," I said. "Let's focus on the here and now."

"Okay," Quinn said, still giggling. "I'm sorry. It's wrong of me, I know. But I can't believe you broke into a locker. Who does that?"

"I do," I said. "But never mind me." Becca rejoined the circle. "Learn anything?" I asked her.

"Yes, and it's weird," Becca said. "It's house paint."

"What?" all three of us asked.

Becca nodded. "The saboteur's paint is the kind of paint sold in hardware stores for painting a house's interior walls. I thought I recognized its stretchiness. It's just like the paint Dad bought for us to paint our living room, except red, not beige."

"Weird. Who would have that here?"

"The park would," Becca said. "Remember all those paint cans in the toolshed?"

"Any of those could be the saboteur's weapon. And Aaron might have access to that shed."

"One more point in his favor. But who's his accomplice?"

"I don't know. But I know what to look for if someone is acting suspicious."

"Then that's your job." Becca handed me her camera. "Take this and get a picture of anyone acting weird. Do *not* delete anything."

"Sure, like I want to go through your righteous fury again," I mumbled as I took the camera.

"And if someone says anything interesting, get a video. My camera has a great microphone."

"I know. You've only tried to use it to tape me confessing a hundred times." I put the camera in my pocket.

"That's an exaggeration. I'm going to go look for Aaron. I'd like to ask him some questions," Becca said. "We better hurry. Your stunt must have hit the rumor mill by now, and the saboteurs haven't struck in a while. They could attack any minute."

"We want to help," Larissa said. "Quinn's a contestant. She could have easily been attacked. That means we're involved."

"You sure?" I asked. "You don't have to."

Quinn smiled. "Let's catch these guys. It'll be fun."

I raised my eyebrows at her. "You aren't mad at me, then? I could have ruined your reputation."

"I think it will take more than one public accusation to change how people see me," Quinn said lightly. "Besides, Larissa gave you a much better punishment than I could have." I rubbed my face. Good thing Quinn was just as mild-mannered as Becca and Larissa had said or I'd be getting slapped again.

"Okay, then," Becca said. "We'll need both of you looking if we're going to find these guys in time."

"Stop," I said. "We don't have time to run around the park. Who knows if we'd even bump into them?"

Becca folded her arms. "Do you have a better suggestion?"

I grinned. "Why chase them when we can wait for them to come to us? We know who else is marked."

She opened her mouth, then closed it, frowning. "I can't believe I didn't think of that."

"We set guards over the remaining art. When the saboteurs come, and they will—"

"We'll have them."

I nodded. "Do you think catching the saboteurs red-handed will be proof enough for your mom?"

Becca grinned. "Absolutely."

My neck prickled. "Then let's go."

WITHIN MINUTES, WE WERE in position. Becca assigned us all places to wait for the saboteurs to strike. Larissa was sent to watch Sandra's sculpture. Becca would hang around near Henry's photograph. Quinn went somewhere she could get a perfect bird's-eye view of the park: the balcony of the art museum.

"It's a good lookout," Becca told me when I'd smirked at her. "You can search for patterns of guilty people."

As for me, I was the floater. I was supposed to wander the park, looking for suspicious activity. We were 90 percent sure Aaron and his partner would attack the marked works; I was to look out for the other 10 percent.

Larissa didn't have a phone, so Becca lent her hers. I gave the sisters Mom's number so we could communicate in some way. "If you see him or if you see anything weird, text me," I'd told them. "Either Becca or I will come to help you."

Since Becca was without her phone, she and I would have to go talk to each other in person if something happened. Inconvenient but necessary. It was better if the sisters could call for help; Becca knew how to take care of herself.

And so we began. The girls laid in wait, and I went on the hunt.

Here's the thing about searching for a single object in a large space: it doesn't matter if it's a missing shoe or a prime sabotage suspect—either way, you have a lot of ground to cover. It's worse when the object you're looking for can move. You have to move too, and do it smarter and faster than whatever you're chasing. I moved at random, taking turns without clear reason, keeping my eyes peeled for Aaron's accomplice (and can I just comment on how gross that saying is? "Eyes peeled"? Who came up with that, Dr. Frankenstein?).

When you're moving that much, you're bound to run into something. For me, it was Case and Hack. They were walking toward the Contestants' Tent, and Case looked irritated.

"Hey," I said. "What's going on?"

"We have to go to the tent," Case groaned.

Hack shook his head. "Case wanted to guard his painting some more. We took your advice, and Case kept guard while I looked for clues. We found nothing, though, and it's time for the awards ceremony."

Awards ceremony? Was it that time already? "So that's it? Everything was judged?"

The danger might have passed, which was good news. But it also meant the saboteurs were in the wind. We'd never catch them.

Case snorted. "You'd think. But the judges were delayed earlier because the police were investigating. There are still some pieces they haven't seen yet. I don't think they've even looked at the sculptures."

"Then why are you going to the awards ceremony?"

"Because it's still at four," Case said, rolling his eyes. "And no one changed the schedule. The rest of us have to keep pretending that this is still okay, that nothing's wrong. We'll be sitting there for half an hour, waiting. Who knows what the saboteur could do with that time?"

"I think he missed his shot," Hack said. "Too many police. If I were him, I'd have something planned to ruin the awards ceremony. I think having to go to the tent is a good thing."

"I think so too," I said. I meant it; if the saboteurs had missed their shot with Sandra and Henry, they might try to ruin the awards. No prizes, no one wins. "Keep an eye out, okay?"

"You too, right?" Case asked. "You're coming."

"I have to do something first, but I wouldn't miss your moment of glory."

Case smiled. "I don't know if I'd call it *glory.* Everyone knows Sandra's going to take Best Overall. . . ."

I waved and raced off. If the judges weren't done with the favorites, the saboteurs still had one chance left to destroy the competition. We had to stop them now.

People were streaming to the tent. The paths were emptying, and empty paths meant more chances for the saboteurs to strike.

That meant Sandra could be in real trouble. I hurried to the sculpture garden, passing that punk Lee with his stupid buttoned-up vest, probably on his way to meet his so-called friend at the tent for the ceremony.

No sign of the judges yet. I admired Sandra's statue again. I could see why everyone thought she'd win; the wax etchings were so detailed. If the saboteurs dumped paint on this, those delicate scratches could be hidden. It would be ruined.

It looked really good, especially sitting right next to a sculpture that looked like a melted Rubik's Cube. That piece was painted in all kinds of colors, using what seemed to be all kinds of paint. I ran a finger over the sculpture. The paint changed texture as I moved from blue to red, from rough tempera to something smooth. Not quite a glaze . . . hmmm.

"Hands off the art," a voice whispered in my ear. I pulled back to see Larissa, wearing a pair of sunglasses and burying her face in a park map.

"I didn't even see you," I said. "Nice."

"Let's hope Aaron doesn't see me either," she said.

"No sign of him yet?"

"Nothing. Though that's not encouraging, since nobody saw anything at Diana's or Justin's paintings."

"Fair point. I'm going to go check with Becca. See if anything happened with her."

I left and speed-walked toward the photography section, thinking about what Larissa had said. No one had seen *anything* when the other sabotages happened. Why? How were the saboteurs doing it?

I was so deep in thought that I almost ran into Becca coming from the opposite direction.

Before I could say anything, Becca said, "I'm not abandoning anything. The judges showed up, judged Henry's piece along with a bunch of other ones, and left. No reason to guard his anymore. They're running really late."

"No kidding," I said. "They got held up by the investigations."

"The park is emptier," Becca said. "Even the volunteers are heading to the tent. The saboteurs have a better chance to attack now."

"At least we have a window to catch these guys. Case thinks the judges haven't seen the sculptures yet at all. *And* apparently, 'everyone knows Sandra will take Best Overall.'"

Becca's eyes widened. "They're going after Sandra. We have to get to the sculpture garden."

"Do that. I want to check on Case's picture first."

"He probably got judged hours ago. He's fine."

"Maybe, but I want to see for myself."

Becca nodded and hurried to help Larissa, and I moved toward Case's painting. There it was, on Wall C, with nothing amiss. Perfectly safe. I heaved a sigh of relief and started walking back to the sculpture garden.

How were the saboteurs doing it? How could they get close enough to the art to ruin it when the paths weren't as empty as they were now? It didn't make any sense.

A couple of volunteers, both teenage girls, were shutting down a snow-cone stand. One of them had spilled some syrup on her vest and was trying to rub the blue out of the orange.

Pressure seemed to build in my head as I watched the volunteers. Vests. Orange vests, like Aaron's, designating them as trusted employees. *Uniforms.*

Have you ever noticed that people in uniform don't get seen? I'd told Becca. *The uniform is seen and processed, but not the face. People in uniform blend into the background.*

That might be it! An orange vest, worn at the right moments, prevented anyone from really seeing or caring what they were doing. It's not strange for an art contest employee to be near the art; no one would think anything of it!

Aaron could have easily walked up to Justin's art and smeared paint on with a sponge. But what about Diana's sabotage? That wasn't Aaron. How did that saboteur escape notice?

The vest was with his partner. His partner took the vest to hide in plain sight while attacking Diana. He must have returned it to him later, before I saw Lee and Aaron talking.

My heart stopped. Lee. Aaron. Talking like they knew each other. Lee hadn't been wearing his gray vest then. But Aaron had been wearing his orange one. I'd never seen the two of them wearing their vests at the same time, not even that first time when Aaron had gotten Becca and me into the tent.

It made sense. Diana had said she hadn't seen Lee, but if Lee had been disguised as a volunteer, wearing the orange vest, Diana might not have realized who he was even if she had seen him near when the sabotage had been committed.

Hands shaking, I pulled out Becca's camera and flipped through the pictures she had taken of the pictures on Lee's camera. Photo after photo of Quinn, and there it was: the picture with them and their art. There was Quinn's hamster painting. And there was Lee with his melting Rubik's Cube.

The Rubik's Cube with the shiny paint. The paint like house paint. *Recycled* house paint, used by an artist with a pricey medium. As discussed in a conversation between two people who weren't supposed to know each other.

I do one favor for the guy and he thinks he owns me, Aaron had said. A favor like sabotage?

Red paint. Orange vest. Gray vest. Two saboteurs. Wow, I can be stupid sometimes.

Lee. Where had I seen him last? Heading away from the sculpture garden, and he was *wearing the vest*. He was going to attack someone. He was going to do it soon.

I had to stop him. I ran through the deserted paths.

My skin prickled. I was hyper-alert, noticing everything

from the wasp sting on a kid's elbow to the way parents have a certain look on their faces when they run into their friends. (The kids have a look too. Theirs can best be described as, "Oh no, this is going to take forever.")

No sign of him. Where was he?

I kept moving. Man, I wished I had some awesome spy music to listen to while I did this. It was so intense, searching for Lee. I had to stop him. *I* did. Becca, Quinn, and Larissa were looking for Aaron, and I didn't have time to warn them about Lee. This one was on me.

Think, Wilderson. He'd been walking *away* from the sculpture garden. Where was he going instead? Was Hack right? Was Lee going to ruin the awards ceremony itself?

I raced past the aisles, looking down each one. It was faster but no more fruitful. Nothing in the paintings, nothing in the photographs—and then I was at the tent, and there he was.

People were talking, walking into the tent, ready for a ceremony that would have to be late. Lee stood outside the tent, to the side, alone. Just staring at his phone. Not typing a message or laughing or anything else people do when looking at a phone. Weird.

This was my chance, while he was distracted. I circled behind him and tugged on his gray vest's collar hard enough to pull him backward.

"Hey!" When Lee saw who I was, he narrowed his eyes. "You. What's wrong with you?"

"I thought I saw a spider," I said. "Just getting it for you."

"Some *detective* you are," he said. "First you accuse two innocent girls of a horrible crime, and now you're seeing bugs where they have no business being." He sounded offended that I'd insinuate that spiders would ever touch him with their dirty little legs.

"My bad," I said. "But maybe you can help me. I have a question for you that may get the Eccles sisters in the clear."

I'd said the magic words; Lee paused and looked at me.

Smiling, I said, "Why is your vest bright orange on the inside?"

20

LEE'S EYES WIDENED AND his jaw dropped. He took a step back, and I moved toward him, smiling. I had him and he knew it. He was wearing his evidence, and I'd bet the phone had some incriminating texts on it. Nothing would stop justice from taking him down.

"We got you," I said. "Come quietly, and don't make a fuss." I reached out for Lee.

Before I could touch him, a crash echoed through the empty park. It had come from the sculpture garden. Lee's mouth curved into a triumphant smile.

Sandra. My head whipped toward the sound, my gaze following volunteers and officials hurrying toward the commotion.

When I turned back, Lee was gone. I saw his back disappear into the twisting paths.

That little monster. I pictured wax slamming against the concrete central area of the park, shattering.

I felt like I'd been punched in the stomach. We'd lost. Sandra had lost.

No. I couldn't accept that. I knew who the saboteurs were. The least I could do was make sure they didn't get away with it.

Moving slowly at first, but gaining speed, I ran into the paths after Lee.

I swear, I heard Becca's voice in my head as I ran: *If you don't catch that little saboteur, I will personally drag you into detention as soon as we get back to school.*

So I did. I ran deep into the photography and paintings, chasing someone who was already too far ahead for me to see.

Maybe I should contact my eyes in the sky. I pulled out my phone to call Quinn. Larissa had sent me messages from Becca's phone. *You have to see this,* she said, and had attached pictures of art carnage. Sculpture pieces lay strewn on the ground.

I stopped and looked at the pictures. Oh, wow. Putting the phone away, I smiled grimly. Lee was going to suffer.

But first I had to find him. I cleared Wall D and dashed into C.

And there he was, standing in the empty path, like he was just admiring the art, his vest hanging open so I could see the orange lining.

"Here to bring me in, 'detective'?" he said, putting air quotes around the word.

It took everything in me not to grab the guy by the collar and slam him up between the art. "How could you?" I asked. "You sabotaged artists. You attacked Sandra. No one deserved to have you or Aaron destroy the art they worked so hard on."

Lee shrugged, totally unsurprised when I said Sandra had been sabotaged. Like I knew he would be. "Why would you care? It's not really your line of work, is it, *thief*?"

Lee was playing with his phone, flipping it over in his hands, unperturbed.

"I'm not a thief."

"Oh, I'm sorry. Retrieval specialist, right? I hear you prefer to be called that."

"What else have you heard?" I didn't like this. Instead of running, Lee was playing some kind of game, and I didn't know what it was.

"Enough to know that sabotage isn't really your area of expertise. I'd understand if you were here to steal back someone's stolen art, but this? Shouldn't you leave this to Becca Mills?"

"What do you know about Becca?" I asked.

"Lots of things. I know she has an impressive case history. Her work with the gum-smuggling ring is inspired. And the mystery-meat recipe case? Amazing."

I took a step closer to him and placed my hand in my pocket. It rested right on top of Becca's camera. "How do you know about Becca? You don't go to our school. Those cases had nothing to do with you."

"Same way I knew about you, though, I admit, I was warned about Becca. You showing up was a surprise."

"Who warned you?"

"Someone who likes to follow your careers. Both of yours. Great work on that Mark case, by the way. Really clever how you tricked him into bringing the key into school in his pocket. Excellent teamwork, I have to say."

"How?" No one knew Becca and I had worked together on the Mark job. *No one.* We made sure no one knew.

Lee shrugged. "You ask the right people, you get the right answers. After I saw you viciously attack an innocent girl and her sister, I became very interested in who this Jeremy really was. A thief who works with a detective. Talk about identity crisis."

"Who did you talk to?" I needed to know. If word was out about Becca and me, if Case and Hack found out . . .

"Someone who knows everything about what happens in Scottsville."

"A name, Lee."

"Not telling."

"That's it. It's over. I know who you are and what you did. Come quietly and maybe the Detectives Mills will go easy on you."

Lee smirked. "I'm not going anywhere. You won't tell anyone about me. You know why?"

This couldn't be good. "Why?"

"You tell anyone about what I've done today, I'll tell Casey Kingston and Paul 'Hack' Heigel who you spent all day with. Yes, my source told me about them, too."

My blood ran cold. Looking at him, his eyes cold like a shark's, I knew he would do it. "I've had it backward," I said. "I thought Aaron was the mastermind. But it was you the whole time."

He scoffed. "Do you really think a *finger painter* could come up with a plan like this? It took foresight and the right connections. Aaron was convenient."

"Right, since he had access to the judges' schedules and the orange vest you're currently wearing. Too bad the schedule got messed up, and that only one of you could have the vest at a time."

Lee nodded. "A problem, but a small one. We had enough time to take out the top painters, like Aaron wanted, and you just heard him finish the job."

"If he's out there now, how come you're the one with the vest? Did your plan get that out of control, or do you just not care if Aaron gets caught?"

He gestured at the empty walkway. "Have you seen how empty the park is now? A bright orange vest would stand out. It's better for him to look like everyone else. Besides, why should I care what happens now that he's taken out my biggest competition?"

I clenched the fist not in my pocket. "*How dare you?* Sandra did nothing to you. You could have won on your own merit."

"You bet I could."

"Then why didn't you trust that to save the day? How did you even meet Aaron?" I sputtered, before I realized. "Your mysterious source. Of course."

"My friend told me about a disgraced painter who might be willing to take out a little of my competition, for the right price."

"What was that price, by the way?"

Lee smiled. "My source gets half my winnings for setting this up. Aaron did it just for the revenge. The torment he's endured over the last year has made him very angry, and I had a need for that anger. The partnership made sense. My friend agreed."

It was my turn to scoff. "Sure, because anger is *always* such a good thing to have. You watch out or my anger is going to be a big problem for you."

He smirked. "Don't make promises you can't keep. Oh wait, that's your thing, isn't it?"

I wanted to hit him. But I held it together. "And I thought sculpture was *your* thing," I said. "That can't be true, though. You don't even trust yourself to win without resorting to sabotage. Wow. What a great artist."

Lee scowled. "You don't know what it's like. Imagine working so hard, just so she—just so you can win this contest. Then you find out the prize is even better than you thought, and you can go to Harris Arts and then . . . and then . . ."

"And then Quinn would notice you," I finished. "That's what this is all about, isn't it? The girl next door? That's why you used your parents' leftover house paint to spice up your sculpture by painting it. That's why you took that same paint and slathered it all over your competition."

"That paint was supposed to help me win the contest," Lee grumbled. "If it wasn't going to work on my art, it could do its job covering everyone else's art."

"And all this for a girl."

"She's not just some girl! She—" Lee bit his lip. "You wouldn't understand."

"So explain it to me. How can a guy like you, using recycled materials in his art, get a girl like that to notice you?"

"By being better! By winning. By doing what it took to outshine everyone else!"

Lee's eyes were wild. I was hitting some pretty raw nerves. I kept going.

"Like getting help, long before the contest even started. Before you knew the prize was going to change."

"The prize didn't matter to me. Winning was the only thing that mattered, right from the start."

"Winning? Not having a good time while still following the rules?"

"Rules?" Lee laughed. "There are no rules in art. There's only what you can do."

I took another step closer. "So what could you do, Lee?"

He looked at me like I had empty tubes of paint for brains. "What could I do? I could talk to a friend and get a partner to help me. I could make Aaron's orange vest reversible so we could use it to get close to the art and then flip it around and hide in the crowds again. I could bring the can of paint my parents used to paint the kitchen and keep it in a toolshed by the tent. I could sabotage Diana while Aaron distracted the crowd, and I could hand him the vest as he went to get Justin."

"Then you could hurry to the tent to make sure you had an alibi," I said, another piece of the puzzle snapping into place. "After all, if Aaron got caught, you could claim innocence and that untalented hack of a finger painter would go down for your dastardly plan."

"Exactly."

I shook my head. "You did all of this, just to get the attention of a girl?"

"Of course I did."

"Well, you got her attention, but not in any good way. Don't you remember? Because of what you did, Quinn got accused instead. You threw her to the wolves. That's cold, man. You didn't even throw blame elsewhere when I accused her."

Lee looked at the ground, nervous or ashamed, I couldn't tell. "I didn't feel bad letting you chase her. I knew it would throw Becca off my trail, and in the end, Quinn wouldn't get blamed. She's too sweet and clearly innocent except to lunatics like *you.*"

"So you win the contest but lose the girl. That sounds like a great trade, all things considered."

"I won't lose her," Lee said. "Because I'm not getting caught. Aaron might be, but not me because you're going to let me go. You won't tell anyone about our little conversation because you don't want your friends knowing that you ditched them all day to play detective with Scottsville Middle's best snoop. What would Casey say?"

Nothing good. But never let them see you sweat. I shrugged, showing more confidence than I felt. "I'm sure Case will understand in time. See, everything I have done today has been to protect my friends. But I've seen how you treat your friends. You are awful to Ethan. As for other people, well, that's obvious. You attacked Sandra. You sabotaged Diana's painting. How dare you stand there and pretend that you're going to get away with all of this?"

"Because I will!" Lee yelled. "Diana, Justin, and Sandra didn't deserve Best Overall; I did. So I covered Diana's art with paint." His eyes sparkled. "And Aaron took care of Justin and Sandra. Nothing stands in my way anymore. I'm going to win."

"Not if you're disqualified. Becca was watching Sandra's sculpture. She probably has Aaron in custody now. He'll talk. He'll tell the cops what you did."

"Weren't you listening?" Lee said, laughing. "Aaron

sabotaged Justin's painting and Sandra's statue. He has things to hide too. He won't say anything."

"Maybe not," I said. "But you've already done it for him. I think I have what I need."

Smiling, I pulled Becca's camera out of my pocket. "How's that for hard evidence, Becca?" I said into the camera's microphone, and stopped the recording I'd started when I'd put my hand in my pocket.

Like I said before, a good retrieval specialist knows that when playing cards (be it Go Fish, Old Maid, or slapjack) or working a job, always keep an ace up your sleeve. Or in your pocket.

Lee gaped, and I carefully but jauntily tossed the camera from hand to hand. "It really wasn't hard getting you going. You sure like to hear yourself talk."

"What?"

"I could have turned you in, but then it would have been my word against yours, and that could have gone on forever, and I have an awards ceremony to get to. So I thought, you know, what's better than a witness testimony? A confession caught on tape. And I got it. Every ill-advised word, every insult to your partner. I can think of a few people who'd like to hear it."

"Give me that!" Lee lunged for the camera, and I pulled it away.

"Nope." I tucked the camera in my hip pocket, and I was sure Lee wasn't enough of a pickpocket to get it away from me.

Lee's mouth opened and closed like a hungry baby bird. "You won't play that file for anyone. Casey and Hack would kill you."

"You get caught as a saboteur planning to stab his partner in the back, and *I* get killed? Can you explain that logic? Don't worry about me. Worry about yourself."

He scowled. "At least I got Sandra's sculpture first."

"Oh, right. About that. I must have forgotten to mention." I pulled out my phone and pulled up the photos Larissa had sent me. "It wasn't Sandra's sculpture that fell. It was yours."

Or, when possible, keep *two* cards hidden.

"What?" Lee grabbed at my phone, wrapping his hand around mine. He turned as pale as the phone's light as he saw the pieces of painted clay scattered across the ground, and in the background, Sandra's sculpture safe on its stand. "No, it's impossible."

I pried his hands off my phone and put it away. "You said Aaron did it for the revenge, right? Well, he had no problem with Sandra; he hated the painters, not the sculptors. And you, well, you treated him like dirt and planned to betray him. Who do you think he'd want revenge on?

He might be *only a finger painter*, but still, somehow, he knew to attack *you* before the judges had gotten to the sculptures."

I smiled. I'd felt such relief when Larissa had sent me the pictures. And I had been correct. Lee was suffering. Served him right.

He turned away from me, shoulders hunched. He kept shaking his head. "You've taken it all from me. All of it."

I tucked the camera away. "No, this one's on you. Now, are you going to come quietly, or should I call the law?"

"You think you're so smart, Jeremy," Lee said. He rested a hand inside his vest. "But you're wrong about so many things. You were wrong to tell me about my sculpture. Now I have nothing to lose and everything to gain, by hurting you!"

With that, Lee lunged at me. I jerked back, but was too late. His hands scraped along my arm, drawing red behind them.

No, not blood. Paint. The same paint as used in the sabotages.

Lee watched me. In his hand was a wide paintbrush, the bristles soaked in red paint. On the ground lay a plastic bag. The little creep must have been hiding it in his vest this whole time.

"If you were so smart, you would have seen where

we are," he hissed at me as he gestured to the painting between us. I stiffened as I recognized Case's seascape.

Lee grinned like a feral cat. "Always have a Plan B in your pocket. In my case, literally." I hate it when the bad guy has the same idea I have.

The paint on me. Leading me away to Case's painting. Lee was going to strike where it hurt: he was going to ruin Case's painting.

No, Case must have already been judged. But if Case won, and got a picture in the paper with his art, and his art was ruined . . . I couldn't let that happen!

Lee smiled that too-perfect grin and swiped his arm at Case's painting. With a grunt I leaped, latching onto his arm. Paint flew, spattering my face and shirt.

Great. Finally wrecked my real shirt. Should have just worn the snot-crusted poncho all day. But I had saved Case's painting. Just barely. At the last moment, I pulled the wet bristles away from the black-and-white seascape.

"Case's art is good enough on its own," I grunted as I hauled on the saboteur's arm. "Doesn't need a touch-up."

For a skinny, weird little guy, Lee was pretty strong. Must have been all that sculpting. He struggled against me, inching the paintbrush closer and closer to Case's painting.

Where were the guards when you needed them? Probably in the tent.

I grabbed Lee's arm with both my hands and resorted to that time-honored tradition of retrieval specialists out of their league: cheating. With a hard tug I dropped to the ground, using all my weight to counter Lee's pull.

Lee came tumbling after me. The paintbrush clattered on the sidewalk, but not before splattering both of us with a fresh shower of red droplets.

The little creep made a grab at the camera in my pocket, which I easily deflected. He scrambled away from me, reaching for the brush. I grabbed him by the waistband and hauled him back.

"What was your original reason for bringing me here?" I asked as I pushed the squirming criminal away from the brush. "Back when you thought all I had on you was an orange vest."

Lee struggled. "F-frame you," he sputtered.

"Really? A frame job? A *frame* job?" I pushed the squirming criminal away from the incriminating brush. "At an *art show*? Are you completely uncreative?"

That must have struck a nerve. Lee lunged again, but this time aiming a fist at my face. I crossed my arms in front of my face, blocking the blow, and screamed as loud as I could, "HELP! SABOTAGE! HE'S RIGHT HERE!"

Bet the smug little saboteur didn't think of *that.*

He didn't. His face paled under the flecks of red paint, and he made another play for the brush. But this time I was between him and his target. I swept at the brush, sending it skittering farther down the path. "Try it again," I said. "Just try."

Lee froze. He was breathing hard. "It's over now," I said. "You've lost."

His eyes widened and then narrowed. Then he took off running down the path.

Oh, perfect. I scrambled to my feet and took off after him.

Case's painting was safe, but I wasn't. Lee had marked me with his paint, and if anyone saw me there, next to the paintbrush, they'd jump to some unfortunate conclusions that would take time to explain away. And I didn't have time. I had to catch Lee.

The saboteur had a head start on me, but I was a track jock in my element. The paths were empty; everyone was at the tent, waiting for the ceremony to begin. Sure, I had to dodge a few passersby, but I could race, unhindered, after Lee. And boy, did I race.

I saw Lee, running hard, up ahead. Pushing harder, I closed the distance. Sixty feet. Fifty. Forty.

We were by the Contestants' Tent. I could hear conversation inside. The ceremony must not have started yet. Good. I'd be able to be there for Case after all this was over.

Thirty feet now.

And then Lee stopped suddenly and faced me. He held out a hand like a police officer. "Stop."

Yeah, right.

Around the corner, walking toward the tent, came a small swarm of judges. They must have finished judging the art and were coming to announce the winners. I skidded to a halt and hunched protectively over the red on my shirt. If they were to see the incriminating evidence on me . . . that was it.

Lee laughed. "Your speed won't help you now, Wilderson."

"Don't call me 'Wilderson.' Only Becca gets to call me that."

He laughed again and disappeared into the paths. The crowd of judges and the need to hide the obvious paint on my shirt slowed me down. A lot. I had to wait for them to pass.

After the judges went inside the tent, I ran ahead, looking for Lee.

I scanned the park. Something, anything, had to give him away. *Come on, think, Jeremy.* He was almost as painted as I was. He couldn't stay where any stragglers could see him. He'd have to be moving away from the main paths of the park. I ran away from the tent, toward the grassy areas.

And there he was, sprinting toward the toolshed where Becca and I had kept our disguises. All those cans of paint . . . we had been right. The paint was with the park's supply in the shed I'd unlocked earlier. Oh, that made a delightful bonus.

He was too far ahead. Even if he didn't stop at the shed, he'd make it out of the park before I could catch him. After he got out, it would be too easy to lose him for good.

I ran harder. Lee looked back and grinned at me. He knew he was in the clear. He passed the shed, still looking behind him.

Running without looking ahead can be dangerous. Lee never saw the hand snap out from the shed and grab onto his collar. He looked shocked as that hand yanked him down into the grass.

I arrived on the scene to see Becca pinning Lee's hand behind him. She was practically singing him his rights. When she saw me, she smiled.

I smiled back. "Nice job."

She shrugged. "What are partners for?"

TURNED OUT, AFTER THE hubbub in the sculpture garden had been taken care of, Becca had used Larissa's phone to call Quinn. Our eyes in the sky had seen me confronting Lee and then chasing him. Quinn and Becca had coordinated to intercept him. But the kicker was that the real lead came from Ethan.

"He told me all about how Lee would sneak off to the shed," Becca said as she pulled out a pair of handcuffs (real ones) from her Mary Poppins–like pockets and cuffed Lee. "He was very forthcoming."

"No, really?" I said, laughing. "After all the nice things Lee did for him?"

"Everyone has a breaking point. Anyway, when the sisters said Lee was headed this way, I knew where to set up. You may be good at running, but not even you can run forever."

"That sounds like a threat."

"Maybe." Becca laughed. Catching bad guys put her in a creepily good mood, which wasn't hurt by the fact that she was right and had caught the saboteur for her mom. "Great detective work, by the way. Figuring out Lee was the other saboteur."

"Thank you." I guess I had managed to put the pieces together and solve the mystery, even though it's not my usual gig. It felt good.

"Oh, and here." Becca tossed me a moist towelette packet she must have been keeping in her shorts. "You have flecks of red on your face. What is it with you and paint?"

I scrubbed my face and looked soberly at the paint on my shirt. "One far-distant day, the best minds in the universe may figure it out. But today we are not so wise."

"Will you two stop flirting?" Lee spat from his place facedown on the grass.

Becca leaned close to his ear. "Nope. Because you are too darn cute. In fact, you're so cute, I think I should introduce you to my mother." Lee visibly shivered and Becca laughed. "She'll have some strong words to say about the attempted sabotage of Casey Kingston's work, to say nothing of the sabotage of Diana and Justin's paintings."

"And the attempted sabotage of Sandra's statue." I leaned toward Lee. "*Attempted.*"

"Too bad about that other one, though," Becca said, her lips twitching.

"Shut *up*," Lee growled. "At least when you bring me in, I'll get to tell Aaron what I think of him for destroying my art!"

Becca winced. "Sorry to disappoint you there, too."

"Aaron?" I asked.

She got somber. "He got away. We did all we could. I'm sorry."

"What happened?"

"Aaron had appeared in the sculpture garden not long after you left," Becca said. "Larissa and I saw him right away. He was carrying a can of red paint, and basically looking really suspicious. He obviously wasn't expecting a welcome committee. We shouted at him and blocked his way to Sandra's sculpture. He threw the paint can at me—good thing it still had the lid on—and when I caught it, he moved toward the statue. Larissa grabbed it to protect it."

"But he wasn't going for Sandra's art," I said.

She shook her head. "He pushed over the one next to it. The crash made us both jump back, and he ran away. You should have seen us: me throwing the paint can aside so I could chase Aaron, and Larissa clutching the statue. I ran after him and Larissa dealt with the adults, but I couldn't catch him. He disappeared."

Lee laughed. "You won't catch him. But wait until I get my hands on him. I'll—"

Becca squeezed his arm, making him go silent. "I'm sure what you're planning is wonderful, but it will have to wait. Right now, you're going to come with me and explain to my mom why you're covered in paint."

"You might also want to have him explain the paintbrush lying by Wall C," I said. "And here's this."

I handed her the camera and pressed play. Lee's confession rang out, and Becca beamed.

"Jeremy, you sure know how to give a girl a present. Evidence doesn't get any better. Mom can't ignore any of this. I call this a good day's work."

"I second that," I said as Becca hauled Lee to his feet. "Come on, Wilderson. Let's hand this creep off to the proper authorities."

"Uhh, about that." It's not that I didn't want to go back to the help office and face down Becca's mom and all the guards I'd seen earlier. It's just that I *really* didn't want to.

"Your witness testimony might be necessary," Becca said.

"I got you the recording. That should be enough."

"But you were part of the investigation. You should be there with me."

"I wish I could." I really didn't. "But I can't. The awards ceremony is happening right now."

Becca nodded. "Casey."

"Yep. I should be there for him at least this part of today." I examined the paint stains and sighed. "You're my partner, sure, but he's my friend. I owe him this."

Becca smiled and glanced from Lee to me. "I get that. See you around, then, Wilderson."

With that, she took Lee to meet his justice and I ran to the bathroom to change into the plaid shirt I'd hidden. It might have been stained, but it wasn't splashed with red paint. I put it on and went to work scrubbing and peeling the stretchy paint off my face and arms. Once the worst of it was gone, I headed back to the tent.

I was late, so I snuck in and sat in the back row. Case was sitting up on the stage with the other contestants. He looked kind of sick. The awarding hadn't happened yet.

"Hey, man." Hack sat down next to me. "Whoa, what happened to that shirt? Why are you late?"

"Trouble hunting mountain lions. Why are *you* late?"

"Checking up on something," Hack said. "Big."

"Get-you-grounded-again big?"

Hack grinned and took his glasses off. "Maybe. Did you hear about the sabotage earlier?"

"Which one?"

"Lee's. Not sure I care about that one, actually."

"Me neither. So what were you checking up on?"

"A hunch. Someone isn't as good as they think they are about covering tracks."

"And that someone is?"

"Let's just say that when the judges came in, I went looking for you. And you know what I saw? A dirty saboteur slinking out of the park, carrying a paint-soaked sponge in a bag. Probably trying to dispose of it. I got a picture and asked around, got a name. Guess what? He stupidly left his real e-mail address in the park volunteer database," Hack said, his voice tinged with venom. "Case and I are going to pay him a visit and make him an offer he can't refuse. You know the key to a good con."

I nodded. "Give the mark what they want. . . ."

"Or, if that doesn't work, threaten them with something they don't." Hack tilted his chair back and dramatically put his glasses back on.

"Nice." I grinned. "So what will you do?"

"Too many people here. Let's just say, for now, that I may have sent an e-mail to this certain someone offering some incriminating fingerprints I found. I may or may not have left out that no such prints exist. Too soon to tell. And when he gets back here for the meeting, Case and I are going to give him some very good reasons to turn himself in."

"Uh-huh." Case, Hack, and I had been tight for a long time, but this was the first time one of them was really scaring me. A forger and a hacker tend not to be the most threatening people, on first thought. They're white-collar troublemakers who work alone with delicate, sensitive instruments. But while Hack was talking to me, I had visions of viruses, compromised security, and false homework assignments. Secrets uncovered, and fake closet skeletons with convincing paperwork to back them up. My friends were bad people to tick off. I had a feeling Aaron was about to discover that for himself.

I was so glad they were on my side. I was also glad that I'd successfully avoided being seen with Becca. The job was done.

So I sat back, watched the mayor finish his speech, and then waited as art teachers from various schools presented different awards. Sandra won Best Overall, Henry won Best Photograph, and the kid who had been muttering to himself in the tent won Best Sculpture for a statue of a dog wielding a lightsaber.

Diana and Justin were in the audience. I watched them, too. During the presentation of the Best Painting award, the mayor made a comment about the unfortunate tragedies of the day and his encouragement to the artists to "remember that art is a prize in itself." At that, Diana looked at her lap and Justin twitched. We all read between the lines and knew they weren't getting anything. My stomach squirmed, like I'd failed a job. This wasn't right. Diana and Justin deserved more.

But that didn't stop me, when they announced Casey Kingston as the winner of Best Painting, from joining Hack in rushing the stage and carrying our friend off in a tide of victory."I can't believe you did that," Case said after the ceremony. "That was so tasteless."

"It's not like they took your newspaper picture right there," I said. "That happens later, with your painting."

"I know, but really? Rushing the stage?"

"Oh, you knew we were going to do it," Hack said. "You would have been disappointed if we hadn't." His phone beeped and he looked at it. "Showtime."

Case nodded, an evil glint in his eye. "Mess with the art show, will he?"

Oh yeah. My friends probably thought Aaron was the primary bad guy. The news of Lee's arrest would have yet to hit the rumor mill. "Go easy on him, okay, guys? He might not be the criminal sludge bucket you think he is."

Case and Hack looked at me, shocked. "Who do you think we are, Becca Mills?" Case asked.

"We have nothing but compassion for kids who turn to crime," Hack added.

"But they don't have to know that right away," Case finished.

They're scary when they do that.

"Want to come? I'm sure you'd love to ream out a criminal."

After doing it twice that day, *I* was a little reamed out. Besides, I had an idea. "Love to, but can't. There's something I need to do. Catch you later?"

They nodded and I ran back to the shed and gathered up all the bits of my and Becca's disguises. Time to return the clothes. It wasn't like they were mine, anyway. The poncho, the muumuu, the hats, and the sunglasses. Even the buttons from our shoes. Everything except the shirt on my back went into a giant wad in my arms.

I must have looked strange as I walked into, around, and out of the art museum's gift shop. The place was busy, so I got a lot of weird looks from shoppers. But I didn't care. I walked through to the Lost and Found, which, despite the shop's busyness, was deserted.

Well, almost deserted. As I set the bundle down carefully, a voice said, "Hey, Jeremy."

I almost jumped out of my skin. I could have sworn there was no one in there! I looked around and saw Larissa by the door.

"I was at the lockers with my family and saw you come in," Larissa said. She reached for the bundle. "Let me help you with that."

I pulled away. "I've got it."

Larissa stepped closer, looked at the bundle, and tilted her head. She reached under the poncho and pulled out two sets of brushes, the kind sold at the art museum's gift shop. Which I had just passed through with a bundle of very obscuring cloth in my arms. "With all these people around too?" she said. "Pretty bold, thief."

I snatched them back. "I'm not a thief. I return what was stolen or lost. Everyone knows Diana or Justin could have won if they hadn't been sabotaged. They were robbed and they deserve something. Last year Aaron had a win stolen from him, and no one did anything about it. Maybe if someone had helped him then, the sabotages wouldn't have happened this year. So, if no one else is willing to give the victims back what they lost, it falls to me."

Larissa didn't say anything. She just held the brushes in her hands. "Or me."

"What?"

"I could give the brushes to them. I have connections through my sister. And since you were the one who took them, wouldn't it be safer for you if you didn't have them anymore?" Larissa stopped. "Unless you want to be the one who gives them to Diana and Justin."

I smiled. Normally I would have liked the glory, but it didn't seem important in the moment and Larissa had made a good point. "Good thinking. You'd make a decent retrieval specialist. But it is a loss, not being able to get attention for this one. What will you give me in return?"

She looked startled. "Uh, what do you want?"

"The painting. The one you made to replace Quinn's real painting. I want that one."

She crinkled her forehead. "You're welcome to it, after everything you did today. But . . . why? It's not that good."

I shrugged. "It's good enough. I like the monster." And more than that, I liked what it meant. Case says art is about subtext, and I would enjoy having a painting with the subtext of a girl willing to do anything to protect her sister.

Larissa smiled. She tucked the brush sets into the waistband of her pants. "I'll deliver these as soon as I can. The painting, *my* painting, is behind the bases in the storage room. I swapped it for Quinn's real painting during the awards ceremony. You can pick it up from there."

"Great."

"Are you going to keep that shirt?"

I looked down at the dirty plaid. "No choice. I don't think whoever lost this would recognize it. If it cleans well, maybe I'll return it when I come back to pay for those art supplies."

"Pay? I thought you were a thief."

"I thought I told you, I'm not. I just didn't bring enough money today."

Larissa nodded and walked to the door. She paused, her hand on the door handle, and looked back at me. "I'll go in with you. On the brushes. I'll pay half."

"You don't have to do that."

"Consider it my thank-you. It was fun, today. Even with the fake accusation and getting lost in the air vents. It was exciting."

I smiled. I knew how she felt. I'd been feeling it since my first job, that rush of adrenaline. "If you liked that, there's a lot I could show you."

"Yes, please!"

"I guess I'll see you around," I said.

"See you around." And then she was gone.

Smiling, I left the museum and headed to the

help-office storage room. Maybe bringing home some art would keep Mom from killing me over the shirt thing.

The door was open, so I just walked in and picked up the painting. The fiery monster glared at me. It reminded me of a warm version of Becca. I tucked it under my arm and left the storage room.

As I returned to the path, Becca burst out of the help office. "Jeremy, wait."

"Gah!" Again, I nearly jumped out of my skin. "You two are so similar."

"We two who?"

"Never mind."

Becca pointed. "Why do you have that painting?"

"Gift from the painter. How's it going with Lee?"

She shrugged, walking down the steps to meet me on the sidewalk. "Not bad. Your recording was very helpful. Exactly what we needed, by the way. Mom saved your file and gave me back the camera, which left me free to catch this on tape."

Becca pressed the play button, and Detective Mills's voice said, "Well done, Becca! You trusted your instincts and let them lead you to the truth. You're going to make a great detective one day."

She beamed and I patted her shoulder. "Good job. So your mom has everything she needs?"

"Oh yeah. This and the paintbrush, and Lee got a lot more chatty when Mom talked to him, but then, Mom usually has a way of getting people to cooperate."

"I bet she does." That time spent with the Elder Mills was still terrifyingly vivid.

Becca got closer. "It would be easier if we had Aaron, though."

"Unless I'm very wrong, you'll be seeing Aaron soon."

Becca tilted her head. "How sure are you?"

"Pretty darn."

"Wilderson, is this some kind of thief thing? What have you been up to?"

Stealing paintbrushes, just like you accused me of this morning. Ain't you glad to be right? "This is harmless, I promise. If you need anything else for the investigation, like my statement or whatever, I live across the street. Just come over and get it from me."

Becca smiled. "Thank you."

"There was one other thing," I said. "Did you listen to the tape?"

"Not all of it. Not yet, but I still have it saved. Why?"

"Lee knew about you. About your past jobs, and that you'd be here, tracking him, at the show. He knew things he shouldn't have known."

Becca furrowed her brow. “Maybe my reputation precedes me.”

“Yes, but not in a good way.” I lowered my voice. “He knew about the Mark job. He knew we had worked together.”

Becca’s lips tightened. “That’s impossible. We covered our tracks.”

“I thought so too. But Lee knew about everything. I think this source warned him about you before he came here today, so Lee knew to try to throw you off by letting Quinn take the heat.”

“That is interesting. How did he get this information? Did he say?”

“Lee told me he had a source who told him everything, but he wouldn’t give me a name.”

Becca nodded. “Lee’s being very forthcoming about sabotaging the paintings, but he hasn’t mentioned any kind of source. It could just be someone from our school spreading rumors. But still. Someone who warned him about me and knows about *us* . . . We should find out who this source is. I’ll try to get it out of Lee. He’s going to have a long, lonely summer. Maybe he’ll be more willing to talk in a few months.”

I shuddered as I thought about Becca’s interrogation tactics. “You do that. I’ll keep my ear to the ground and see what I find out.”

"Be careful. This person knows about you, too. They might know other things that you won't want anyone else finding out. Your past jobs come to mind."

That was a scary thought. "Still, I'll see what I can turn up."

"Let me know as soon as you find something. And, again, thank you for all your help today." Becca pushed some hair behind her ear. "It meant a lot to me. I mean that."

I smiled back and stuck out my hand. "What are partners for?"

Becca shook my hand. Her grip was firm and warm.

A sound like someone choking made me drop that hand and turn around.

Oh no. No. No.

Forget Lee. Forget his friend's impossible knowledge. Forget Becca and Detective Mills. Forget Mom and Dad and Rick and everyone who had ever or could ever make my life difficult. This was a hundred, million times worse.

Case stood there, looking like he had swallowed his tongue. Hack stood beside him, cleaning his glasses so hard he was going to etch the glass with his shirt. Aaron was with them, apparently of his own accord, looking scared. As my friends gaped, he hurried into the help office.

"Uh, hi, guys," I said. "Uh, how long have you been standing th—"

"Partners?" Case spat. *"Partners?"*

"That long, huh."

Now Lee's mysterious friend wasn't the only one who knew about Becca and me. My own friends knew. Oh man. If looks could kill, they'd have blasted my remains into dust by now.

Becca patted me on the back and walked into the help office. I was left alone, clutching a painting and staring at my two best friends. No explanation, no matter how clever, could take away the truth they had just heard.

My heart sank, lower and lower through my stomach on its way to my feet. Lee wasn't the only guy who was going to have a long, lonely summer.

ACKNOWLEDGMENTS

Somehow, and with much help, I managed to complete another book. I didn't run an official contest, but if I did, these people would be the winners:

The Best Agent award goes to Lauren E. Abramo for being there for me and for taking care of business like a boss. Thank you for all your help and support.

Best Editor, Amy Cloud. Thank you for taking my goofy stories and helping me make them something special. I've loved working with you on these books.

Best Copy Editor, Jen Strada, for her careful, detailed copyediting that put the final polish on the book.

Best Artist goes to Matt David, and Best Art Director to Karin Paprocki, for yet another cover illustration. I can't stop smiling at Jeremy with his green mustache!

Love and gratitude to my best and only family, for believing in me and in my dream of writing. Grace, thank you especially for being a great reader and for listening to me as I discussed my plans for Jeremy's continuing adventures.

Thanks also to Madeleine, Jenna, Kiersty, Bekah, and all the other readers who helped me smooth out the rough edges of this book, trim down the garbage, and perfect the ending. I couldn't have done this without you.

TURN THE PAGE

FOR A PEEK AT THE FIRST BOOK ABOUT JEREMY'S ADVENTURES:

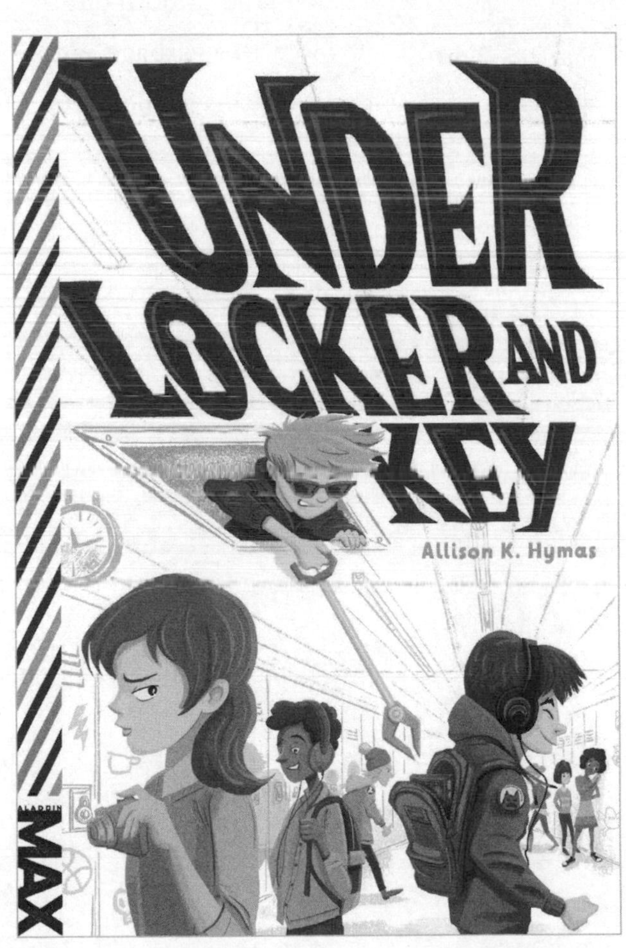

FIRST OFF, I AM NOT A THIEF.

I am a retrieval specialist. Big difference. Thieves take what doesn't belong to them. They *steal.* Me, I take back the things thieves steal and return them to their rightful owners. The job runs everywhere from crazy to boring to dangerous, but someone has to do it. Kids need protection from the jungle out there.

If you've ever been in middle school, you know what I mean. Bigger kids rip sixth graders off for lunch money, new shoes, whatever. Even teachers contribute to the problem by confiscating cell phones and iPods. I have the highest respect for teachers—my mom is one—but they don't always understand that the cell phone belongs to your dad, not you, and that if you don't give it back right after school, you're grounded.

So I step in. One meeting with me over a cafeteria

lunch or before class and I guarantee to return your stolen property before the late bus leaves. No payment needed—I just ask that you pass my name on to someone else who needs me. And don't tell the teachers that I retrieved your stuff. Or Becca Mills. Especially Becca Mills.

Still convinced I'm a thief? Read on. After you become more familiar with my method, you'll change your mind. Where to begin? How about somewhere exciting . . . ?

The tiles froze my bare knees as I knelt in front of the backpack. I'd like to tell you my heart raced and sweat dripped down my forehead, but I never get nervous on a job that routine. If anything, I felt annoyed at the school for pumping the boys' locker room full of icy air. Why can I almost see my breath in the one room in school where people strip down?

Anyway, the bag didn't belong to me. But the Hello Kitty wallet shoved at the bottom sure didn't belong to the owner of the tough-looking blue-and-black backpack with the X Games key chain.

The client: Carrie Bethesda. First-chair trumpet in the concert band. Sixth grader with a habit of carrying multiple twenties in her wallet. Her parents trusted her with a month of lunch money at a time—a bad idea, as it turned out.

The mark: Adam Lowd. Nothing out of the ordinary: eighth grader with a taste for after-school pizza that left him constantly short on cash. He'd lifted Carrie's wallet during a scuffle in the lunch line, or so Carrie suspected.

She was right. I found the wallet crammed between Lowd's history textbook and a wad of old vocabulary tests. A quick check verified that all $43.75 was still there. This girl was loaded. All that cash might have tempted a real thief to pocket it and leave the client destitute, but I tucked the wallet, bills and all, into the pocket of my hoodie for temporary safekeeping.

My watch beeped. Ten minutes until the end of eighth-grade gym; the students would come back at any minute to change out of their uniforms. Gotta love gym—the only class where you have to leave all your belongings in a room with minimal security. No one's around while class is in session, and half the time, people forget to lock their lockers. On top of that, the gym lockers are so small that backpacks have to be left in the open, like Adam's was. It's like the school *tries* to make my job easier. I zipped Adam's backpack and then left, one hand in my hoodie pocket, resting on the retrieved wallet.

And because it's written in the fabric of the universe that no job can go off without a hitch, with the whir and click of a camera Becca Mills stepped in front of me in the hall outside the gym. "Jeremy Wilderson," she said, twirling her little silver camera by its strap. How did such a tiny girl manage to block the whole hallway?

"Hi, Becca. Shouldn't you be in class?"

"Shouldn't you?"

"Ms. Campbell let us go early after we promised we wouldn't get into mischief." A true statement. That camera wouldn't give her anything on me.

Becca smiled like I imagine a cobra would, if it had lips. "Breaking promises now?"

I raised my hands. "Hey, I'm clean. No trouble here. Why don't you go investigate Scottsville's illegal gum trade? I swear there was some under-the-desk dealing during homeroom."

The twelve-year-old detective stepped closer. Her dark hair gleamed in the June sun coming through the dirty windows. "If there's any illegal gum trading, I bet you're jaw-deep in it."

"After your last three investigations, I'd think you'd know gum trading is not my game."

"Right. Thieving is." Becca's lip curled. "You disgust me."

"Disgusting? Me? I'm a picture of cleanliness, both physically and morally."

"If you're so 'clean,' where is your backpack? Why

were you in the gym locker room right now when your last class of the day is science?"

I sighed. I should have remembered: She'd memorized my schedule back when a history teacher's test answers disappeared between fourth and fifth period, and Becca was certain I'd stolen them. It wasn't me; the teacher remembered he'd left the answers in his car. The way Becca acted, though, you would have thought my innocence personally offended her.

"Like I said, I got out of class early," I said. "It's a nice day. I thought I would put my stuff in my gym locker before I go outside so I wouldn't have to carry it around until after track practice."

Becca's gray eyes narrowed. Her hands lifted, reaching toward the slight bulge in my hoodie pocket. An actual frisking? Really?

"Whoa," I said, backing away. "I know I have an athlete's body, but hands off the abs. People will talk."

Becca drew away. "You *disgust* me."

"You already said that." I shoved my hands into my hoodie's large front pocket. "Now, if you'll excuse me, the sunshine calls."

As I walked away, Becca said, "Your thieving will catch up with you, Wilderson. I'll make sure of it, even if no one else does."

I turned and saluted her, which, judging by her scowl, she did not appreciate.

The bell rang, and I hurried away down halls beginning to crowd with kids. I had to steer through the mess like a getaway driver at rush hour to get back to my locker and retrieve my own backpack. Yeah, I lied to Becca. I wouldn't have to if she would loosen up and see that I provide a necessary service, instead of trying to put me in detention for the rest of my middle school life.

Carrie was waiting outside the instrument room, fussing with her ponytail, biting her lip, and actually *pacing*. I shook my head. I had told her to go about her classes like normal, and she had to act like she stole the principal's car keys (much easier than it sounds, by the way). What if Becca or Adam saw her like this? I beckoned her to follow me into the instrument room.

The loud, busy instrument room makes a great place for handoffs. I use it a lot—band kids need my services more than most people. Instruments have so many loose parts, like reeds and slides and buttons, which have a knack for disappearing just before the winter or spring concert. In return for my help finding mouthpieces that cost way more than a month's allowance, the band kids grant me a certain amount of discretion when I show up in their room. No one bothered me as I leaned into a corner and brought Carrie's wallet out of my pocket.

"You got it!" Carrie said. Or at least I think that's what she said; some trombone player took that moment to run a scale.

"It *was* Adam. He had it in his backpack. You should stop carrying all that money," I said. "Leave some at home in your sock drawer."

Carrie smiled. "I'll do that. I owe you one."

"If you hear of someone who needs something retrieved, send them my way," I said. "But if you feel the need to pay me with something a little more . . . physical, I like chocolate cake. You know where to find me at lunch."

Before I could move, Carrie hugged me. When she let go, I spun on my heel and walked away. It happens a lot. A guy like me—athlete, hero—girls can't resist.